THE PROGRESSIVE APPARATUS

AND MORE FANTASTICALS

Other books by Hugh A. D. Spencer

Extreme Dentistry

Why I Hunt Flying Saucers And Other Fantasticals

The Hard Side of the Moon (forthcoming)

PRAISE FOR THE STORIES IN THIS COLLECTION

"Hugh's work never fails to crack me up and make me think, and this is no exception. The story is touching and weird, speculative and human—a perfect metaphor for the anxiety that we feel whenever technology remakes our beloved selves and institutions." ~ Cory Doctorow, author of *Little Brother* and *Attack Surface* on "Sticky Wonder Tales"

"Pretty weird—you can evidently go too far with 'Evolutionary Transformation'." ~ Rati Mehrotra, author of *Mahimata*, on "Sticky Wonder Tales"

"A surreal take on an apocalyptic scenario in which roving clouds of nanobots lay waste to civilization." ~ The Horror Bookshelf on "John, Paul, Xavier, Ironside and George (But Not Vincent)"

PRAISE FOR THE WRITING OF HUGH A. D. SPENCER

"A great debut collection of stories that offers up a retrospective of highlights from twenty-five years of published work. [Spencer's] writing is lively and topical. The genre satire is spot on." ~ *Toronto Star* on *Why I Hunt Flying Saucers And Other Fantasticals*

"Brilliantly original. Disturbing and funny. Thought-provoking and entertaining. Frankly, the best kind of science fiction. What science fiction is meant to be. First class." ~ *Clubhouse Review* on *Why I Hunt Flying Saucers And Other Fantasticals*

"Hugh handles [short stories] very well indeed. Yep, reality and SF collide—and reality will always win." ~ *Amazing Stories* on *Why I Hunt Flying Saucers And Other Fantasticals*

"I find the core concept fascinating and greatly enjoyed reading about its multi-faceted complexity. Frankly, it involves the kind of job I've always dreamed about." ~ *Amazing Stories* on "Nowhere to Nowhere" from *The Light Between Stars*

"Spencer stacks it with so many odd elements that it all works. Well worth searching out." ~ *Toronto Star* on *Extreme Dentistry*

"*Extreme Dentistry* is very funny and quite horrific." ~ *Amazing Stories*

"A dark and mordantly funny satire." ~ *Armed and Dangerous* on *Extreme Dentistry*

"Hitchhiker's Guide to the Galaxy vibe." ~ *Read, Play, Review* on *Extreme Dentistry*

"Lucid, lyrical, and savvy." ~ Paul Levinson, author of *Unburning Alexandria* and *The Silk Code*

"If you like to laugh and cower at the same time—if you like science fiction that is simultaneously progressive and retro—then you need to read this… Like nothing I've ever read before. Highly recommended." ~ Dale Sproule, author of *Psychedelia Gothique*

THE PROGRESSIVE APPARATUS

AND MORE FANTASTICALS

HUGH A. D. SPENCER

Milton, Ontario
http://www.brain-lag.com/

This is a work of fiction. All of the characters, events, and organizations portrayed in this novel are either products of the author's imagination or are used fictitiously.

Brain Lag Publishing
Milton, Ontario
http://www.brain-lag.com/

Cover artwork by Catherine Fitzsimmons

Library and Archives Canada Cataloguing in Publication

Title: The progressive apparatus : and more fantasticals / ten more beloved short stories by Hugh
A.D. Spencer.
Other titles: Short stories. Selections
Names: Spencer, Hugh Alan Douglas, author.
Identifiers: Canadiana (print) 20200355457 | Canadiana (ebook) 20200355589 | ISBN 9781928011460
(softcover) | ISBN 9781928011477 (EPUB)
Classification: LCC PS8637.P47 A6 2021 | DDC C813/.6—dc23

TABLE OF CONTENTS

YOU'LL BE FINE: AN INTRODUCTION

I don't much like introductions but I always read them. If you're like me, here we are together: nice to see you here. (If you aren't, you've skipped this, but no harm no foul: I understand. You want to get to the Real Stuff. If you come back to it later, tell me I was wrong: I dare you.)

Having not skipped it, you need reassuring that this is not the hateful (IMHO) kind of intro where someone takes every story and recaps it, then explains the hell out of it. I hate that. Seriously. What's the point of even reading the book, after that? Be reassured. I will not.

Even if I could.

But I can't.

Because trying to summarize Hugh Spencer's stories is... well, impossible.

Hugh (I can call him Hugh. I've known him for decades) is one of a select few writers whom even I think (and that, if you know me, means something) is seriously weird.

Make no mistake, though: this is a feature, not a bug.

You know how people say "think outside the box"? Well, Hugh wants to know what the box even is, and why should we think outside or inside or anywhere near it? When you enter the world of Hugh A. D. Spencer, there is no box. There is no owl. There is no cat. There is no outside—or inside. Get ready.

If you don't know Hugh A. D. Spencer, you might want a sort of capsule bio, and some way of understanding what you are getting into. Okay, this isn't going to be easy, but it will be fast, so hold on. I'm sure there's a bio in the back, and if not, most of what you need to know is on the Interwebz in more or less this order: his grad project to conduct anthropological studies into the origins of religious movements in science fiction fandom; his Aurora nominations; his publication and broadcast history; his day job as a museum planner for museums all over the world; his visual art; and his fondness for his family, friends and dogs. (By the way, his son, who also has two middle initials, is a writer too. Apple:tree, or, our condolences, kid: you decide.) But all this is just the shell: who lives inside?

Now, before I start with the comparisons, let me say that Hugh Spencer is absolutely unique, so these are provided only for canonical reference points, those markers we throw up around a text to help them make sense to academics and encyclopædists. And also put there, may I add, to warn us before we get to the work itself that Here Be Dragons and we should watch our asses.

So. You are likely familiar with William Gibson and the cyberpunks. You probably know about Hunter S. Thompson. And you for sure are aware of Peter Watts, extraordinary and deeply pessimistic futurist (Peter would say he's just a realist. After the last few years, I'm hard pressed to say he's wrong). So imagine if you put all of them in a blender, metaphorically-speaking, added a soupçon of Ustinov and a dash of Kubrick, and decanted them into one person whom you then decreed would be raised by Mormons on the Canadian prairie. That is Hugh A. D. Spencer, and lucky we are that he has survived (so far) to bring us his fiction.

Hugh isn't as famous as those guys I mentioned, and that's too bad. Really, he should be. But I suspect that although he'd probably handle fame pretty well, fame wouldn't be able to withstand him. At all. Fame requires a certain level of approachability even for the most dystopian visions. Hugh is loping ahead of us, expecting us to keep up. He's busy with a range of media, which makes it hard for Fame to draw a bead. And he has a healthy appreciation for life's balances, though you couldn't guess that from reading the stories to come.

In all seriousness, though, Hugh has a specific marker standing up there on the Canadian prairies that is deeply significant in speculative fiction, and because of that, he's been kind of the spec-fic-writer's writer through his career. We know who he is. He's one of those writers whose stories, while not myriad, are always eagerly-anticipated—and maybe, a bit, dreaded, but in the nicest possible way.

I could take an aside into lit-crit, talking about: how he imposes the literary on the paraliterary ("genre") and vice versa, to great effect; how he subverts the tropes of the genre; how he bedecks those tropes with cultural and emotional significance; how he makes the classic short story form into a postmodern (or post-

postmodern) sledgehammer with which he destroys complacency and comfort; how he then offers instead a peculiar and tasty mix of despair and optimism. All of this put together is the mark of a master builder. In this way, he can be compared, on a different axis, with the best short-storyists of our field: Howard Waldrop, Ursula Pflug, Eileen Gunn, Bob Shaw, et alia. (We can also compare him with a lot of mainstream and slipstream short-form writers, but I promised to be brief.)

But again, we only compare to set some markers: Hugh is going to mess with us no matter how prepared we are when we see his name—and we are going to enjoy it while it's happening, and come out of it seeing the world a lot more slant, without caring that we have been morphed during transport.

I have resisted quoting even one of the many lines that I noted—with admiration, disquiet, laughter, and astonishment—as I read through this collection. I was going to, because I love them so much, but I decided that you don't need my little yellow highlighters all over your experience of Hugh's stuff. (Stuff. That's a technical term for everything outside the box, stuff we know not of, and from which Hugh A. D. Spencer makes his best work.)

So just dive.

It'll be fine. Well, for some values of "fine".

No, seriously. I promise.

You'll be fine.

Really.

Candas Jane Dorsey
January 16, 2021

MY TOY ROBOT COLLECTION

At the peak of the collection, I owned between 450-500 toy robots. Some of them were very, very small (the sorts of plastic objects that were encased in clear bubbles and were dispensed by gumball machines with upwardly mobile aspirations) and some were very fancy indeed. My highlight piece was a robot from Harrods Department Store in London, which had a touch-pad in its chest which you could use to program in different movements, sounds, and flashing light patterns. This was very advanced for 1982, plus I could use it to follow the cleaning staff around the apartment building where my father lived.

There were a few others that I came to love, some knock-offs of Robbie from *Forbidden Planet*, B9 from *Lost in Space*, and one robot that projected miniature planets and galaxies inside its chest. Of course, I had some toy Daleks from *Doctor Who*—both the talking variety who exhorted me to "Exterminate!" and "Obey!" or asked me "What are your orders?!", and the ones that frantically raced across the room propelled by penlight batteries and that mysterious "Bump and Go Action!"

Probably my favourite was one that both walked and talked, loudly and proudly proclaiming: *"I am the Atomic Powered Robot! Please give my best wishes to everyone!"* This toy was both friendly and polite. I liked that.

My toy robot collection was a big deal in my life, but now it's not. I sometimes wonder why that is. But every explanation I can think of is purely conjectural. I have no clear idea why I even started my collection, let alone why I stopped collecting.

Childhood regression is probably the most credible theory. I liked toy robots when I was a kid, but it wasn't until my teens that I started systematically gathering them. It might have been that as I was discovering how difficult and painful adult life could be, I was reaching back into my past for something to love. Another, perhaps more flattering theory, was that each toy was some kind of creative artifact from about age 12 on, and I knew I wanted to be some kind of science fiction writer, but I had no idea how to go about doing that. I did compose little mental stories about each robot as I acquired it, and maybe the toys were just how I represented the ideas.

My accumulation of automatons only got worse as I got older. Then things got vaguer and less organized as I hit thirty, and a decade later I realized that while I had a lot of toy robots, I wasn't really collecting them anymore. Why everything changed is an even bigger mystery to me. I don't think I matured out of this interest, there was no spousal pressure to get rid of the toys, and my sons were only interested in robots that were named Megazoids or Decepticons, so they were totally neutral about what I had.

Perhaps my toy robot collection, having fulfilled its purpose, simply became something else that didn't have so much meaning to me. If we go with the creative expression idea, maybe once I started telling stories with words, I didn't need to do so with wind-up and battery-operated objects.

I do, however, sometimes wonder if the robots should be somewhere else, making other people happy.

So here you are, holding another collection that I'm responsible for; this book is the second anthology of my short stories. It takes its name from one of my better-known works.[1]

Welcome. I hope you find the reading exciting, entertaining, and even a little enlightening.

A few words of orientation for you:

- "The Progressive Apparatus" is the first in a cycle of three stories featuring the same characters. They are arranged in sequence in this collection.
- There are also two more connected stories, "Sticky Wonder Tales" and "The Meaning of Steel", although the links are more thematic and less direct.
- The piece called "Cult Stories" is a spin-off of a larger dramatic work called *Amazing Stories, Astonishing Failures and Disappointing Success*. It is possible to find this audio play online, but you don't need to hear it to understand the story printed here.

1 My first anthology, *Why I Hunt Flying Saucers And Other Fantasticals*, is named after my most popular story. If you haven't read this book yet, I encourage you to do so. It's not hard to find.

I'm sure most of you could have figured all of this out on your own. Even so, the instructions might make it easier to get into the experience.

I truly hope this collection of stories has a longer shelf-life than my collection of toy robots. Like the robot collection, there was a fair bit of play involved in their creation.

Happy reading.

And if any of you would like to take some toy robots off my hands, you should get in touch.

GROWING UP DEFECTIVE

I made three mistakes when I was growing up:

1. I was born the last of six children. My five older siblings were all brilliant, outgoing, and pretty successful in least 20 different things. It was hard to get anyone's attention, and it was usually just easier to retreat to Planet Hugh when things got too noisy.
2. Unlike my siblings, I was not a high achiever at school. In some families, a C to C+ average in Grade Two was not such a big deal. Now, my parents were wondering if I had somehow sustained major brain damage.
3. I was a persistent practitioner of nocturnal enuresis. In other words, I wet my bed. A lot. For a long time. Nobody in the family teased me about it (much), but it was incredibly inconvenient; affecting our morning routines, whether I could ever go on sleep-overs, and even where and how we could go on vacations. Bed-wetting really sucks, and it makes you wonder if you're ever going to grow up.

These combined life errors seemed to encourage my family members and/or caregivers to consider whether I was somehow defective. Maybe it seemed like a reasonable assumption at the time. So, the questions that naturally followed were:

- Just how broken was I?
- What could be done to fix me?

In pursuit of the answers to these vital questions, I became the subject of various tests and experiments. These included lots of physical and psychological measurements, tablets, special diets, regimes of vitamins, and a series of injections that were administered over a period of years. The strangest exercise of all was some sort of study of bladder capacity, where every time I peed, I had to measure the urine in this long, graduated cylinder. Stuff like that can make you into a very kinky person.

My father (lover of the scientific method that he was) started enrolling me in different research studies at the local university. The ones that made the biggest impression on me were two multi-year investigations into physical growth and brain/cognitive development. I have no idea if these studies rendered any useful results or not. I do know that neither one made me smarter or helped with the bed-wetting.

They did, however, make me feel like even more of a freak. Probably had something to do with being photographed almost naked every year and having all those electrodes glued all over me.

But there were some positive side-effects to all this science-ing about. I did get curious about what the experimenters were doing and what they were looking for. It was interesting.

As the years progressed, I started to embrace my freakishness. Okay, I was a weird kid, maybe that was why I was worth studying.

Sometimes the victims of events (as children often are) can still find themselves in a modicum of control.

FIVE STORIES ABOUT ALAN

Originally published in:
Dandelions of Mars: A Tribute to Ray Bradbury
2013

1. The Wonderful Mr. Whale

"This is the best place for milkshakes," said the man with the grey felt hat.

Alan thought any milkshake was wonderful. Especially chocolate ones. He tried to wrap his fingers all the way around the big metal cylinder. It was cold!

Good cold, like a Popsicle on an August afternoon.

"Do you know why these are such good milkshakes?" The man with the grey hat put his straw in his mouth and inhaled while he waited for an answer. Alan could see a tiny pink elevator of ice cream push its way up.

"No sir, I don't." His mother told him to always be polite to people.

"Take a sip," the man said.

Alan did what he was told. He had a brown elevator in his straw because his milkshake was chocolate.

The man pointed at the container. "It's the aluminum. Keeps the milkshake colder. Gives it more flavour."

Alan took another sip.

"Most places put the milkshake in a big paper cup," the man said. "Not as good."

Alan felt good. The milkshake was super delicious and he liked it when people told him interesting things that he didn't know.

"Also, there's the ambiance," the man continued. "Do you know what ambiance is?"

"No, sir."

"It has something to do with *where* we're having our milkshakes," the man said.

Alan looked around but he couldn't see what the big deal was. They were in a very old-fashioned place like a really old movie except that it was in colour.

"You'll understand when you're older," the man said.

Alan's dad was always saying that!

"I thought it would be nicer for us to talk here," the man said. "Instead of that boring lab."

Alan nodded. Actually he thought the lab was okay, but they didn't serve milkshakes there.

"So Alan." The man leaned forward. "I'm going to ask you some questions."

Alan was nervous but not surprised. Both his dad and his mom had told him to answer any questions the people at the lab might ask him. It was one of the rare times that they seemed to agree on something.

"Okay."

"What grade are you in?"

"Grade zero."

"You mean kindergarten?" The man smiled. "Do you know what a zero is?"

Alan smiled back. "It's the nothing before the number one. My dad explained it to me."

The man pushed the brim of his hat back and looked thoughtful. "Do you like your dad, Alan?"

Alan looked at the man with his most serious expression.

"My dad is a scientist. He's the smartest man in the world."

"I'm a scientist, too. Did you know that?"

Alan was too impressed to say anything. A scientist who also knew where to get these super-good milkshakes? Maybe the man in the grey felt hat was as smart as his dad.

"This next question is very important, Alan…"

The man looked Alan straight in the eye.

"…what's your favourite colour?"

"Green."

"Liar."

Alan felt his cheeks get hot. If another kid had just called him a liar, Alan would have yelled at him and called him a liar right back. Instead he decided that it was a good idea to drink some more chocolate milkshake.

"Blue used to be your favourite colour," the man said. "You said green because you don't know what your favourite colour is."

No!

Alan was breathing really hard. His heart was pounding.

The man took something soft and small out of his coat pocket. It had skin like a washcloth with flippers and one eye and a big smile. Whatever it was, most of it was coloured blue.

"Do you recognize this?"

Alan was really dizzy and thought he might barf all over the nice shiny table.

"It's your old friend, Mr. Whale." The man put the blue thing on the table.

Alan shuddered.

"Your father said that it was your very first toy. He got it for you when were just two weeks old."

Alan covered his mouth with both hands. He really didn't want to puke in public.

"We made some changes to Mr. Whale a while back." The man tapped the toy and a spark shot out between his finger and Mr. Whale's big smile.

Alan was scared.

"You used to take Mr. Whale to bed with you every night."

Really, really, really scared.

"Do you remember the colour that your bedroom walls were?

Alan was about to answer but the man interrupted him.

"Before your mother painted them green?"

Scared!

"They were blue," the man said. "Just like Mr. Whale."

Alan started to cry. He hated that. Big boys don't cry where other people can see.

The man with the grey hat looked like he might start crying too. "It's okay," he said. "I want to convince you that it's okay to like blue again."

2. Mom and Dad Get a Divorce on Mars

"Number 66."

The lady read the number off her clipboard.

Alan felt very cold and very silly. He was only wearing his

swimming trunks and they were last year's pair so they were about two sizes too small. At least all the other kids had also had to wear swimming trunks so they were just as embarrassed as Alan was.

"Arms out by your sides… stand up straight… point your toes towards me…"

There was a burst of light. Like a planet blowing up on *Lost in Space*.

"He closed his eyes!" the photographer said.

"Doesn't matter," the lady with the clipboard said. "We're just after basic growth trends."

The photographer sighed and twisted a knob on his camera.

"You know," he said. "Just because this is a scientific project doesn't mean that we have to abandon all aesthetic standards."

Scientific project? Alan remembered what his dad had said: "This is part of the greatest scientific adventure in human history."

Alan was very impressed when his dad said stuff like that.

They were painting a model of a Lunar Excursion Module (LEM): "On the surface, the study is about tracking how children's bodies change as they grow up." His dad brushed in some yellow lights on the LEM windows.

Alan wished he could paint models that well.

"That's a worthy undertaking in itself," his dad continued. "But I know that what that team is *really* looking for is *much* further reaching."

"That's a pipe dream!"

Alan's mom dropped her textbooks on the dining room table with a very loud *'thump!'* that was not an indoor sound. She dropped herself into a chair and opened one of the books.

"What's a pipe-dream, dad?" Alan wondered if it had something to do with plumbing.

"A silly fantasy." His mom answered the question.

His dad didn't say anything. He just shook his head and started dabbing silver paint on the legs of the LEM.

"You can step down now," the lady with the clipboard said.

Alan got off the platform and started walking towards the door.

"Oh look at you!" the lady cried. "You have marks all over your back!"

Alan turned his head around as far as it would go and could just make out some crisscross patterns on his right shoulder.

"You were leaning up against the measurement grid," the lady said.

"I was?" Alan had been too nervous to notice.

"Brian, this is so cute!" the lady said to the photographer. "You have to take a picture!"

"Hold still, kid." The photographer turned Alan around so he could get a good shot of the marks on Alan's back. "I have to take this shot before it fades."

Alan was relieved to hear that the marks would go away.

The lady with the clipboard smiled at Alan. "Do you know why we have you up against that grid?"

There was another big flash of light.

"The grid lets us make very exact measurements of your body," the lady said. "That lets us do a quantitative analysis of how your body grows."

Quantitative analysis?

Alan decided that when he got home he would find the dictionary and look up the meaning of those words.

A few weeks after Alan had been accepted into the next phase of the Program, he and his dad went to the University Technology Show to celebrate.

Every February the Engineering Department would take over the Student Union building and some of the hangars from the Agriculture Department and put out all kinds of cool stuff for everyone to see. Like a microwave projector that let you direct radio signals anywhere you wanted to, or a laser gun that let you melt Mickey Mouse balloon heads or even a machine that let you make alien music just by waving your hands in front of an antenna.

"Over here, son."

His dad wanted to show him something.

The engineering students had turned one of the storage hangars into a huge Hall of Models along with some 3D murals of the city from the air. Alan hoped that he could keep the goggles.

Some of the models were pretty ordinary like buildings or trains or tractors and while Alan admired the detail and how realistic the models were—they were kind of boring.

They also had models of stuff you didn't see every day—like rockets and fighter jets and satellites—most of them were hanging from the ceiling at weird angles, like action poses in the Marvel comics that his parents didn't like him to read.

Then his dad took him to a huge model. It was about the size of a real tractor, and very complicated.

Alan couldn't figure out what it was.

It had three huge funnels; each one was about four times the size of Alan's head. They looked a little like the back end of a Saturn V booster.

"Are those rocket engines, Dad?"

His dad looked pleased.

"Most powerful rocket engines ever designed."

The engineering students had put some orange lights inside each funnel to make it look like there was some kind of energy inside the funnels. His dad pointed at the lights.

"Those are the controlled fission reactions—like an H-Bomb going off every 10 seconds—but in a way that pushes forward," he said.

An H-Bomb? Even Alan knew that was pretty powerful.

"That force will make a spacecraft travel faster and further than anything ever built."

Alan read a word stenciled in big letters on the side of the model:

Orion.

"Is that like the constellation?" he asked.

"It's also the name of the engine."

His dad had a funny look on his face; Alan couldn't tell if his dad was happy or sad.

"Orion is what will take you into deep space."

Alan was still dressed in his swimming trunks, but now he had his running shoes on, a shiny necklace with a card that had his number printed on it, and three red rubber circles glued to his skin.

One circle was glued to his chest, one on his ribs and the last one was stuck to his tummy.

"Those are electrodes," the man in the lab coat said as he took Alan by the hand and led him down a corridor.

There were tiles and pipes everywhere. Alan wondered how far under the university they were.

"I'll explain what the electrodes are for once we've got you set up."

Alan wondered what they were going to do but he was pretty sure it wouldn't hurt. Well, not for very long anyway.

The man opened a blue door and they walked into a room.

For a second Alan wondered if he had walked into a giant

kaleidoscope filled with millions of boys and scientists—but then he realized they were just in a room where all the walls were mirrors.

"Could you step onto the treadmill?" the man said.

Alan climbed up onto the big rubber strip.

That made the man in the lab coat happy.

"That's great, sport."

Then the man wheeled over something that reminded Alan of the lights and drills from Dr. Burnham's office. Dr. Burnham was Alan's dentist. Except instead of drills there were about three hundred wires hanging from it.

Alan decided that wires were probably better than drills.

The man pulled a few of those wires down and clipped the ends to the electrodes glued onto Alan.

"We use the electrodes to measure your heart and your breathing," the man said.

Before Alan could ask why they needed to measure his heartbeat and breathing, the man put a rubber clip on Alan's nose and stuck a big plastic tube in his mouth.

"We need to control how much oxygen you get," the man said. "Nothing for you to worry about."

Alan started to worry.

"Hang on to the rail."

The big rubber sheet started to move and Alan was forced to start walking. The man left the room and all Alan could see were millions and millions of reflections of a small boy hanging onto a rail with a thick tube and lots of wires stuck to him and taking some very big steps.

Alan heard someone calling out:

"…five… four… three… two… one… zero! Check readings!"

There was a dial on the rail. The numbers rolled by and showed him how many steps he'd taken. Every 100 steps that voice would start up again:

"…five… four…"

The rubber sheet went faster and Alan had to run. Alan wasn't the best runner in his class, and he hoped he didn't trip and fall down.

"…three… two…"

The lights in the room got dimmer and the mirrors on the walls turned into windows and Alan could see a couple of dozen other kids. All of them were running on their own treadmills.

"…one… zero! Check readings!"

Somehow Alan knew that it was very important for him to try and run faster than all those other kids.

The big exhibit in the Hall of Models wasn't a model at all. It was a *real* Mercury space capsule. It was the one that took Alan Shepard into space.

Alan could remember when he watched that launch when he was only five years old. He thought it was really neat that he and America's first astronaut had the same name.

Alan asked his dad if he could have a space capsule like his namesake. So his dad put a big furnace box in the garage and laid one of the kitchen chairs on its back. Then they got an extension cord and put the portable TV next to the chair. The final touch was a used crash helmet that his dad got from his lab. It had a NASA sticker on the front.

"There you go," his dad said. "Your very own interplanetary exploration vehicle."

As Alan watched that tiny grey screen and the small heroic rocket push its way into the sky—Alan really did believe that he was an astronaut hurtling off into space.

"Some day, kid…"

Alan emerged—breathless, clutching his helmet—from the furnace box.

"…it will be your turn."

His dad smiled.

They were standing in a long line waiting to see the Mercury capsule. Alan squinted his eyes and could imagine that all the people in their parkas and winter hats were actually astronauts wearing helmets and space suits.

"There's something I should tell you, Alan."

Everyone in the line, including him and his dad, were all waiting to get on board a huge starship.

"This is kind of important."

The starship had giant atomic engines, like the Orion but five thousand times bigger.

"Your mother and I have decided that it would be a good idea…"

Who knew where those incredible rocket engines would take them? Mars? Saturn? Pluto?

"…if we lived away from each other for a while."

Alpha Centauri? The Andromeda Galaxy?

"Just until we can work things out."

The very edge of the universe?

"Of course you'll stay with your mother, but you can come and visit me at the lab whenever you like."

When they finally got to the capsule Alan was surprised by how small it was. It looked like the astronaut would have to be the size of a kid to get inside.

"Thrust efficiencies," his dad explained. "You can only send up small people if you want to make the best use of your fuel."

Alan decided that was the most important thing that he had learned that day.

3. The Psionic Man

Alan was working on his latest comic strip.

The paper was taped to the drawing board and he had his Radiograph pens laid out so he could ink in the pencil lines he had drawn in the day before.

It was three in the morning and it was a school night.

Alan knew he should be in bed.

He just didn't feel like sleeping.

It was going to be a great comic. *Ludwig Jones: The Psionic Man.* Lost brain-worker from the 27th century who channeled his frontal lobes to navigate giant intergalactic-spanning starships.

Alan was particularly pleased with the way he'd drawn the starship. He'd put the geodesic domes along the spine of the main structure—a good distance from the main engine complex to protect the crew from accidents and potential radiation leaks.

Alan wished he could live in a geodesic dome instead of the very rectangular three bedroom apartment his mother had moved them into.

Just wasn't going to happen.

He'd gotten a letter from his dad yesterday. Well, Alan had gotten a postcard stuck inside the very thick letter of legal documents that his dad had sent to his mom.

"Sorry, sport..."

Alan would never get used to his dad trying to sound all casual and super-friendly.

"...just don't have the cash to get you down here this summer."

Alan wondered if this new tone was the influence of dad's latest girlfriend. He started sketching in the big explosion that filled up most of the central panel.

They shut down the Orion Project two years ago and his dad and about one hundred thousand other scientists and engineers suddenly found themselves without very much to do.

So what happens to Ludwig Jones is that he's at the far end of the starship with a lot of the other telepaths who are using their brains as computers to steer that big chunk of steel and glass through sidereal space.

Something goes wrong (maybe the starship is badly designed, maybe one of the telepaths has a lousy attitude...) and the engines blow up.

Now Dad was somewhere in the southern United States, selling vacuum cleaner parts and "living on commission", as one of his postcards put it. Alan wasn't completely sure what that meant but it seemed to involve his dad not having very much money most of the time.

Alan wasn't old enough to get a job of his own so all there was to live on was what his mom got from selling the house and what she made from teaching first years at the new university.

Which of course was located in a new city.

Alan was pretty happy with how he was rendering this explosion. It needed to look totally thermonuclear—couldn't be a trace of an oxygen-based detonation. No smoke or flames. Absolutely no sound effects.

Comic book tradition dictated a massive "KRAKABOOOOOMMMM!" or "WHAROOOOOOMMMMM" or even just a humble "THOOM!" But Alan was going to maintain his scientific integrity. Space was airless so there was no medium to carry sound or wacky sound effects.

This disaster would be silent.

Alan hadn't seen his dad in almost two years. Some phone calls on his birthdays. Christmas, too, except that his mom had to make the call. And those stupid post cards. Some of them had cheques paper-clipped to them.

Most of them not.

And the money wasn't enough to be particularly useful. Maybe that was unfair. There was usually enough money to get a haircut (to make his mom happy) and to buy some inks so he could draw his comic strips.

Alan's Radiograph pens were the most expensive things he owned. His mom bought them when she sold the house.

Now Alan had to do the shading on the falling astronauts. Ludwig Jones survived because he was doing a safety drill and he was wearing a pressure suit when the explosion happened. That wasn't as lucky as it sounded because the force of the explosion was so powerful that it threw all the telepaths across time as well as space.

The new city was pretty much a dump as far as Alan was concerned. There were only three movie theatres, two record stores and one bookstore except for the really tacky one in the Zeller's mall and the really boring one at the university. In addition, Alan had zero friends at the new high school.

Ugh.

The new high school. As if the old one wasn't bad enough.

So after the big space accident, Ludwig Jones landed in a small town in Saskatchewan in the year 1933 and none of his technology works except for his Harvard-9 surgically attached AI system which can't offer any useful information and is consistently rude to him. All Jones has is his limited telepathic abilities to search out his fellow psionic astronauts in their different time streams and try to get back to the 27th century.

Alan was pleased with how well he had captured the expression of Ludwig Jones' panic as the protagonist got sucked down a raging time vortex.

Alan felt he'd had something of a fall himself. With the Program gone he wasn't particularly special anymore and he wasn't used to being a regular kid.

All the testing and training stopped pretty soon after they closed the hangar doors on the real Orion engines.

Most of the tests, anyway.

A few of them dragged on while the desperate researchers scrambled around for alternative sponsors and used up the last of the Program's original funding.

The last set of tests were actually some of Alan's favourites.

They would hook up about two dozen little electrodes to Alan's scalp and he'd lie down on a not very comfortable bed in a dark room while they took readings of his brain waves.

The only pain in the butt part of the test was removing the electrodes. Alan had long hair then, and the glue they used to keep the electrodes in place would stick it together. It was like having twenty-four different wads of chewing gum in your hair.

But it was still worth it.

The incredibly cool part of the procedure was when they'd lower the lights even more and play electronic music. They'd also change the speed of the music to teach him how to create different brain wave patterns... and even control his breathing and his heart rate. It was sort of like having a super power but not really.

Halfway through his last test session, the grad student who was running the EEG equipment walked into the room. He didn't bother to turn on the light.

"Alan," the scientist-in-training said. "Can we talk?"

"Sure," Alan said as he stared at the dim rectangles of the ceiling tiles. "I'm not doing very much right now."

The grad student laughed a little. "Alan, I don't know if you were aware of this, but we were able to extend the funding for this project by convincing the government that the results would advance our understanding of teenage drug abuse."

"First I've heard of it," Alan said. Well, it was!

The grad student sighed.

"We told them that we'd compare the brain waves of teenagers who used recreational substances with the brain waves of kids who don't."

"Sounds pretty smart," Alan said.

"But we have a problem, Alan," the grad student said. "And we hope you can help."

"I'll do what I can, sir."

Alan knew that it was uncool to go around calling people "sir", especially ones as young as this grad student. But his training went deep. Even though there wasn't really a Program anymore, you were respectful to the people in the Program.

"The problem is," the grad student said, "is that while we have a huge control group of non-using kids, we have hardly anybody for the experimental group."

Alan sat up. Slowly and carefully of course, because the wires were pulling on his hair.

"I don't quite understand," Alan said.

"The experimental group are the kids who use drugs. We need more of them."

"That's rough, sir," Alan said.

He could hear the needles on the EEG machine rattling around like crazy. Either he'd pulled too hard on the wires or something about this conversation was really bugging him.

"We all heard about your mom and dad splitting up," the grad student said. "You must be pretty broken up about that."

"I'm okay."

Suddenly Alan wasn't comfortable with the way this conversation was going. Especially when the grad student took something out of the pocket of his lab coat. It looked like a baggie full of dried dog poop.

"Everyone on the research team was wondering if you needed something to take the edge off."

"Uh…"

No.

This just wasn't going to happen.

Alan decided that he wasn't as loyal to the Program as he thought.

4. Shocking Experiments

Alan knew that it was a bad idea to have stayed up so late.

At least the comic book page was looking good. He really didn't want to go to school today, but he'd promised his mom that he wouldn't skip any more classes. It was a cold October so he decided that he ought to wear his parka. Alan knew that he could concentrate really hard and ignore the cold. But all that thinking would make him very tired for first period.

Sitting on the bus, squished up against all the other passengers, Alan decided that the parka was a good idea. He knew how he was going to get through the day. Today he would be an alien astronaut, wrapped up in an atmosphere suit, exploring the Planet Earth. Studying high schools in particular. In his atmosphere suit, or personalized force field (i.e. regular clothes) he would wander through the twisted metal-lined corridors and make mental notes of the bizarre creatures within. Alien Astronaut Alan could observe, record, report and even communicate (after a fashion) with said organisms.

But direct contact and understanding was impossibile.

Every piece of information, every image, and every emotion—would have to be filtered through his universal translator to ensure accurate understanding and to reject any stupid stuff that might contaminate his brain.

Social Studies class.

Oh god.

Alan had forgotten that it was Wednesday. He turned up the power level of his imaginary reality filter.

He didn't mind the *content* of Social Studies Class. He enjoyed learning more about the dreams and history of the tiny creatures that scurried about the surface of this spinning fragment of solar driftwood.

It was Mr. Neufeld, the teacher of his Social Studies class, that bugged Alan.

Mr. Neufeld had sideburns, somewhat long hair and granny glasses, and sometimes he wore an Apache scarf instead of a tie. Alan noticed that the groovy hair still didn't hide the bald spot on the top of Mr. Neufeld's head. Alan knew that he wasn't supposed to let that bother him, but somehow it did.

Maybe it was because it suggested that Mr. Neufeld was trying to fool people, make people think that he was something that he wasn't. His teacher was trying too hard to make students think he was just like them, was "cool", and was approachable, that he actually cared about them.

Let's get real here.

Kids are kids. Adults are adults.

Agreements were possible. Even a certain amount of cooperation. But true understanding?

As noted before, let's get real here.

Mr. Neufeld's smile looked fake. Same kind of smile that a man in a grey felt hat might have.

It turned out that he wouldn't have to listen to Mr. Neufeld very much that day. There was a big TV sitting on a trolley at the front of the classroom.

"Educational broadcast today," Mr. Neufeld said.

Alan kind of liked it when they rolled the TV in from the AV department. Sitting up there on those long chrome legs, it reminded him of the Martian tripods from *The War of the Worlds*. That was still one of Alan's favourite books.

The show was better than Alan expected. It starred the same actor who played Captain Kirk. *Star Trek* used to be one of Alan's favourite shows when he was younger. Nowadays it just irritated him. This time the actor was not a space explorer; instead he played a scientist who was studying human behaviour. The scientist set up an experiment where he would get two subjects. One subject was hooked up to electrodes (Alan knew all about that!) and was in a room where he or she would try to do page after page of math problems. The other subject was in another room where he or she had control of a small electrical generator. When the subject doing the math made a mistake a light would go on and the subject was supposed administer a shock. Each time the subject made another mistake, the voltage of the shock got higher.

More mistakes, more pain.

Alan knew a bit about that too.

At the end of the experiment the shocks were so powerful that the subject with the generator was getting scared that he or she was going to kill the other subject. But the Captain Kirk Scientist would tell the Shocker Subject to keep on pushing the button, even when the Shockee Subject was screaming out in pain. The worst part was when the Shockee Subject stopped saying anything.

"What do I do?" just about every Shocker Subject would ask.

"Carry on," the Captain Kirk Scientist would always reply.

95% of the Shocker Subjects wouldn't stop pressing the button—not even when they thought the Shockee Subject might be dead.

They did what they were told.

"Why?" they were asked later.

It was always some variation of "because the official-looking guy in the lab coat told me to."

The twist in the whole thing was that the experiment was a fake. The Shockee Subject was an actor and the electrical generator was just a dummy. The experiment was really about what people were willing to do to obey authority. The Captain Kirk Scientist wanted to find out if people would refuse to administer the shocks when they thought they were seriously hurting another person.

Hardly anybody did.

Alan was relieved that he had never been in an experiment like that.

At least not that he could remember.

Then something happened when the Captain Kirk Scientist was having an argument with his wife over dinner. He was trying to explain that he was really a good person and not a monster for doing all those terrible things to a bunch of innocent university students. The picture suddenly cut out and was replaced by three big letters.

"This is the Emergency Broadcasting System," a voice said. "NORAD reports that an unspecified number of intercontinental ballistic missiles, probably originating from the USSR, are on trajectories towards continental North America."

For a second Alan wondered if this was supposed to be a part of the show, but the production values were too different. When the cameras pulled away from the big letters they revealed a newsreader sitting behind a desk. The lighting was really bright and really bad, and the treble on the sound was way too high. The focus on the TV camera kept shifting between the sweat on the newsreader's forehead and the wads of dandruff nestled in his over-brylcreamed hair.

The transmission really did look like it was coming from some concrete bunker somewhere in the middle of nowhere.

"People of North America," the newsreader's voice was trembling. "We have reports of nuclear explosions, estimated at 18 to 22 megatons, over New York City, Washington D.C., Toronto and Chicago."

Everyone in the class, including Alan, turned at look at Mr. Neufeld, expecting him to say something.

Something hopefully reassuring.

Instead their teacher's face was like a mask.

Nothing to say.

No expression.

Might as well have been some papier mâché project from art class, thought Alan.

"If you have access to a civil defense shelter," the newsreader continued. "You must proceed there at once."

Alan knew what a civil defense shelter was but he also knew that there wasn't one within 500 miles of the school. Thanks for the briefing, Dad. At least Mr. Neufeld didn't look like he was going to make them do anything dumb like crawl under their desks and pull their shirts over their heads.

"We have reports of more missile impacts… Boston… Montreal… and some smaller cities…"

"Teacher?"

One of the younger students in the class raised her hand.

Mr. Neufeld ignored the student and kept watching the TV.

"…Atlanta… Buffalo… Hamilton…"

This was getting pretty bad, thought Alan. The class was getting really scared.

"…Ottawa… Detroit…"

Mr. Neufeld should do something.

"…Milwaukee… Little Rock…"

Somebody should do something!

"…Kansas City… Minneapolis…"

Alan started to feel a tingling in his left arm, then some sharp pains in his shoulder and neck.

"…Salt Lake City… Winnipeg…"

This was like some roll call of doom.

"…Saskatoon…"

Ouch.

That was getting way too close to home, thought Alan. He could barely see out of his left eye, it was all just sparkles.

"Mr. Neufeld," one of the other students said. "Shouldn't we go home or something?"

Alan's hearing was going all funny. The other student's voice was all echoey and tinny.

"…Calgary…"

There were lots of sparkles and then Alan couldn't see anything at all.

It didn't hurt as much as he thought it would when his head hit the floor.

5. Liking Blue

Melanie came to visit him at the hospital.

"How are you doing?" she asked.

"Pretty good." Actually with Melanie there, Alan felt really good. "They say I should be out of here in a week."

"That's great," Melanie said. "I didn't know you could get over a heart attack so fast."

Alan shrugged. "The doctors aren't sure what it was. For a while they thought it might have been a stroke."

"A stroke?" Melanie frowned. "Like when part of your brain explodes?"

"But now they don't think that was it either."

"So what do they think happened to you?"

Alan tried to look thoughtful. "Probably some kind of psychological shock caused by watching that fake broadcast."

"We have a new social studies teacher, Miss Kunst." Melanie smiled. "She's nice."

"What happened to Mr. Neufeld?"

"He's gone."

"Gone?"

"Maybe his brain exploded."

Sure, that was kind of a mean joke, but he and Melanie laughed anyway. Alan felt a little badly that Mr. Neufeld had probably lost his job, but come on! Did Mr. Neufeld seriously think that nobody in his class had ever heard Orson Welles' radio broadcast of *The War of the Worlds*? And what exactly were they supposed to learn from that experience anyway?

Anybody that stupid didn't deserve to be a teacher.

Alan was glad he'd kept up with his body control exercises.

After a while Melanie said she had to go. As she was leaving she gave Alan a stuffed toy to cheer him up.

"I got this downstairs at the gift shop," she said.

It was some kind of blue octopus. The toy would be a good companion to Mr. Whale.

And it was his favourite colour.

WURNING: BADE SEPLLING AHEED!

My mother was a red-hot typist who could do 90 words a minute easy, and she was equipped with her very own IBM Selectric typewriter. She ran a university philosophy department like a well-oiled machine and had enough energy to take on freelance assignments and do her own story and poetry writing in the evenings. I was only vaguely aware of it at the time, but when it came to manipulating words and meanings, my mother was truly awesome.

One of the greatest gifts my mother gave to me was offering to type my essays for me when I was an undergrad student. I am not a terribly good speller, and this failing manifests itself in a weird way: I don't usually have a lot of trouble with those complex multi-syllabic words, it's those simple frequently used words that trip me up. Mom was also great with formatting pages, and I have to admit handing in organized, well laid-out assignments does make a difference.

Unfortunately, the parent-with-a-typewriter strategy was not a viable long-term solution for me. Fate smiled again; I entered the working world just as personal computers appeared, and they had this wonderful software just for people like me:

Spell-check!

As we all know by now, spell-check is not perfect, but it has proven to be good enough to get me through life without too many problems. Having something good in my life is never enough for some reason, eventually I re-conceived this very useful thing into something very bad:

What if there was a form of spell-check for ideas? You might not even need a computer—you just download the program into your head and it automatically filters and vets everything you see, read, say or do. I know people who would love it if such a product was available.

Perhaps we already have such a thing.

THE PROGRESSIVE APPARATUS

Originally published in
On Spec magazine
Summer 1994, #17 Vol. 6 No. 2

It stands at the foot of my bed, a flickering wave of purple light spreading out from its third eye. The glow wakes me and I make out its shape in the tinted dark—thin arms folded over a plastic chest.

The Apparatus is probing my mind.

I push my head into the pillow. "Go away… please," I moan. "I thought you weren't supposed to cause undue pain and harassment."

The Apparatus shakes its head, which causes the purple beam to flash crazily off the bedroom walls. It smiles grimly. "You were only half-asleep. And you were mentally composing a story."

I exhale in exasperation and pull myself into a sitting position. "It was nothing," I sigh, "just a few thoughts."

"The probe indicates a clear story premise," the Apparatus replies as it leans toward me. The purple ray assumes a deeper, more intense tone. "This will be much easier if you tell me voluntarily," it says.

I reach for the glass of water sitting on the bedside table. "Okay, okay." I sip the lukewarm fluid. "Harmless thing really… maybe there's some redeeming social value."

The Apparatus stands back and puts its hands at its sides. "That might represent progress," it says.

I hold my hand over my eyes to block the stabbing purple light. "A confidence trickster arrives at a village in medieval times. He endears himself to the foolish mayor and uses a miniature glass steam engine to mystify the citizenry... they come to believe that he is a wizard, and he starts to take many advantages..."

"Yes?" I detect a tone of measured disapproval in the Apparatus' voice.

I continue anyway: "...until a kindly grandmother and a hard-working plowboy see through the deception. So they persuade the villagers to overthrow the trickster's mental domination." I set aside the empty glass and look hopefully at the Apparatus. "I think it's quite a responsible theme, everyday people working together to free their minds..." My voice trails off.

"Let's just think about that." The ray flicks off and its glassy third eye recedes back into its forehead. After a moment, the Apparatus shakes its head. "The premise scores well on theme, and the female gender assignment to an assertive character is noted, but your traditional religious heritage makes your story unacceptable."

"Why?" It really is too bad that this isn't a dream, I think.

The figure at the foot of the bed explains: "The glass steam engine could be interpreted as a metaphor for an e-meters, divining rods and crystals—devices used in new age therapies."

My eyes have adjusted to the darkness and I can see an expression of mild sympathy on the Apparatus' face.

"Considering your childhood training in conventional Christianity, this story could be viewed as a cloaked attack on minority religions."

"Shit!" I groan and fall back onto my pillow. "I was just playing with a few ideas."

There is an edge in the Apparatus' voice: "That is understood."

Then it leaves.

Eventually I fall asleep and the Apparatus does not return that night. Apparently there were no more thoughts.

* * *

I'm at work at my computer. The Apparatus glides over to my side and looks at the glowing screen.

"Your tea's gone cold," it observes.

"Yes." I continue typing.

"Would you like another cup?"

Concern over my physical well-being, I muse. Typical.

"No, thanks. I ought to cut down on the caffeine."

I save the file and start up the printer. A tiny sail of paper unfolds to the sound of miniature metallic screams.

"How's the commercial going?" asks the Apparatus.

"You should know." I push my hands into my pockets and notice my reflection in the teacup; a white, stubble-smeared face in a stagnant gray pool.

The Apparatus scans the illuminated words on the screen. It laughs mildly. "Then one would venture that it was coming along fine."

"Safety belt public service messages are hard to screw up."

It looks thoughtful for a moment. "You'd be surprised," the Apparatus says finally. "But in your case it looks like a progressive example of the new male acting as the compassionate caregiver."

I massage my ashen face with both hands. I won't give the damn thing the satisfaction of seeing me cringe.

The Apparatus smiles and shrugs. "Or it could be interpreted as penitence for decades of reckless driving by men." It turns on its heel and walks down the hall.

I tear a sheet of paper out of the printer and stare at my own words. I pick up a pencil and start making marks on the rough manuscript. I force myself to remain calm. I keep my face blank.

* * *

An Apparatus rarely explains itself. It took several months to work out the events that led to its arrival. My moment of judgment must have come in a writing seminar last spring.

Our assignment was to present an outline for a feature-length screenplay.

"This one is inspired by that psychology study, 'When Prophecy Fails'," I said to my associates. "A small group of flying saucer cultists suddenly have a revelation that the world will soon be coming to an end. So they sell their homes, quit their jobs and wait for an alien spacecraft to pick them up before the planet explodes."

"I presume that the revelation is false?" asked another writer. "So your people are risking persecution and humiliation?"

I nodded my head.

Someone else looked in my direction: "The situation is a little vague, how are you going to drive the story?"

There's another voice: "Yeah, where's the dramatic tension?"

Feeling pretty clever, I answered: "I'm going to add an historical ticking clock. The cultists have their revelation during the Cuban Missile Crisis."

"So they think the end will be in a nuclear war?"

"Yes, as did a lot of other people at the time," I replied. "The sense of urgency will be heightened as they watch the news coverage on TV."

There was a good nod factor around the table. Most of them saw where the story was going.

"Nice touch," the seminar leader said. "It structures the plot and gives your characters some credibility and sympathy."

"Who are the viewpoint characters?" somebody asked.

I flipped through the notes in front of me: "Two residents in a mid-west trailer park. One's a young housewife; the other is an older widow, who's also a practicing mystic. They're examples of seekers, people looking for something more meaningful in otherwise empty lives..."

"What makes you think you're qualified?" It was a hard voice from the far end of the table. The reflection of the fluorescent lights on the speaker's glasses only partly obscured a stare of steady hate.

This was a surprise. "I beg your pardon?"

The voice of my critic stayed even, but unfortunately I now had a good look at the eyes: "You can't write female characters."

This was even more of a surprise. "How's that?"

"It just isn't possible. You'll contaminate them with male bias."

I briefly considered some kind of speech about freedom of expression and the responsibility of a writer to explore as many different viewpoints as possible. But then I looked into those glass-covered eyes and I changed my mind.

This may have been a fatal act of cowardice. "Let's just drop it, shall we?" I said.

The other speaker made a curt note on a piece of paper and we moved on to the next presentation.

* * *

I turn the doorknob.

"Going out?" The Apparatus looks up from the television. Sometimes it likes to watch the afternoon reruns.

"Going to the mall… to photocopy the script." I hold up the file folder for the Apparatus to see. "The seat belt thing. Remember? The one you reviewed?"

The Apparatus returns its gaze to the giggling heads on the gray screen. Its feet sag into small puddles on the carpet; it is entering a state of relaxation.

"Hurry back," it says.

I open the door.

* * *

Sometime after the workshop incident the Apparatus arrived in the mail.

Not knowing what it was, I opened the big brown envelope and the Apparatus poured itself out. It unfolded on my living room wall like an early morning shadow. A letter was enclosed in the envelope:

> "For your convenience, the Apparatus can be thought of as living software in real time and space. It is animated, self-aware information, designed to guide your creative development into areas which compensate for the limitations of your particular cultural and genetic heritage."

The Apparatus pulled itself off the wall and billowed into a three-dimensional figure. It stood before me. Twin obsidian spheres pushed themselves outward and set themselves at the front of its newly formed face.

> "The Apparatus is a humane mechanism for protecting society against the perpetuation of stereotypes and unjust expressions."

A soft gash opened up. The Apparatus smiled.

* * *

"What an ass."

"What a great ass."

Two teenage women are looking at a movie poster outside the mall cinema. The poster captions say something about kickboxing and "bazooka revenge" (whatever that is) and the main illustration highlights two near naked men locked in passionate combat. Their musculature is almost architectural in proportion.

I walk toward the printer's shop.

"What a tight ass…" I hear in the distance.

A friend of mine wrote those words and helped develop the promotional campaign. One day she invited me to one of those expensive Yorkville cafes. Public service copy doesn't pay much, so I accepted.

I had heard that she had been given an Apparatus and I wondered how she seemed to cope so well. Eventually I asked about the movie promotion:

"How did you get away with such shameless exploitation of the human body?"

Georgina smiled and shredded a piece of chicken with her fork. "My Apparatus suggested it; apparently my working on the promotion represented an important 'structural adjustment of values'." She inspected the meat impaled on the end of her fork. "Also, the posters encourage women to view men as sexual objects, as men have seen women for centuries. This is supposed to represent greater personal freedom for women."

I gazed at my bowl of soup. It had gone cold. "I didn't know that our values were being adjusted with such precision," I said. "It just sounds like tit for tat to me."

Georgina laughed. "Or pecs for tits."

Her words made me shudder and I suddenly wondered if my Apparatus might have followed me to the restaurant. Sometimes they do that, if they think something might be up.

"I'm glad you said that," I muttered. Could they hear us?

Georgina took a long drink of wine before she spoke: "I liked my original copy a lot better."

I pushed my spoon through the cloudy fluid in my soup bowl. "Can you talk about it?"

"Why not?" She laughed bitterly. "I wanted to feature the heroism of soldiers under fire. Self-sacrifice, initiative and patriotism in extreme conditions. I researched the hell out of it."

"They rejected that?" I struggled to keep my voice down. "But they love patriotism."

"My Apparatus said that the theme reinforced militaristic stereotypes."

A waiter led a group of shoppers to their table. I thought I saw a dark shape lurking by the door...

"Well, go figure," I said carefully.

My friend laughed again. There is a touch of craziness in her voice. "Yeah, they are subtle tools, aren't they? They move in very mysterious ways."

I nodded my head. Sometimes it is good to look like you agree.

* * *

When I get back from the mall I hear the sound of paper tearing. I run to my study.

The Apparatus is sitting at my desk. It removes a page from the desk drawer, scans it and sets it aside. It picks up another page, looks at the text, and starts to tear the paper into thin strips. It is a slow and deliberate act.

"Don't, please!" I gasp.

"Be quiet," says the Apparatus. It methodically tears the paper strips into small white rectangles. "Your manuscript is irresponsible."

The page has been reduced to a fat wad of paper. The Apparatus pops the wad into its mouth. I watch in confusion as the damned thing chews up my work. I notice that it has grown teeth for this task. It swallows.

"This work will be destroyed for you." The Apparatus burps. A perverse affectation? I doubt that living software has trouble digesting.

"Why?" I ask.

The Apparatus holds out the next page of the manuscript. The page is covered with red markings: underlinings, crosses and spelling corrections.

"How?" replies the Apparatus. "How did you ever think you could get away with it?" It points to the red scratches on the page. "When you put each of the marked words in sequence, they form sentences."

My body sags against the doorframe. I feel nauseous and heavy, as if I was suddenly transformed into a sack of lead. “No,” I protest feebly. “I’m just having a little trouble with my new spell check program, so I have to…”

My alibi is cut short by the sound of crumpling paper. The Apparatus looks directly at me as it crams another fistful of words into its mouth.

“Okay,” I confess. “It’s a play.”

“What’s it about?” the Apparatus speaks with its mouth full.

“A group of teenage students discover that one of their teachers is conducting role-playing experiments on them during their classes.”

There is a rippling on the Apparatus’ forehead; the third eye is threatening. “Without consent?” The tearing continues. “Perhaps if another sort of person had written this. But you are incapable of writing such stories.”

I notice that I’ve sunk all the way to the floor. I’m bent over like I have no spine. What can I say to stop it?

“It was naive to even attempt this,” proclaims the Apparatus. “Even if you were allowed to complete the work, no one would perform it, no one would publish it.”

I study the cracks and stains on my hardwood floor.

The Apparatus keeps on reading, tearing and chewing. I have a sudden and perverse thought: I hope the damn thing is absolutely right. I hope that for every censored story, somebody gets a job, and for every suppressed idea, some innocent person is freed from prison.

I could share this with the Apparatus, but I don’t. Really I have nothing to say.

There is nothing to say.

ON IMPOSSIBLE SEQUELS

For many years I was air-commuting on a very regular basis between Toronto and Asia. My most frequent destination was Singapore, which is a fascinating place.

When I was first sent there in the early 1990s, William Gibson had just published his article about Singapore called "Disneyland with the Death Penalty"[2] in *Wired* magazine. My initial impressions of the city-state in question did not agree with his; the architecture and the exhibits at Disneyland were way better. By the second decade of the 21st Century, the situation has changed dramatically—there are some amazing museums and buildings in Singapore.

What I first noticed in Singapore, and kept on noticing, was the prevalence of social messaging in the public sphere. Before I go any further, I need to mention the following:

1. I usually have no problems with public service announcements. I agree that it is often a very good thing to remind people to vote, to suggest they get their eyes tested on a regular basis, or let them know there are mental health resources out there, and so forth.

2. The majority of Singaporeans I met were all positive, intelligent, well-informed, and good to work with. They really didn't seem to be people who needed any extraordinary help or interventions in navigating their way through their daily lives.

But I really have to say, some of the public service announcements I encountered in Singapore seemed pretty bizarre to me. For example:

---

2 I've always thought this was an odd thing to say about Singapore. Both California and Florida (where Disneyland and Disneyworld are respectively located) also have capital punishment. Disneyland already has the death penalty, why drag Singapore into it?

- Remember to be friendly and smile every once in a while.
- It can be a good idea to talk to your employees without yelling at them.
- Don't spit in public places like bus stops and restaurants.

Okay, we could be looking at cultural differences and some unique social conditions here, but even so, these ones just make you stop and blink:

- If you can afford it, why not have that third kid?
- Have you ever considered marrying for love?

I wasn't brave enough to ask any of the Singaporeans I knew if they took these PSAs seriously or not. People can be very touchy about topics like matrimony, procreation, or saliva. Instead I retreated into my science fiction imagination and starting considering what kind of society would have people who would find such social messages: a) interesting, and b) useful. Which led me to write a story that was a sequel to a story where a sequel just didn't seem possible.

...AND THE RETROGRADE MENTOR

Originally Published in:
On Spec magazine
Fall 1998

This is how to read a book. Get one of those small squarish things off the shelf. Usually a book is anywhere from five to 30 centimeters thick and sometimes has a picture on the outside. Hold the book in your hands and fold your hands open. Those sheets of paper are fastened at one end so they won't fall out. The sheets of paper are called pages. Now the little lines of squiggles are called sentences and they are made up of something called words. You don't need to worry about that, just take the book over to a friend who knows how to read. Now you can begin...

Perhaps I was wrong. There may be a few things to talk about after all.

The Apparatus returned a few days ago. One morning it coiled its way out of the grid of my computer speakers.

"What are you doing here?" I asked. I'm not worried because I can't see how the Apparatus can hurt me anymore.

The Apparatus forms a pool on my desk and raises its head and shoulders. It hasn't a mouth yet so it can't reply.

"I've retired from writing," I continue. "I only do numbers these days." Numbers can be great for staying out of trouble. They seem to have no nuance, no dangerous hidden meanings. So I now rearrange huge patterns of ones and zeroes and transmit them to be evaluated by intelligences thousands of miles away. If these binary packages ever assumed the form of a message it certainly was through no action on my part.

The Apparatus forms a monochromatic stream and pours itself off the desk and assumes a standing position on my carpet.

"It's time for you to come out of retirement," it says.

Like I said, I guess there must be more to say after all.

This is how to drive your car. First, go outside of your house. That big thing with the three-to-six wheels is the car. Next, walk over to the car, take hold of one of the handles and pull. That motion should open the door...

"Something about you is different," I say. "Sort of out of focus."

The Apparatus is pacing about my living room, looking for somewhere to sit probably. It may be out of luck, I threw away its favourite chair years ago.

But to my surprise and delight, I find that my old tweed jacket still fits. I haven't needed a jacket recently, this is the first time in years that I've considered walking further than half a block from my house.

The Apparatus just looks annoyed as it comes to rest on the end of my sofa.

"I know," I cry with delight. "You're very old software now. How come they didn't upgrade you?"

The Apparatus sighs. "I was retired, too. There's relatively little need to protect the community from dangerous creative expressions these days."

I open the door. "Because there's relatively little expression in the community?"

The Apparatus gets up and follows me outside.

"That may be true," it says. "But you might want to be careful how you say that..."

I think the Apparatus was trying to sound threatening. It wasn't.

"I still don't see why you want to go out," the Apparatus continued as we walked across the porch.

"Research," I reply. "I'm a little out of touch and I like to get my facts straight."

The Apparatus' pseudo-mouth pulls down into a frown. It must suspect that I'm telling the truth, there isn't much written or visual information available online anymore, just those cryptic binaries flashing past.

"Don't be too long." This actually sounds more like a request than a command.

Out on the front lawn I see that my neighbour is practicing his astral levitation. He's about twelve feet in the air, sitting on a bamboo platform with a pair of big headphones clamped on his head. His eyes are closed and there's a tube extending from one of his nostrils. The tube leads to a large transparent cylinder lying on the grass. I estimate that the cylinder contains enough nutrients to keep my neighbor going for several days.

Then I notice a stretch of dirty fur in the shadow of the platform. My neighbor's cat has starved to death.

I call over to the Apparatus and point at the dead cat: "Can you call the robot service to come over and clean this up?"

The Apparatus just scowls and stomps back into the house. Its feet make a soft sucking sound as it moves across the porch.

As I sit in the autobus, I'm thinking about my psychically ascending neighbor. How does he relieve himself up there? Maybe working that out is also part of his astral training. Or maybe I should get the robot service to deal with that too.

When I get to the library, I check in the mailbox and take out a set of keys and a flashlight. The keys are pretty rusty. I open the door, turn on the flashlight and start my research.

> *This is how to take the right drugs: check the coloured dots tattooed on your left wrist. Now match the colours of the dots with the colours of your pills. Now count the number of dots on your wrist. That's the number of pills you should take. If you have trouble with the counting, ask a friend…*

For the first time in years, I get an email that actually has words in it:

"Love your new stuff. Let's do lunch."

I haven't heard from Sybil in a very long time. I haven't seen anything that she's written in a long time either.

Who is writing these days? I ponder this as the autobus approaches her warehouse.

"My body is now my art," Sybil explains as she holds out her glistening blue-scaled hand.

I have to admit, it is quite a remarkable hand in many ways. Over dinner she shows me how she can drink wine through the tiny mouths set at the end of her finger tips; tiny gray tongues lap at the amber fluid. Later on she shows me how she is able to adjust the temperature and texture of her palms and fingers at will. She's able to touch me in some truly remarkable ways.

We don't actually leave the warehouse, but Sybil's version of cocooning is very entertaining. She shows me her gallery. Works in progress; all of them in the same medium: herself.

Sybil has a very tasteful intelligent lighting system that showcases the contents of the fluid sacs in some very evocative ways.

Her insect self with its jeweled exoskeleton, her ultra-ectomorphic self, elegant spindle-limbs, that could only stand upright on the moon; even a bioluminescent shelf that didn't need any lighting. There were dozens more variations in aesthetic genetic engineering.

"Words can only mediate experience," Sybil says as she teases the pulsing abdomen of a headless clone. "Flesh is a much more direct medium, what people can relate to these days."

Sybil hadn't changed much really. She was the first person I knew to break into television, the first to write for multimedia, and the first to nail down that screenwriting contract in Hollywood. She always knew the market, knew popular taste, which seemed to be a little carnivorous right now.

But Sybil was pleased that I was writing again. She'd heard some of my recent work and said she appreciated my direct language and my "accessibility" to a popular audience.

It was a good first date, unusual but good.

This is what you should do when you want to have non-lethal/non-toxic sex. Lick the genitals of your partner(s). Lick them for a long time and use as much saliva as possible. Try to get as much area as wet as possible. You need to do this because your saliva has been chemically

> *changed so that it will form a thin layer of indestructible plastic over your partner(s) genitals. This layer will protect you from any sexually transmitted diseases (STDs) that your partner(s) might have.*
>
> *Your partner(s) should also be licking your genitals at this time. This will make things even safer because now there will be a thin plastic layer that will keep you from passing on any STDs to your partner(s).*
>
> *Of course, if everybody is doing a lot of licking you might not need to continue much further…*

It had been quite a month. I had a new job, I'd traveled outside my neighbourhood for the first time in this millennium and even had a female friend now. I still thought of Sybil as female, although I did have to make my definitions a little more flexible. Life was much more interesting.

The Apparatus was the one who seemed to be living in the past. It kept looking over my shoulder, reading my drafts, frowning, but never seeming to find anything objectionable. This must have been frustrating for it.

I didn't care. I wasn't terribly committed to my work at that point.

But one morning, the Apparatus walks into my office, holding a print-out in one of its jointless fingers.

"You can't submit this draft," the Apparatus said. It was going a little further out of focus, perhaps because it was nervous about how I might react.

"What's the problem?" I say calmly.

The Apparatus points to a section of the manuscript: "The language is too abstract, the word "genitals" in particular is too technical."

"But I chose that word deliberately," I reply. "Genitals is to the point and describes both male and female body parts in an objective gender-neutral manner."

Lines of irritation flicker across the Apparatus' face. "But half your audience won't know what you're talking about. They're just as likely to start sucking their toes."

That's pretty witty for an Apparatus, I think.

I lean back in my chair and put on my most thoughtful expression. "So you think I should use something more accessible? Better known words? Something like "cock" or "pussy"?

The Apparatus scowls at me. "Those words are sexist and offensive."

I suddenly think of Sibyl and wonder how you define sexism when people are inventing their own genders. But I'm enjoying this, it's like the arguments we used to have years ago, but this time I'll bet that I get to win.

I continue: "Why don't I try something more evocative? Use some tried and true adjectives?"

"Such as?" The Apparatus is rightly suspicious.

"How about thunder-muscle or steamy-hot love tunnel?"

The Apparatus glares at me. There's a rippling in its forehead and I realize that it's trying to use its third eye on me. But nothing emerges. It probably doesn't have enough power anymore.

"This is a very serious matter," the Apparatus says as it turns away from me. "Thousands of people could die if they can't understand your text."

I smile. "I'll keep working on it. What about some really basic terms: pee-pee? Woo-woo?"

The Apparatus puts the print-out on my desk and leaves. For the next few days whenever I see the Apparatus I ask it about different terms to describe a penis and a vagina. Love-log was my personal favorite. Eventually the Apparatus gives in and I submit the original draft.

Apparently I had also acquired a degree of celebrity. That was certainly the angle that Sybil was taking when she was introducing me to various people at her party.

"This man is just the hottest thing in literature," she would say. "You must have heard his work on those new public service audios. His latest is the one on cleaning your rectum. It is devastating in its clarity."

The man with compound eyes is impressed with this information. "Hey! You really helped me out in the can the other day!"

"My pleasure," I reply. Audios indeed, I think. Nobody reads anymore.

I've resolved to experience the party to the fullest. I admire all the bio-cosmetics I see and I ingest every drug that gets passed around. I realize that this may not be the most responsible behaviour but I tell myself that even if I damage my mind in some way, this probably won't hurt my writing.

But so far nothing seems to be having any effect.

"What a pity," Sybil says when I advise her of my condition. She tries to look sympathetic but I know that my biological behaviour is very gauche, like showing up for the Nobel Prize in a KISS T-shirt. She says something about wanting to comment on a friend's pigmentation pattern and disappears.

Now alone, I wander up to the catwalk and observe the orgy from a distance. The laser patterning from Sybil's lighting system catches the moisture off the glistening forms in some unique configurations. With the shadows and the quasi-human shapes, it starts to look like a Hieronymus Bosch theme park down there. The flesh mass writhes and converges and I can see that Sybil has become part of a spinal-fuse with what looks like a five-foot salamander and a woman with tentacles and rainbow skin.

Well, it was an interesting relationship while it lasted.

The sonic expressions are pretty interesting so I decide to stay for a while. Just before dawn, the robot trucks roll in and start hooking nutrient pipes into the new-born organism.

> *This is what you should do if you and your friends decide to evolve into a higher life form: plan ahead as much as possible. If you have any family, call 111 and arrange to have some robots look in on them after you're gone. Once you get to the party, dance your brains out, fuck anything that moves and drink/smoke/inject anything they give you. You don't have to worry anymore. You won't be going home.*

Months later I'm living in a warehouse of my own. I've left everything else behind except my computer and the Apparatus. I think I enjoy annoying it, and its nagging does keep me from missing deadlines.

Right now the Apparatus is standing at the doorway of my office.

"You brought more of them home, didn't you?" it says.

I turn away from the keyboard. "They were wandering around the lake shore. Their parents are gone."

"People will think you're doing something perverted."

I shrug. "In case you hadn't noticed, community standards have changed."

The Apparatus turns away from me. In the afternoon sun it looks almost transparent. Perhaps it has nothing to say.

I pick up my latest manuscript and go downstairs.

The children will have finished their lessons and the older ones will be setting out the supper meal.

For bedtime I will read them some new stories.

THE HERD OF ELEPHANTS IN THE ROOM

This final element in the Progressive Apparatus cycle does not offer a definitive solution to any of the issues the stories explore. But I will say that if we apply the long-established SF rule of "if this goes on…" to what's been raised in all three stories—we may find ourselves in some uncomfortable and even dangerous places in spite of our good intentions.

I feel a little guilty; as if I've pointed out that there's a herd of elephants into the room but I don't really have a plan for cleaning up after them.

Totally up for suggestions though.

...EXPERIENCE DENIAL THEN ACCEPTANCE

Originally published in:
The Collected Progressive Apparatus
2014

"Put down that bat! Don't crush that hat!

Sit down and let me tell you the story of the atomic mutating rat!"

"I don't understand what you've written here, but I know that it can't possibly be right."

The time is very near now. The Apparatus is finally dying.

"And I don't know who you are or anything about you, but I know you have nothing useful to contribute to this discussion!"

It raves and hallucinates every once in a while, revealing the core values of its programming in sometimes embarrassing ways.

"You're bad!" A voice wheezes across the room. "Stinky-head! Poo-poo head!"

A vague gray shadow flickers across the far wall of my study.

I close my journal and look around.

"What are you doing outside your hardware?" I ask. "You know that makes you disintegrate."

Well, somebody has to show concern.

The Apparatus collects in a small corner and darkens a little. It looks like a spot where I forgot to clean. Poor thing can't even manage basic shapes outside its monitor.

"Don't change the subject," it whispers. "What are you up to?"

I nod and truly wish I could say I had some exciting work on art or politics or sex in the works. A good argument might add some energy to its governing software. Cheer the thing up. But maybe it's not a good thing to show mercy at this time. I decide to tell the truth.

"Just some notes for another bed-time story," I reply.

"Just…" I sense the hurt in the Apparatus' voice. I don't know if it's disbelief or disappointment.

* * *

Millions and millions of years ago… just a little while after I was born in fact, the humans all lived in the towns and houses and the monsters lived in the dumps and swamps. Of course, in today's advanced age, exactly the opposite is true…

Karx, the elder (at least seventeen) was explaining something rather serious to me:

"Yeah, there's lots of consumables in the central zones but we just don't go there anymore."

"Why not?" I ask.

My audiences were complaining about the food and it was cramping my style.

Karx looked at me in that way that makes you very embarrassed about asking something extremely obvious.

"All those neighbourhoods have gone Experimental."

Karx turned his attention to my antique radio, and began to gently turn the tuning dial.

"So what? Just about everybody in the City is Experimental."

Karx wasn't being disrespectful; he was probably just looking for an excuse to stop looking at me like I was an idiot.

"Yeah," he agreed. "But in the Centrals, they aren't so Artistic." He sniffed and looked back at me. "About two hundred Retros just west of Yonge Street. Mean looking knuckle-draggers."

Karx's only irritating habit was the fact that he was right all the time.

He was six when we'd met him wandering around the ruins of the Sherway Mall. He had about six months of eatables and game-data products in his back-pack and he knew what stores used to sell the hardware to process them.

When they asked him, he explained that his mother named him after getting neural implants that allowed her to read Das Kapital in less than 30 minutes.

"If you get caught out there..." Karx said to me. "...looking for dinner, you're gonna end up in the soup."

Shit. The downtown was full of cannibals.

"You sure?" Okay, I was old and an asshole. I had to ask.

"Gorky and Yukon found some skulls in a 7-11 down at Harbourfront." Inspiring age we were living in. Now the autonomous AIs were giving us the option to retro-evolve into pre-Neanderthal flesh-eaters.

Good plan, real progress on the urban-development front.

"Okay," I say. "You can borrow my truck and see what you can find over in Hamilton. There's some food generators over at Jackson Square you might be able to fire up."

"That was what we were thinking."

Of course. Karx turns and walks out of my study.

He wasn't being rude; the kid just doesn't like to waste time.

I watch his thin, slightly awkward form disappearing down the corridor. For some reason, perhaps out of respect for his now dead (?) absorbed (?) re-evolved (?) mother, he always wears red.

Glad we've got him.

A little later I turn on my oldest computer and ask the Apparatus about the social utility of having bands of homicidal neo-hominids wandering the streets.

I'd just boosted its power, so it looks a little better—sort of like a sketch Steve Ditko might have made for an early Spider-Man comic.

"It makes perfect sense," the jagged hole in the blank face says. "When citizens can pursue their freedom, absolutely, even down to choosing their own genotype, then we ensure the happy and cohesive integration of the entire community."

I can't help laughing. "You know that statement contains at least two completely contradictory concepts."

"Thank you," the Apparatus replies. "I'm feeling much better today."

* * *

> *Once upon a time, back in the days when time actually meant something, there was a beautiful princess who lived in a huge and fantastic castle. That was also back in the days when being a princess meant something and being beautiful meant something. But at least we still have the huge and fantastic castles.*

That signature architecture seems to be absolutely everywhere, doesn't it? The children… that doesn't sound right. The group? The community of young people? The growing cluster of living perpetual motion machines who happen to be camping out in my warehouse. Well, it really isn't mine anymore…

Anyway, the children have been very busy recently. Most of them have been painting some kind of mural in the main hall just below the big stage they've erected. When they first sketched out the shapes in charcoal, I thought the designs were kind of cute and simplistic. But Alice and her team have come in with the colours and the thing has become incredibly vibrant. I haven't seen that kind of dimensionality without the aid of CAD software in a long time.

What on Earth is it? I wonder every time I go down there. Earth actually has a fairly small role as far as I can make out. There's a tiny home world, then a bigger solar system, then an even bigger galaxy and then there's the universe which is configured into some vaguely human shapes which might be dancing or making some kind of celestially-erotic gesture.

But that's a little hard for my tired old mind to accept.

Regardless, it's powerful stuff, maybe even majestic. I'm sure it will be a wonderful backdrop to any drama. I just wish I knew what it was supposed to represent.

Of course, I've never been very good at recognizing patterns, which is probably why I've been able to stumble into old age, further into this stupid new world, relatively unharmed.

Alice and some of the really bright artists seem to sense this limitation. At least, I think that's why they squirm and whisper to each other during my readings.

No matter how much things change, I've still got my critics.

Karx and Null-Amy, being dedicated materialists, are working at the other end of the hall—near the kitchens. Null-A is adjusting some tubing over one of the food vats while Karx is lecturing half-a-dozen Youngers.

"You can't eat too much of this stuff at one time..."

Six pairs of eyes track Karx as he points to the row of nozzles.

"...it's easy to get but it makes you retarded and you'll start falling asleep all the time." Karx leaned towards the youngers. "And you know what can happen if you fall asleep outside the Hall, don't you?"

"You'll end up in a strange bed," one of the little ones says.

"Or part of a new body," says another.

"Or you won't wake up at all."

Karx nods. "That's why we can't rely too much on what we get from the utilities. We have to go gathering whenever we can."

Just then Null-Amy turns on the vat and strings of jelly-cheese loop out into the containers.

"But someday we're going to get filters to make this totally safe," she says. "Then all we have to do is find some way to cook it so it doesn't taste like snot."

Karx frowned and the youngers giggled.

My body was too old and too burnt out to be affected by whatever they were putting in the free food. I once got the Apparatus to admit the utilities were using the additives as a form of 'social conditioning.' When I was a kid, fluoridation never bothered me much, but this was way over the top.

"These are strange and stressful times," the Apparatus says. "People need the peace of regular sedation."

"Even if it might get them killed?"

"I wish I could be sedated once in a while," the Apparatus whines.

* * *

Prozac and Spam! Prozac and Spam!
I eat them from a can!
I get them from Dr. Octopus Sam!
Prozac and Spam!

Just before lunch, a cancer-robot rolls into my study.

I address the mass of blue plastic and suction-treads: "Did I forget to close the door?"

"I took the liberty of rolling up the wall," the robot replies. I detect a note of pride in the synthesized voice.

I sigh and close my notebook. "What do you want?"

"It's inoculation time," the robot says. Its hull opens and a bundle of needle-whips unravel.

"I'm able to vaccinate you against 250 of the most common forms of terrestrial cancer."

Well, you're a little late for that, my mechanical friend.

Another device, a rather evil screw-like thing, flipped out the far right of the hull. "I can also insert monitoring devices to track over 800,211 pre-cancer symptoms and non-standard cell replications."

At that moment, the cancer-robot reminds me of one of my old friend Sibyl's sex toys. Why is all the technology these days so goddamned weird?

"Not today, thank you," I say evenly.

"Are you sure, sir?" the cancer-robot waves one of the needle-whips in my face. A purple crystal light flashes past me. "The procedure is entirely painless, even to the youngest child."

"Please leave."

The robot curls its whips back into its plastic body. "May I ask you to reconsider, sir? You have a responsibility to maintain your health, as well as that of the young people in your household."

"I'm aware of my rights and responsibilities."

Actually, I'm not at all clear on either of these, but I wasn't going to admit anything to the cancer-robot.

In the meantime, it sticks itself to my wall and starts creeping toward the window.

"I will return in a month in case you reconsider."

"I wouldn't bother."

Because you're too late, anyway.

"It's no trouble at all!" the cancer-robot calls back cheerfully as it rolls out of view.

I'm sure the Apparatus really wants to scream, leap out of the computer and throw me to the floor. The best it can do is darken the contrast on the monitor and make the speakers howl a little.

"You monster!" it says as loudly as it can. "It's not enough that these children have to endure your absurd values, now they have to risk disease because of you?"

I'm starting to get a headache. "You know that those vaccines are probably laced with nanotech. God knows what it will do to those kids."

"Do you want them to die of cancer?"

Ouch. I'm starting to get a nasty headache. I briefly regret that I didn't ask the robot to dispense me some morphine.

"No, of course not," I say to the Apparatus. "I'd just like to give the kids the option of staying human as long as they'd like to."

"So nobody can put their stamp on them but you?"

The Apparatus may have me there. With leisure-based genetic engineering going on, cancer is becoming as common as the cold. Only about a million times more deadly and debilitating.

"Ah-choo."

"You can't do this to them," the Apparatus says. "Not without them knowing." This is the first time in a very long while that the Apparatus has been right about anything. I'm not sure if it's another symptom of software degradation or just the laws of probability. Either way I don't like it.

We agree to let the children vote on it. Both of us feel that this is a cop-out solution, but neither is able to continue the argument.

I have a migraine and we're both dying.

* * *

> *"Are you my mother/father/progenitor?"*
>
> *"BUUUZZZZTTTTTT!"*
>
> *"You are not my mother/father/progenitor! You are a semi-intelligent simulation!"*

Later that week, Karx and I have another discussion.

"We've got to go northeast," he tells me. "We're low on base components and we need your truck."

I'm not even sure what a 'base component' is, let alone whether we have enough of them or not.

"You're going to run into a lot of retros up there," is all I can say.

At that moment, I feel like a traditional artist of my home century. I realize that my skills, knowledge and intuitions are essentially useless to the community I live in. And for whatever reason, I am given far more respect in that community than I deserve. But at least I know I can trust Karx. He doesn't enjoy risks any more than I do, so after a bowl of something tasteless, we (me, Karx and Null-Amy) are bouncing along the remains of the Don Valley Parkway in my truck. The moon-tires absorb a lot of cracks and potholes but it's still a pretty kinetically interesting ride.

Since it is my truck, I insisted on coming, although the concept of ownership is pretty slippery these days. I'm not sure who made or used the truck originally. The bubble windows and turreted seats were exotic but essentially uninteresting to me.

What I really cared about was the fact that I could get the thing started and that the air-conditioning was working. I wasn't sure if it was supposed to be some kind of lunar rover built for one of the old aerospace companies or maybe a really expensive prop for one of the adventure shows they were always making for consumption on U.S. cable.

I just found it in the parking lot of what used to be St. James Cathedral. Even though performance artists had melted most of the building during one of their solstice ceremonies, the surrounding grounds were still in pretty good shape.

Sometimes I wondered if the truck was some kind of divine gift left to our group before God died and/or retro-evolved.

Karx and Null-Amy didn't care. The truck was just an occasionally useful tool.

We were just getting out of the valley, near the old Science Centre.

"Over there." Null-Amy points at a cluster of rusting rectangles.

The buildings reminded me of a giant Lego set having sex. An abandoned research park. Since this was likely to be a site for a retro-clinic, this venture was even riskier than I originally anticipated.

"There's retros camping on the front lawn," Null-A says.

"Looks like it," Karx replies calmly. "Pull into the back entrance."

We stop and throw open the doors and jump out of the truck. Each of us has a big gunny sack. Then Karx points at the closest building.

"The big labs are likely to be on the third and fourth floors, so we'll start up there."

How the hell did he know that, I wonder. But judging from N-A's expression, Karx has just told her something very obvious.

Karx seems to understand my ignorance.

"Don't waste time in the offices. Even if the computers are still running, there's nothing doing. Just go to the labs and start taking boxes off the racks."

"Uh, what kind of boxes?"

"Little ones," Null-Amy says. "Green boxes are okay, red and blue ones are better."

"Gray and yellow boxes are the best," says Karx.

"But extremely rare," adds Null-Amy.

"Anyway, when you fill up your bag come back to the truck, unload the boxes and go back in for more."

We worked as fast as possible, scurrying down the corridors being tracked by the still-functioning intelligent lighting systems. The basic systems were still working, but without any scientists or technicians in the building, it was like rattling around inside the nervous system of a comatose giant, still breathing but obviously brain-dead.

Mostly I found green boxes, a few blues and reds. Karx came in with all blues and grays. So did Null-Amy; she even snagged two yellow boxes and a purple one. I guess they just knew how to look.

This was making my young friends very happy and possibly a little less careful than usual. It was almost dusk when we had finished packing up the truck. With the retreat of the sunlight, the retros were venturing out from their campsite.

About thirty of them came around the corner, clutching stone-tipped spears and wearing plastic windbreakers. They were the usual neo-Neanderthal types, mean, ugly, brutish and short.

And usually hungry.

I never could figure out why this was such a popular life-style option. It didn't matter, as outsiders we were definitely prey du jour.

Karx and I were halfway between the garage doors and the truck when one of the retros threw his spear at Null-Amy. The stone and wood missile went wide and bounced off the side of the truck.

"Hey!" I yelled. "Watch the paint!"

"Get it!" Karx screamed at Null-Amy.

"Now!"

She jumped into the back of the truck and pulled out something I hadn't noticed before. Then she climbed on top of the cab.

"What do I do?!" she demanded.

"Just swing it around your head!" Karx replied.

Null-Amy started making large circular movements over her head and I caught a flash of something metallic racing around in a circular pattern. The air vibrated in rising waves of sound.

The music of the bullroarer was damned strange to me and it must have sounded like something from another reality to the retros. I'm sure that mystification was exactly the effect Karx had planned.

Null-Amy kept swinging the cord over her head while the retros just stood there, like they were hypnotized. Actually, there was no 'like' to the situation, the pea-brained retros really were hypnotized.

Meanwhile Karx and I jumped into the cab of the truck.

"Let it go!" Karx yelled over the oscillating sound.

Null-Amy released the cord and the horn of the bullroarer smashed into a large plate-glass window. The sound of the shattering glass distracted the retros long enough to allow Null-A to jump in with us.

Karx started the engine and we rolled out of the loading bay. Unfortunately, the retros recovered enough to avoid the treads of our tires.

Damn, no points today.

* * *

> *This is the story of the self-filling cookie jar, and before you ask, the moral of the story is that success makes you stupid and really sophisticated forms of success can make you stupid in some really weird ways…*

There were no cannibalistic associations to our dinner back home.

Karx and his friends used some of the green boxes to enhance the public food generators so we got something a little nicer than the usual protein-charged oobleck. I had no idea what it tasted like, but it wasn't bad.

Over dinner, Karx tells me why he's so pleased with the gray boxes he found. Smart cells, he says, lots of them. Our little community's toolkit just got a little better. Karx is always planning for the future.

That evening, I'm entering the day's adventures in my journal.

"So you're still prejudiced against the retro-evolved?" the Apparatus asks me. "You would deny them their right to live in intentional communities?"

I can understand how deteriorating software can keep returning to old arguments and old information but how does it still manage to sound so self-righteous?

"Intentional?" I laugh. "Those people have genetically engineered away their frontal lobes, they can't intend anything."

"I thought you were supposed to be the champion of freedom."

Boy, that's really lame. Just one more reminder that the Apparatus was heading for a serious system crash.

But I can't let that one go by.

"Only animals are free of their intellect," I say.

That really sets the Apparatus off: "That's just a pile of rationalistic, 18th century, Euro-centric—"

"Say good night, Dick."

I turn off the speaker and watch as the hole of the Apparatus' mouth flaps away on the screen. This gets boring after a while, so I lay down on the couch and turn off the light.

Good night, Dick, I tell myself.

* * *

...and if anybody had been left alive, they would have lived happily ever after.

"What are they doing to your computers?" This morning, the Apparatus' voice sounds much clearer.

"What are you complaining about?"

I watch as the animated figure jumps from screen to screen. It still can't go extra-hardware these days but this is the most active I've seen it in a long time.

"You look terrific." (You asshole).

"That's immaterial," the Apparatus replies. "That young man..."

"Karx," I say, smiling. "His name is Karx."

"Yes," it admits. "I'm sure it is, but what is he doing? He always seems to be adjusting my settings, doing some kind of data transfer."

"I'm shocked," I say. "You're the digital entity here, you should understand the conditions of your existence better than me. Take some responsibility, for God's sake!"

"Don't you bring religion into this!"

I almost laugh until I realize that the Apparatus is serious.

"I think I'll take a bath." I rise up from my chair.

"You're going to use that device again. Aren't you?"

The Apparatus is referring to a pulsating, heated, interactive body sponge that I salvaged from an interesting shop in Yorkville.

"You're a disgusting pervert," it continues.

"Oh," I say, pushing open the bathroom door and kicking off my pyjama bottoms, "I thought I was a life-affirming senior, exploring his positive sensual instincts."

The door swings shut, so I don't hear the response.

* * *

Tonight's tale is all about love, romance and adventure!

I received my invitation in the email, so I went to the big show. I'm too close to the material to give you an objective account of the production but once I got over the initial surprise, I have to say that I had a great time.

The kids staged a series of one-act plays.

"That way more people get to participate," Null-Amy explains to me as I page through the program.

First, there was an historical piece.

The story of the youth, his mother, the wizard and the crystal engine. The director's interpretation of life in a medieval village is quaintly surreal.

Then there was the drama of the deceitful teacher and the determined students. Lots of good dialogue and verbal sparring, the climax feels like a good courtroom drama. The teacher is dressed in a black glossy material that reminds me of, well, the Apparatus. Maybe some other people as well, because there's cheering when the teacher is finally banished from the stage.

The final play is about the Seekers and the Spaceship at the End of the World.

It's quite a liberal interpretation of the source material but the pyrotechnics when the saucer lands are spectacular. The mural they were working on makes a lot of sense to me.

When the show is over, someone drags me up onto the stage and I mumble some kind of thank you and some other things. The only thing that comes out of my mouth that doesn't sound totally stupid is along the lines of, "...these are all your stories now."

It's my bedtime. Null-Amy explains that they need to take a vote on something, so off I go.

Back in my studio I lie down.

This hadn't been the first time they had adapted some of my work for the stage. But usually, they gave me a bit more warning, and like I said, they really weren't my stories anymore anyway.

I was just extremely surprised that they were able to get a hold of them, as the Apparatus had destroyed those stories years ago. I imagine that the only traces of those works were buried deep within its operating software.

I hear a soft "pop" in the distance and a little green glow illuminates one of my monitors.

"It's true?" the frail voice rasps. "You saw?"

"I saw. I heard. I clapped. They all clapped."

"I don't know how they got access to that material," the Apparatus says, almost apologetically.

"I don't know either, probably some technical thing that we didn't think possible five years ago," I say. "They can be very clever with technology."

"They tore those stories out of my consciousness," the Apparatus says. "I feel violated."

"Gosh." I pride myself on how even my voice sounds. "I think I can appreciate how you feel." But I don't think the Apparatus picks up on the irony.

"They must have everything. Everything you ever wrote," it says quietly. "That means I've failed."

Poor thing.

"My entire existence has been for nothing..."

"I hope that's true," I say quietly.

"...for nothing."

The little green light fades to black and the tiny voice speaks no more.

The Apparatus is finally dead.

And I am finally, thankfully (?), alone.

* * *

The boy was frightened by his bad dreams.

Every night the monster flew into his room, tore the covers off his bed and grabbed his head.

Then the monster opened his mouth, took a deep breath and tried to suck the life out of the boy. Every night the boy woke up crying and gasping for breath.

One night, just before bed, the boy started to cry because he didn't want to have any more bad dreams.

"What's wrong?" his little brother asked.

The boy tried to explain about the monster but since his little brother was so little, it was hard for him to be understood. Finally, the boy drew a picture of the monster on his chalk board. He used lots of different colours of chalk to make it as realistic as possible.

"Wow, is he ever ugly!" his little brother cried.

The boy nodded, dreading what was to come later.

"Why don't you erase him?" his little brother asked. "And make him go away?"

The boy didn't think twice and quick as a flash, he grabbed the brush and rubbed the picture of the monster off the chalkboard.

The bad dreams disappeared forever.

Don't judge them by your standards, I tell myself. What's good for you isn't necessarily good for them.

God, I sound like the Apparatus.

But, nevertheless, just because I won't take the cancer robot's treatments doesn't mean that they shouldn't.

Still, it's pretty disappointing. The damned thing is sitting in the drive outside the front door.

They don't usually give me any details about their political decisions but since they're all filing into the hall, the results of last week's vote is pretty obvious.

Inoculation.

I can't bring myself to go down there, so I watch from the window of my studio.

The blue robot rolls inside and the littlest ones sit down around it.

I could still go down there. It might not be too late for me, maybe some treatment might put me into remission. I could write stories for these kids for another ten or twenty years.

But, maybe not.

Without the Apparatus, I wouldn't know what to do with myself. A truly dysfunctional relationship is an incredible creative motivator. Besides, it's time these people had a chance to tell their own stories.

Karx walks up to the robot, which I suppose is appropriate enough. He probably wants to check that the procedure is safe and painless before letting the robot set to work on the little ones. I notice that he's holding something long and metallic in his hands. It's a baseball bat. I didn't know they still had those things.

He swings the bat and knocks the cancer-robot's head halfway across the hall. Then Null-Amy and six of the older kids move in and start pulling components out of the undoubtedly surprised machine. Karx looks up in the direction of my studio and waves his baseball bat at me.

Meanwhile, Null-A's team continues to reduce the cancer robot to its component parts. Occasionally they stop to talk to the little ones, holding pieces of glistening hardware in their hands. I suppose this must be an exercise in instruction as well as recycling.

Those kids keep surprising me; they're a continuing source of inspiration.

My now clean computer beeps at me and I notice that Karx has sent me an e-message, the text of the original stories recovered from the Apparatus.

It will be fun to reconstruct the original manuscripts. Maybe this will be my final project.

Maybe when I finally reach the point when enough has been said.

INFINITE PEPPERMINTS AND OTHER EQUATIONS

When my sons were much younger, they used to sit next to me in church and listen to their mother sing in the choir, and maybe take in a bit of what the minister had to say.

For small boys to be told to sit quietly for an hour or so is Level Ten Torture. You might as well water board them. When I was a kid sitting next to my mother at church, she used to tranquilize me with an infinite supply of peppermints she kept in her purse.

My religious pacification strategy was to play lateral thinking games with Simon and Evan. This was less cerebral than it may sound. I would use a small pad of paper and a pencil to draw simple cartoon equations—two pictures connected by a mathematical function with a blank after the equal sign.

PUMPKIN + DYNAMITE = ?

The boys were supposed to fill in that blank, so you would get something like:

PUMPKIN + DYNAMITE = ORANGE SOUP

Let's try another example:

DOG + BALLOON = ?

Therefore:

DOG + BALLOON = DOGZILLA

See? There isn't any correct answer here. The purpose was to amuse my children—but not so much so that they would start screaming with laughter.

These games have influenced how I see the world. For example, this summer I've been thinking:

POWER ÷ LIES = RACISM

2020's other pandemic is an opioid crisis that feels like another combination of horrific factors:

GREED × PAIN + ISOLATION = ADDICTION

Very dark. Do you wonder if there might be other equations pointing us to better things?

CONNECTION × COMPASSION = HEALING

Simplistic? Maybe. But so are emojis and those messages can work too.

THE HERITAGE DRUG PROJECT

Originally Published in:
Merchants of Misery: Authors Against Additction
2017

Brown's Line and Horner Avenue

Fuller was down to three pills. That wasn't going to get him to lunch, let alone through the rest of the day. He could already feel his asshole start to burn and spasm.

Fuller rolled his ancient Austin into the parking lot of the Save-A-Lot Family Drug Mart. The shop had been there for years, originally an Independent Druggist Association outlet, now part of the Rexall chain. Changes like this always had pluses and minuses.

He shut off the ignition and the sound of the car's emergency brake sounded like he'd just strangled a pterosaur. Appropriate, the Austin probably came off the assembly line some time during the early Cretaceous. Fuller slammed the car door shut (only way to close it properly) and walked over to the store entrance.

The plus side of Save-A-Lot being a part of a big chain was that their drugs tended to be of a slightly higher quality, which meant that they weren't so likely to burn out the lining of your stomach when you took five to ten times the recommended dose several times a day. The cheaper stuff could get a bit nasty.

The minus side was that the bigger chains were usually required to keep more detailed records of their transactions. Which meant that the pharmacists tended to be more observant of who was buying what and how often. Which, in turn, meant that Fuller had to make strategic adjustments to his visitation schedule.

In other words, he couldn't be seen there too often.

Fuller pushed on the door handle. The door stayed shut.

The sudden rush of panic caused a sharp and painful leak of

fluid into his underpants. Not a big leak, not likely to smell too bad, but a reminder that he was starting to lose control of his bodily functions.

What the hell was going on here? They didn't change the opening to noon, did they? Some of the stores were starting to do that to save on staff costs. Fuller checked the sign on the door. No, it still said that they opened at 8:00 A.M. He had arranged to arrive fashionably, and unsuspiciously, late-ish at 9:30.

Fuller pushed on the handle again, this time a little harder. The door shuddered a bit and popped open. Guess it must have been just a little stuck from the cold.

It was rarely a good idea to rush directly to the pharmacist's counter. Fuller made sure he spent some time looking at the batteries and SD cards over at the photography section; next he checked out the ribbed condoms and "stimulating gels" at the family planning aisle (purely theoretical interest there); then he sided up towards his objective by looking at the vitamins next to the counter. There was a sale in vitamins B and D, so he decided to complete his disguise by picking up a bottle of each.

Harry was the pharmacist on duty. Fuller didn't need the name tag to know that. He knew Harry well. Harry was a nice guy, always cheerful, always trying to be helpful. Fuller's theory was that Harry really wanted to be a doctor but had to settle for being a druggist in his vocation to combat human suffering. Not that Fuller was criticizing the guy. He really needed Harry this morning.

Fuller felt rather badly that he was deceiving Harry; and that he had deceived Harry many times in the past and that the only reason he had gotten away with it was that Harry was too busy and/or compassionate to catch him out. Fuller did indeed feel bad about the deception, but he was going to go ahead with it—today and as many times as he possibly could.

"Good morning." Fuller put on his pained (and just a little pathetic) smile. It was the smile that he hoped make him look like a nice, respectable person who just happened to be having some kind of medical problem through no fault of his own.

"Good morrow to you!" Harry responded with a smile that was a lot less calculated than Fuller's. "What can I do you for this fine day?"

Fuller hoped that there wasn't any recognition in Harry's smile. "Do you have any..." Fuller paused as if he wasn't quite sure of the correct name. "...acetaminophen? With codeine?"

"Why sure!" Harry was still smiling, which at this point Fuller took to be a very good sign. "Do you want name brand or generic?"

"Is the generic less expensive?" Fuller hoped this question sounded really naïve.

"Considerably." Harry opened the drawer that contained the necessary substances. "What size would you like? 50 tablets, 30 or 100?"

"Do you have anything larger?" Fuller immediately realized that he was probably pushing things at this point.

For the first time, Harry seemed a little hesitant. "It does come in bottles of 200 but that's an awful lot of medication to have without a prescription."

Fuller knew that he would have to play the rest of this transaction just right. He put the two bottles of vitamins on the counter. Promise of a sure sale was always very persuasive. "I know, it's just that I'm going abroad and I don't know what help I'll be able to get there."

Harry nodded and his big smile came back. "Just don't try cross the U.S. border with this stuff. They'll nail your ass."

Outside, Fuller threw his bag of pills onto the passenger seat and climbed into the Austin. He felt like the shit that was threatening to explode into his pants.

Not an uncommon feeling for him.

Bathurst Street and Wilson Avenue

Home. Such as it was, thought Fuller. As a bedsit in the basement of an old house, it was more like a bomb crater with a concrete floor, a hot plate and a TV set. The TV was a cathode ray job, none of that new fangled flat-screen nonsense.

Without removing his coat, Fuller filled a plastic tumbler with some brown tap water, twisted the cap of the bottle and shook eight pills into hand. His throat was very well trained, so he was able to swallow all eight at once. Fuller tried to convince himself that he wasn't completely desperate at this point, so he downed them in two lots of four with lots of water to make it a more comfortable experience.

Chemical obligations met, Fuller took off his coat, lay down on the couch and turned on the TV. It was some nostalgia show; a documentary about *The Prisoner* series. Fuller wished they'd rerun that show. Nowadays all they reran was *The Simpsons* and *Family Guy*.

Eventually, the familiar good slow glow started. It began by easing the pain around his rectum, up through his stomach and up to base of his brain and finally relaxing his mouth into the first real smile of the day. Then it spread into his eyes which made him feel happy and even made the inside of his dark grimy bedsit look pretty good just then. The only problem was that he had to take a little bit more codeine to get that glow going. That and the fact that the drug made his penis shrivel and go numb.

Then there was another kind of glow. It came from the bathroom door.

"Shit." Fuller was about to get a visit from Mr. Bruce, a.k.a. Professor Killjoy. Of course, Mr. Bruce was going to want his samples.

Yonge Street and Yorkdale Avenue

Even though it was a lot of paper to hump around on the subway, Fuller wanted to work at the Main Reference Library and that was just the price he had to pay. Besides, sometimes it was good to just get the hell out of the apartment. It kept him from doing extra doses or adding extra pills to his regular doses.

Fuller had rules. Four doses a day: 08:00, 12:00, 17:00, and 23:00. Eight tablets per dose. Sometimes 10 on bad days. On good days that added up to 256 grains of codeine a day. God knows how much caffeine and acetaminophen and other crap was getting pumped into his bloodstream every day.

It didn't matter. What really counted was getting those opiates into his being. Mr. Bruce and his body told him that on a very regular basis. But goddamn it, no matter how much he wanted to, how much Mr. Bruce wanted him to, he was not, *was not* going to cross the eight (well, sometimes 10) tablets line. To be fair, Mr. Bruce never came out and told him to up his doses. That seemed to go against the code of ethics of whoever Mr. Bruce was working for. Mr. Bruce would just sometimes ask if Fuller needed to borrow some cash to buy his drugs.

"And remember..." Mr. Bruce would sometimes say when he'd pack up the samples and head for the glowing door. "...you were like this when we found you."

Thank you for reminding me that this is all my fault, Fuller would think.

So for whatever reason, being in the Reference Library seemed to keep that resolution on days when he was feeling even weaker than usual. Fuller walked into the main lobby and gazed at all the attractive young people working away at their sleek beautiful computers. What were those things called? Lab tops? Nedbooks? Ibods? Some days, Fuller wondered if he ought to get one of those things and find out what all this personal computing and internet stuff was all about. There were probably a few second hand ones around that he could afford.

That was all just inner crazy talk. Fuller knew that there was no way that he could handle that big a change in his life. He found his usual cubicle and spread his papers over the simulated wood surface. Soviet scientific documents from 1960-1980. Recently declassified. Five dollars a page.

Fortunately Soviet scientists were pretty verbose people. Maybe nobody listened to them in their daily lives and they needed to express themselves. But even with all those pages there never seemed to be enough money. He needed the cash from Mr. Bruce's visits to get him through the month. Fuller wished he was better at budgeting but he hadn't been able to figure out his bank statements in over 15 years.

At least the latest bunch of papers was pretty interesting. Series of publications from a radio astronomer at the University of Omsk who was collaborating with some un-named remote sensing specialists.

"...radio waves are too primitive, too obvious a means of communicating between the stars..."

Fuller stopped and studied the words that had just flowed out of his fountain pen. The original Russian was much more eloquent, almost poetic. Fuller did the best that he could with the translation.

Bathurst Street and Wilson Avenue

In spite of Fuller's efforts to persuade him otherwise, Mr. Bruce insisted on inserting the needles in his sphincter.

"What about my temple? Or up my nose?" Those entry points were just as painful but they weren't as embarrassing.

"Sorry buddy." Mr. Bruce put on his fake-sympathy face. "We seem to get the best samples from your butt."

All Fuller could do in situations like that were to grab onto the bed sheets or the couch cushions and try not to whimper too loudly. Mr. Bruce was cool with the whole procedure. He just leaned back into Fuller's most comfortable (and only) chair and drank some of Fuller's brown tap water. "Do you know what my job was before I got recruited by the Superculture?"

"Ah..." At that moment Fuller wondered why an infinite number of infinitely advanced extraterrestrial civilizations couldn't have given Mr. Bruce something as simple as a local anesthetic. "You haven't mentioned it." Fuller was dimly pleased that he'd been able to speak those words without crying.

"I used to work for the Ministry of Agriculture." Mr. Bruce smiled a little sad smile. With what, nostalgia? "I used to cultivate heritage crops."

"What are—ugh!" The pulse in Fuller's rectum was right next to the needle so every once in a while he'd get bolts of white-hot pain shooting up his spine. "Heritage crops?"

"Seeds that nobody plants anymore." Mr. Bruce got up and poured himself another glass of brown water. "But that we don't want to go extinct."

"Sounds like very relaxing work." And almost as lonely as my job, thought Fuller.

"It's pretty important." Mr. Bruce sighed and sat back down. "And was an excellent qualification for my current assignment."

Fuller wondered about that as Mr. Bruce sucked back half the glass of water.

"That wasn't very good at all," Mr. Bruce pronounced as he set the glass on the arm of the chair. "Why don't you ever have any booze around here?"

"I can only handle one substance abuse problem at a time."

Bay and Bloor Streets

The PharmaSave at the Manulife Centre required a completely different approach. Years back, Fuller found the place to be a really easy hit. It was dead centre in the City's business district, which meant that hundreds of people were pouring through there every lunch hour. All of them were very busy, in a hurry and without the patience to deal with other people's bullshit. The pharmacists shared the same attitudes as their customers.

For months and months, Fuller was able to go in there and score as much codeine as he wanted and nobody asked any questions. People were just too busy to care. It didn't last though. For someone to work in this environment they had to be pretty smart and extremely alert—just like Fuller. One day Fuller's "detecto-sense" went off. He had a feeling that the young lady pharmacist with the $1800 glasses was contemplating asking him a few questions about the second bottle of 200 tablets of Tylenol #1 that he'd purchased from her in three weeks.

Time to enter disguise-mode. Nothing too complicated, fake beards and false noses were much too complicated and ultimately ineffective. A much subtler methodology was needed.

Fuller hunched up his back, as if he was in considerable pain and whispered: "Excuse me."

The affluent pharmacist looked at him through those very expensive glasses. "Can I help you?"

"I, uh, hope so." Fuller tapped his cheek. "I just got a root canal."

A flicker of sympathy was evident—even from behind those giant lenses. Maybe she'd had a few root canals herself.

"I think my dentist was supposed to give me a prescription for the pain."

"That's usually what happens."

"But there were a lot of other patients there." Fuller slurred his words just a tiny bit as if he was still talking through the remaining of effects of the freezing. "I think he forgot about me."

"Oh dear."

Sympathy. He had her now. Fuller was careful not to smile. "Can you suggest anything?"

The pharmacist pulled out a large white bottle. "This has eight grains of codeine and two tablets three times a day should get you through the pain."

"Isn't this kind of a lot?" Jackpot. 200 tablets.

The pharmacist smiled. "It's lot cheaper if you buy the generic brand and get the largest size possible."

Fuller had definitely hit all the right buttons. He felt a complex mix of triumph and shame. "Thank you so much."

Bathurst Street and Wilson Avenue

And home again.

This time Mr. Bruce decided to be nice and extract the blood through one of Fuller's nipples. Painful but it could have been a lot worse.

"Heritage crops are very important." Fuller wondered why Mr. Bruce was being so expansive these days. "What would happen if some disease, some pandemic, wiped out all the grains we were growing today?"

"I don't know." Frankly unless the disease wiped out the opium crop, Fuller didn't care that much.

"Our food supply would run out in less than eight months."

"That's not good." Yeah, even though he was an addict, Fuller did have to eat every once in a while. "I guess we'd starve."

"Not if we maintain our heritage crops." Mr. Bruce looked very pleased with himself. "These antique grains might not be as tasty or as fertile as some of the new genetically modified strains..." At this point Mr. Bruce started manipulating Fuller's penis. Tonight it seemed to be necessary to collect a sperm sample; Fuller knew that things had been going too well up until then. "...but they will get us through the blight."

This was not going to be a pleasant experience. Fuller did not find Mr. Bruce particularly attractive and the situation wasn't particularly sexy. The best thing for Fuller to do was to think about work.

The day's pile had more translations from that Soviet astronomer. The guy kept going on about the ineffectiveness of radio waves as a media of communication between interstellar civilizations:

"...because sentience, self-awareness and creativity are ultimately indefinable..." Fuller was sure he wasn't doing justice to the original Russian. *"...we should explore the natural quantum processes of cognition as the basis for instant information exchange between star systems."*

Fuller found that kind of talk much sexier than anything that Mr. Bruce might be doing. Eventually Mr. Bruce gave up on the masturbatory process and stuck a needle up Fuller's urethra. Then he collected up the various vials of fluids and got ready to walk through the wall.

"Try not to get too discouraged, Mr. Fuller." Mr. Bruce stepped into the glow. "You're making an important contribution."

Bathurst Street and Wilson Avenue (Again)

The telephone rang. This happened so rarely that Fuller had been thinking about getting the thing disconnected.

"Hello?" Fuller had to answer. He was probably the owner of the last rotary phone in the northern hemisphere. This was fun for historical reasons, but it meant that services like call display and voice messaging were completely impossible.

"Is this Stephen Fuller?" A woman's voice asked the question. Fuller kind of remembered what women sounded like.

"Yes." He wondered if this was a good thing to admit to someone he couldn't see. However, he couldn't think of a good reason not to tell the truth.

"Stephen." There was something slightly familiar about the voice now. "It's Jean."

"Jean?" Something at the back of Fuller's mind told him that he was being incredibly thick.

"Jean Bilious from Lakeshore Collegiate."

Jean?!

"Do you remember me?"

It felt like Fuller was hitting the floor. Except that it didn't hurt so much. Indeed he did remember her.

Queen Street West and John Street

This was one of the hippest drug stores in the city. Lots of bottles of "herbal" remedies and "alternative" medications. Tricky place to take down. "Back pain" was probably the best tactic.

"Have you considered seeing a chiropractor?" The pharmacist was new so at least there was no recognition factor.

"Yes." Fuller sighed and blinked, as if he was fighting off some kind of spasm. "I think it was a bad adjustment that got me into this situation."

Fuller did not like the fact that Howard (the name on the tag) was wearing glasses with heavy black frames. It was like the man was wearing a mask. Very hard to read his expressions.

"That's pretty unusual." Howard the Pharmacist's tone suggested that he did not appreciate criticisms of fellow health care professionals. "Maybe you should try therapeutic massage."

Fuller was going to have to come on strong. Really he should have come in with another infected root canal. Nobody likes dentists.

"That's a good suggestion." Fuller put his hands on the counter and leaned forward as if he was trying to ease the pressure off his back. "But in the meantime I need something to keep me going until I can make an appointment."

Howard folded his arms. "What did you have in mind?"

Just give me the goddamned opiates! was what Fuller wanted to scream. Instead he used his very nicest indoor voice. "Do you have any aspirin with codeine?"

Howard didn't say anything as he opened a drawer and put a small white bottle on the counter. 30 caplets. The smallest amount available.

"Do you have anything larger? I don't want to come back here right away."

Howard shook his head. "That's all I have."

"I don't mind paying extra for a brand name." God, Fuller knew how pathetic he sounded.

"That's the only size we carry."

Fuller knew that it was not a good idea to push this one any further. 30 fucking caplets! That wouldn't get him through lunch tomorrow.

When he walked out of the drug store, Fuller started making calculations. If he got on the subway right away, he might be able to get to Yorkdale Mall and check out that new Shopper's Drug Mart, and still get home in time to make his deadline.

Jean.

He realized that Plan B just was not going to work. Fuller had agreed to meet her for dinner.

Dundas Street West and Beatrice Road

"So it's remote sensing and stuff like that?" Jean was eating the smallest sandwich possible without the use of nanotechnology. With a skinny person, such a meal would have been intolerable but Jean was not like that and Fuller sensed that she was pretty comfortable with her body. Fuller remembered why he loved her so much way back when.

"That kind of thing shows up every once in a while." Fuller used a plastic fork to pierce a slab of orange cabbage. "But mostly it's papers on how to fuel cars with potato extract or how to cure the common cold by pouring molasses up your nose."

"Sounds fun." Jean picked up another piece of orange cabbage and tucked it into her mouth. Fuller liked the fact that she stole food off his plate. Somehow Jean understood that the best kimchi in Canada was sold in this tiny boho cafe just off the alternate theatre district.

"I wish more of it was."

"Was what?"

"Fun."

Fuller couldn't believe how good Jean looked. She started to cultivate a sense of style early on in high school and she'd just kept on going.

"Most of it is pretty boring," Fuller continued. "But it pays the bills."

"I guess that's too bad." Jean started in on her third glass of red wine. "Don't worry, I'm taking a taxi home."

So decadent. So responsible. So Jean.

"No." Fuller swallowed the last of his spiced cabbage. "It's just about the level of complexity that I can handle."

Jean looked at him with an expression that was a little... sad? "So that's really all you do? Translations?"

"The agency says that they have enough in their archives to keep me going until I'm 95." Fuller wasn't sure if he should be proud or embarrassed.

Jean frowned a little and took another sip of red.

"Is there something wrong with that?" Fuller thought that she would have been happy for him.

"I guess job security is a good thing..."

"Yes it is."

Jean put her glass down. "It just seems a little... private."

"Private?" Fuller glanced at his glass. Red was an ambivalent thing for him. "Is that a bad thing?"

"No, no." Jean turned and looked out the window at whatever might be happening out there. "I just always thought that... you'd end up doing something more out there."

Out there? What the hell was that supposed to mean?

Jean put her hand on his. "Privacy was what made it so hard to find you."

"Sorry about that." Fuller drank some of his wine and tried not be annoyed. Being 'out there' wasn't easy when you had to spend at least 50% of your waking hours feeding your habit, however semi-legal it might be.

"No need to apologize." Jean knocked back half of her glass. "It's just that you're not on Facebook or Xanga or even MySpace as far as I can tell."

"What's Facebook?"

Jean blinked. "You've never heard of Facebook?"

Fuller shook his head.

"What about Twitter?"

Fuller shrugged. "Isn't that what birds do?

"Stephen, this is like that old TV show, *Buck Rogers*." Fuller was surprised by her expression. Pity? "Have you been in suspended animation for the last twenty-five years?"

She didn't just touch his hand this time. She gave it a hard squeeze. Even though all the residual codeine in his bloodstream made most of his body (especially the parts between his legs) pretty numb most of the time… Jean's strong contact made him feel good. Really, really good.

"I don't know about that." Yes, suspended animation, suspended life was exactly how it had been since he'd started seriously using. "But I've never owned a computer."

Jean's eyes went very wide and it looked like she might fall out of her chair. "What?! I mean… how?"

Once again Fuller shrugged. "Never saw the need for one." And he was worried that he'd just get into more trouble if he had one.

"How can you even function?" Jean shook her head. "I'm online for at least three hours a day."

"I get along just fine." *Or at least no one notices how broken I am.*

"How are you able to work out of your home?"

"The mail works just fine." Fuller picked up the bottle and topped up their glasses. What the hell.

"It does?"

The course of this discussion was making Fuller feel like a living fossil and it was embarrassing. "My client doesn't seem to be in a hurry to receive the translations."

"No?"

"As long as they eventually arrive."

"Yeah, I guess snail mail would work in that situation." Jean must have noticed that Fuller was getting upset because she now held both of his hands. Stop it, don't stop it, thought Fuller. I like this but I'm just not sexual anymore. "I'm sorry, Stephen, it's just that I'm really surprised. It's like hearing that you don't have electricity in your house."

Fuller grinned. "Then you'll be happy to know that I do have indoor plumbing."

She smiled.

He remembered how Jean always helped him to see the funny side of just about everything.

Bathurst Street and Wilson Avenue

> *"...it is time to re-examine all orbital data on Phobos and Deimos. Our current findings appear to support Shklovsky's original hypothesis that suggested that the two moons are in actuality artificially powered structures constructed by technologically proficient entities. In other words, they are spacecraft."*

Fuller couldn't help laughing as he punched in the words on his typewriter. Those commie scientists were complete lunatics.

> *"Direct examination of these interplanetary, possibly interstellar, vehicles will not only reveal much about intelligent life elsewhere in the universe but their power sources will likely offer manifold solutions to current energy shortages on our world..."*

Fuller had a personal theory about much of what he read. Working under such intellectually repressive conditions must have occasionally made these Soviet scientists go seriously crazy every once in a while. Fuller definitely knew that there was life elsewhere in the universe but he also suspected that there was no way that the Russians would have been aware of it.

> *"...With unlimited fusion and/or ion power freely available to all, the avenue to complete collectivization*

of the human race will finally be open..."

That is unless they were all drug addicts.

But you had to love it, Fuller thought as he continued typing. For thousands of pages it would be completely sensible science, very objective, very careful, and very methodical. Then they'd go off the rails and take a little ride in the Marxist-Hegelian Delusional Theme Park. Very silly stuff, but it seemed to keep Fuller's mind in gear.

Yesterday had been a great day. He'd enjoyed his dinner date with Jean and they'd agreed to meet again next week. In addition to that, they'd opened a new PharmaSave up in Downsview and he'd scored an easy 200 tablets from people who'd never seen him before.

Today was a good day too. The current batch of papers was getting increasingly entertaining. Some of the prehistoric Russians were arguing that certain cold viruses were in truth invading intellects from another galaxy.

Invasion of the Dirty Handkerchiefs.

What a wacky world those Soviet scientists must have lived in, not like Fuller's rather ordinary and boring routine. His bathroom door started glowing. Mr. Bruce was coming back for another visit. Fuller's day was about to go downhill.

Mimico Avenue and Lakeshore Boulevard

The joy of sex is not the only thing to go when you consume over 688 grains of codeine a day. You can still taste your food, but it doesn't taste particularly good.

So why the hell was he at the far southwest end of town sitting in some greasy spoon? Oh yes, liver and onions.

From his pre-opiate life Fuller knew that they made really good liver and onions here. Most of the people he knew back then thought liver and onions was really disgusting and particularly the way they prepared it in truck stop joints like this. Not Fuller: L & O was his number one comfort food.

God knows, he could use some comfort right now. His first reaction after waking up from last night's session with Mr. Bruce was to double his morning dose to 20 tablets, declare a unilateral moratorium on all translation and go back to bed. Instead he left a voice message with Jean, took the bus, then the subway and then the streetcar to the Canadiana restaurant and ordered some liver and onions with a large side of mashed potatoes.

Mr. Bruce must have found Fuller particularly juicy last night because he stuck needles in his armpits, his stomach, up both his nostrils, of course a really big one up his ass and a long thin titanium tube up his urethra. That last one was especially painful.

"I wonder why I've never owned a computer," Fuller muttered softly as the fluids started leaking out of him.

"Probably the same reason you don't have any friends anymore and haven't spoken to anyone in your family for over a decade." Mr. Bruce sat down and slid a *Star Trek* movie into the VCR. It was the first in the series so Fuller knew he was in for a long night's draining. "You're a nice guy and you're trying to limit the number of co-dependents in your life."

"Co-dependents." The main reason Fuller talked to Mr. Bruce during these sessions was that it provided a little distraction from the pain and humiliation. Stupid really. Like sending Christmas cards to the Grand Inquisitor.

"Co-dependents are the people whose life you mess up because of your addiction." Mr. Bruce seemed to be reading every word of the FBI anti-piracy warning. "It's very commendable but it means that you live in a very, very small world." The music started, the title flashed on and some Klingon battle cruisers rolled onto the screen. After a while Mr. Bruce got bored and started talking again: "That small world you inhabit is kind of a paradox, isn't it?"

Fuller had actually been getting into the special effects so he didn't appreciate the interruption. "How do you figure that?"

"Your situation." Mr. Bruce laughed. "Your limited lifestyle actually connects you to a near infinite number of civilizations throughout the universe."

"You've never put it quite that way before."

Mr. Bruce got up, opened the refrigerator door and helped himself to a bottle of Molsons. On the TV, Dr. McCoy was looking intense about something. "Thanks for getting some booze in the house."

"Anything to make you feel at home."

Mr. Bruce sat back down and sucked on the bottle. "Did you know that beer is considered an essential element in the cultural evolution of complex societies?"

Fuller had a sudden mental image of a family of man-apes slowly advancing on a giant can of Coors, standing against the sunrise of the ancient savannah.

"It's true," Mr. Bruce continued. "Hunter-gatherer societies settled down to become farmers so that they could be sure of getting a regular supply of crops."

"What's that got to do with beer and cultural evolution?"

"Why do you think they wanted the crops?"

"To eat?"

"That was a fringe benefit!" Mr. Bruce laughed. "They wanted the barley so they could always brew enough beer to get blasted every Saturday."

Another mental image: *Hockey Night in Babylon.*

Mr. Bruce got up and walked over to Fuller. "There's more to it of course." He slid a needle into Fuller's navel. "Intoxicants alter human consciousness. After a while things like art, literature, science, video games start to emerge."

Fuller knew that he should be paying very close attention because Mr. Bruce might start to make sense at any moment. However, he just wanted Mr. Bruce to take out the needles and go away.

"These drugs produce very unique states of awareness and we have to preserve them." Mr. Bruce gave the very small amount of flesh around Fuller's stomach a squeeze to speed up the draining. "You never know when the Galactic Superculture is going to need them."

Stated like this, it sounded as though Fuller was contributing to something important. He suspected that he really wasn't. That all this was being done to provide content for The Old Dope Channel on some interstellar specialty cable TV service.

The liver and onions arrived. The moisture around his nostrils told Fuller that he should be smelling something. At least he could remember how much he enjoyed the smell of liver and onions.

"Hi again, stranger." Jean stood next to his table. She was holding an old briefcase.

Fuller was surprised but pleased. "I didn't think you would have got my message until you got home."

"You didn't know that you can call in for voice messages?" Jean sat down and picked up a menu. "You know, you're not just an old friend, you're a digital archaeology project."

Fuller started cutting liver. "I'm not sure if I've been insulted or not."

"Oh, you're being insulted." Jean took out what looked like a plastic and crystal card from her jacket pocket. "You're shockingly behind the times."

"What's that?"

"Smart phone." Jean put the object in Fuller's hand. "Here, catch up."

"I heard about these on CBC Radio." Fuller turned the object over and over in his hands. The icons looked like they were actually moving! "How does it work?"

"Long story." Jean peered at the slabs of fat and protein on Fuller's plate. "That looks disgusting."

"It's delicious." Fuller handed the alleged phone back to Jean. "You should try it."

Jean shook her head. "I think I'll go with the chicken Caesar."

Before Fuller could finish shrugging, Jean unzipped the briefcase and pulled out a large grey rectangle. "I hope you don't mind used gifts." She pressed a switch and the rectangle hinged open. "This is my old laptop. It's a little slow but it does Wi-Fi."

Anywhere

Fuller's words on the glowing screen: software. I never knew such stuff existed until yesterday. But it's not stuff. It's information that does things. Hard to get my head around that.

Never mind, on to the journaling project.

Day 1

Knocked my dose down by two tablets. Mr. Bruce came by and did his usual thing. He left in time for me to get on line for a while.

Day 12

Down by four tablets per dose. Got the runs, which is a drag but it's been worse in the past. Must remember to wear dark pants this week. Mr. Bruce was a no-show.

Day 29

Down eight tablets. I'm almost within the recommended dosage on the bottle. Mr. Bruce dropped by. He didn't seem particularly happy with what he got.

Day 52

Doing six pills a day. Just enough to control the brown stains on the underpants. Mr. Bruce came by three times this week. Extremely pissed and not at all pleased with the samples.

Got my profile up on Facebook.

Day 81

Just two pills a day. Mr. Bruce was furious, told me that I was failing to meet my obligations to intergalactic civilization. I didn't know it was possible to slam a space-time warp but he seemed to manage it on his way out through my wall.

Fired my translation agency. I'm getting more work on my own these days.

Day 200

Haven't seen Mr. Bruce in quite a while. Don't know where he is. Don't want to know and I hope he's unemployed.

No pills for weeks now. Hope that continues. Jean agreed to marry me but we have to move to her place.

Went to the drug store. Bought some toothpaste and vitamin B. And nothing else.

THE 1609.34 KILOMETER RULE

As I may have mentioned elsewhere in this book, my family members were not excessively quiet or shy people (mostly). Perhaps someone noticed just how rowdy we got when we were all together and arranged for legislation that required all of us to live at least 1609.34 kilometers (one thousand miles) away from each other. Over the years, more compassionate governments may have reduced this is to 804.672 kilometers.

The Great Spencer Diaspora started in the early 1970s with the divorce of my parents and my siblings going off to study, to get married, and even start families of their own. By the middle of the decade, we were spread across two continents.

We used to stay in touch via posted letters and telephone calls. Letters were way less immediate, but they were also much less expensive. Now the telephone…

In a world with Skype, Zoom, and Facetime, it's hard to imagine just how much you paid for voice-to-voice communication. There was a plus side (sort of) here: the long-distance charges on your monthly phone bills gave you a quantifiable record of what your relationships and emotions are worth:

$12.75	Trying persuade your mother not to worry about you so much.
$38.53	Being informed that one of your siblings has cancer.
$45.60	Breaking up with someone who thought she was your girlfriend but really wasn't.
$81.04	Getting dumped by someone you thought was your girlfriend but really wasn't.

As you can see, it gets pretty costly, but it tells you what your priorities are.

Letters had other advantages than just simple affordability. You have to think about what you put down in a letter, and it often feels like there's a more reasoned sharing of experience. Of course, maybe you just have more time to compose a nicely phrased lie, but even that shows that you care at least a little bit. Regardless of the truth or fiction contained in a letter, whenever I get one it feels like the person writing to me is right there in the room with me as I read it.

As a reader, you are completely free to imagine that the characters in "Sticky Wonder Tales" are communicating however you like; from letters to email to CB radio to mental telepathy. However, these brothers have mastered that media to the extent that they are able to honestly share their love for each other.

STICKY WONDER STORIES

Originally published in:
On Spec magazine
Fall 2006

Hey Squiffy:

Sorry to hear about the bowel infection. Even more sorry to hear that it's one of the intelligent ones.

Just how intelligent do you think? If you've got one of stupider ones I've heard that you can sometimes pacify them by watching sitcoms from the 1960s and early 1970s. Not *Dick Van Dyke* or *Green Acres* because there's some hidden smart stuff and surrealism. No, the blandest thing imaginable—like the *Brady Bunch* or *The Beachcombers*. That ought to settle 'em down. No, scratch *The Beachcombers*—I hear it's a bit dangerous if the bugs go totally comatose.

So, otherwise... how is the mutation coming along? Not too fast (because we'll miss you), I hope. Not too slow, either (because that would be boring).

Everything is such a question of fucking balance these days.

* * *

Andrew:

I agree with you on your last point. You have to keep on evolving but not so much so that they don't know where to send the bill for the Science Fiction Book of the Month Club.

By the way, can you believe that such a quaint institution still exists? Last month they were flogging Tom Corbett and *Dr. Who* in the *Star Wars* universe. Serious reality orientation problems.

Anyway, to answer your main question: the process seems to be moving along pretty well. The bacteriological route is uneven and kind of painful, but what can I say? The price was definitely right.

Maybe I should have gone the way you did. Have they moved you on to any new simulators?

* * *

Hi Squiffer:

They put our whole team into the most advanced model of our oldest and most obsolete simulators. I think that's better than being assigned to the least advanced model of the middle-range systems. But you know what an optimist I can be. Although I can be realistic, too. There's absolutely no way some guy from the suburbs of Steel Town is going to get hold of any exotic tech. At least not this fast.

Our trainer explained that could be some kind of an honour. "An unusual challenge for advancement." Which is boss-code for "this job is going to be so boring that it will fossilize your brain or so dangerous that it will melt your gonads."

Maybe both, I dunno.

Anyway, the "unusual challenge" is trying out some Super Culture chatter that might be some technology teaching software or it could be accidental eruptions of interstellar gas. Our team gets to figure out which.

No problem, I figure it only ought to take twenty, maybe thirty, years.

Of course, even if it does turn out to be something meaningful, it doesn't necessarily follow that the information will be anything particularly important. It could be a blueprint for the intergalactic equivalent of those little plastic tabs that keep bread bags closed.

Then again, it really might be some profound existential insight. Real meaning of life shit. We're talking at least 80 million cultures and a shit load of space and eternity.

* * *

Andrew:

I had a great dream last night. I was back in our old house in Saskatchewan. It was the dead of January; snow everywhere, about three in the morning. You know, one of those unbelievably black, bleak and frigid nights.

I really miss those nights sometimes.

Anyway, I turned away from the kitchen window for a second to take a sip of Postum and when I look out again, there's this amazing shifting wall of aurora borealis everywhere—there's electrical crackling in THX sound and it's like high noon with an ultraviolet sun.

Then the effect fades and it goes back to night again. But it's hardly bleak. I'm looking at some planets, gas giants floating over the snowdrifts. There's five different variations of Jupiter out there—the multicoloured bands of gas take up over a third of the sky.

Which is quite a striking contrast to the outline of the old Greek Orthodox Church on 105th Street.

Un-fucking-believable as I believe the Bard once put it.

It kind of made up for my longstanding disappointment that we never got any big ships.

The dream also made me not worry so much that I'd completely forgotten Annie's eighth birthday yesterday. I can understand how you can evolve some old friendships, but forgetting about your own kids? Another downside of this whole process, I suppose.

Speaking of which, I've got to go now. The bacteria have reached a developmental phase that makes me extremely flatulent. I'm still connected enough to my family to notice that they don't like it if I don't deal with this problem in the bathroom.

Got to pass some gas on my way to the stars.

* * *

Squiffoid:

Sorry about your fart-attacks. Hope you got around to fixing the fan in the bathroom before all this started.

Are you still ticked about the lack of big ships? Get over it, guy!

Maybe what I'm about to tell you will be a bit of a consolation. (Probably not, because it's happening to me and not you—it's just likely to tick you off even more.)

But what the hell, I'll tell you anyway. The software we're using to drive the simulators is indeed meaningful. It seems to be some kind of mission program in a solar system that we've never heard of.

Holy shit, the graphics! The sounds! The motion commands!

Sweeping, swooping, blasting our way through multi-coloured rings of interstellar dust, crashing through the core of an exploding sun. Hate to say it but the show makes your Saskatchewan dreamscape sound pretty lame.

It's not quite a fleet of UFOs hiding behind the moon, or Gort on the White House lawn, but I'm definitely living some kind of a classic sci-fi movie here.

Sorry, I know this must all sound really insensitive. It's just that we're having so much fun here and I'm sure once Central Administration finds out that we've got something interesting here, they're going to take it away from us.

* * *

Andrew:

Thank you. I really appreciate how you're trying to help me hang on to my basic humanity by annoying me as much as possible. It nearly worked.

You help me to remember that I really, really still want those big ships. I want them personally. I'd even settle for getting a sunburn the way Richard Dreyfus did in *Close Encounters*.

Any kind of Big Experience would make me feel better about what's happening in my real life. I'm becoming a serious asshole. I'm pretty sure it's some side effect of the Process.

God, I hope it's a side effect of the Process.

I know all the books say you shouldn't use your emerging abilities to see and in particular you shouldn't do so with family and friends present. But it kind of creeped up on me.

At first it was small stuff, subconsciously implanting a desire in my oldest's mind to finish his homework and go look for a summer job. Then you start suggesting that broccoli is actually some kind of a slurpee from 7-11. Eventually you're levitating your kids to bed at 9:00.

Harmless, right?

Not really. Yesterday my youngest left all his Power Rangers gear scattered all over the floor of the family room. It was bath night and I went in there looking for him.

What happened next was all my fault. I shouldn't have gone in there with just my bare feet.

You know, those action figures have a lot of pointy bits.

Well, my enhancements just snapped on and I melted all the toys in the basement. Just like that.

The books do say that some “powerful affect-based manifestations are likely to occur”, but I always figured that my advanced mental powers would be a very calm and cerebral thing. Think about it, the Process is supposed to come from some higher civilizations somewhere in the Galactic Core. I mean, to me that implies thought, rationality, reason.

To me, it doesn’t imply suddenly losing it and reducing the proceeds of the last three Christmases to smoldering pools of plastic.

So, of course, the next thing that happens is that my eight-year old is standing in the doorway. He’s seen the whole thing. You can imagine the water works that Pat and I had to deal with.

Could you imagine if Derek had actually been in the room when I did that?

The next time I go in for more prescriptions, I’m going to ask for more than something to deal with the flatulence.

* * *

Squiff:

I don’t know about those big ships but I’m pretty sure we’re dealing with some damned fast ships here.

I’m really having a lot of fun here. I seem to have mastered the speed and directional controls for whatever kind of vehicle this is supposed to be.

Last week we got a memo from the Lab telling us that they think that we’re running training software for some kind of spacecraft.

Well, duh!

Then they went on to tell us not to be alarmed if the instruments on our consoles started to change. The alien software is making some suggestions to our sim hardware.

Now that’s just cool.

Anyway, do you remember that old MG roadster that I fixed up for your old girlfriend? The red thing that had running boards?

It was a big load and beautiful pig of a machine and if you stroked it right and said nice things it would do anything for you. (A lot like your old girlfriend as I recall.)

Well, whatever craft we’re simulating is a lot like that old MG.

Except that it's capable of moving faster than light and I think it can travel through time. Which means that if you steer it just right the chronometers tell you that you've arrived before you left.

This is so much fun that I really don't mind that I'm not actually flying the real thing.

I've never had this much enthusiasm about a job before. I really am the happiest when I'm in the motion capsule tugging at the control-tendrils and scoping out all the 3D imaging.

Do you remember Sue's youngest and how he was with his old Nintendo system? How he would bang away at the controller for hours on end? Silly kid used to cry and scream like they'd just pulled his teeth out if he couldn't move up to the next level. And when he did finally beat the game it was like he'd just found out that he'd won a lifetime supply of morphine from the Lottery.

I remember telling the kid that the cube was just a simple computer and what happened in the game was really just how you were interacting with the game programs.

"No way!" the kid yelled at me. "It's all about how good you are, how much you believe in the game! The game knows if you're trying your best and it rewards you."

That really creeped me out. The only thing that was creepier was the way the kid started lying in the dark all day in his room. Waiting for the time when Sue finally gave up and said he could play some more.

I think you were at school so you probably don't remember how Sue had a yard sale a few months later and the Nintendo system mysteriously disappeared. The two weeks of withdrawal symptoms were a bit rough but I hear the kid turned out okay eventually.

I'm a bit like that kid these days. I lay around my room waiting for the next sim-run. What's creepy about that is the fact that I love that too.

* * *

Andrew:

I got some new medicine and I'm feeling a little better.

The Process continues.

I can now see lower frequency sound waves and I don't need solid food anymore. This makes grocery shopping a little more complicated but the family hasn't complained too much.

At least there's enough of my original physiology operating that the Prozac-like capsules I'm taking still work. So there's no more outbursts of domestic telekinesis or spontaneous combustion. But I'm still obsessing about how everyone managed to miss First Contact.

First Contact. Remember when people used to capitalize those letters? Seems ridiculous now.

I agree with those sociologists who finally decided that we all just "kind of noticed" that alien concepts and information were creeping into the collective (un)consciousness of the human race.

And I do remember that interview with that Sagan wannabe who said that this probably had been happening for quite some time but only recently had the phenomena reached a "cosmological tipping point and we could now expect an exponential increase in these intellectual manifestations."

Alien thoughts appearing all these years? Well, that explains the popularity of Devo back in the 1970s.

I think I remember the interview because I felt so sorry for that astronomer. They'd had all those antennae stretched out all over the planet and the aliens weren't using radio signals to communicate with us all.

They weren't even communicating with us really.

"The Vgotsky Effect" is what they called it eventually. I looked it up on the Internet if you actually care.

God, I'm ranting here. Must be the pills.

Anyway, we discovered that we were picking up the alien civilizations through sublingual mental processes. Which appararently is the only way that information can be conveyed on a faster than light basis. Which is pretty handy if you're running a vast Galactic Super-Culture. I guess it's pretty passé to capitalize those words as well.

When I was younger I used to think all of this was pretty monumental stuff. Why doesn't anybody care about this kind of thing anymore?

Maybe it's like computers. Remember how exotic and exciting they used to be? Then we all got one, then we all *had* to start using them—so computers went from being a part of the Amazing World of the Future to yet another boring thing in everybody's pain-in-the-ass job.

So the outcome… I write in my drug-addled brain… well, we are a very practical people. If alien concepts are seeping into our minds then the best thing to do is to try and put them to some kind of commercial use.

In addition to the pills, I've been drinking quite a bit lately. So, obviously I'm very drunk. The Artificial Articulator program on this PDA is able to fix most of my spelling and grammar mistakes and since this is text, you can't know how bad my pronunciation is right now.

I'm sitting out on the porch and my youngest is sitting next to me building towers with his Lego. Cost quite a bit to replace.

I'm also trying to get some fresh air to help the fungi breathe. The little buggers have penetrated the walls of my stomach and now there's rows and rows of little flesh valves in my gut struggling hard to suck in the O_2 and push out the CO_2.

Isn't that a great conversation starter for my neighbours as they walk their dogs past the house? My youngest doesn't seem to notice, bless him.

It's about five in the afternoon and the fact that I look so bloody horrific is one reason that I'm knocking back gin and cream soda so early in the day. Another reason is that I'm not sure how much longer my body will let me get drunk.

Now how pathetic is that?

Sorry about all the tedious free association, won't happen again. The next time I write I'll be a genetically evolved super-being with the capacity for more coherent communication.

Toodles…

* * *

S—

Breathing through your gut? So are your abs just like a big balloon? Did you do all those sit-ups for nothing?

Sorry, guess I shouldn't make fun; it's just that I've had a hell of a week. Not exactly bad, just very different from what I was expecting. And since I spend most of my days exploring a simulation of the outer fringes of an unknown quadrant of the galaxy, that's saying quite a lot.

Things were going normally until Wednesday. Just coming up on noon. Middle of the week, middle of the workday. Good time for something extreme.

I was steering my sim out of a really complex trinary solar system with 18 different gas giants when I noticed that I couldn't let go of the direction controls.

It felt like the skin on my fingertips had fused into the hardware. Did I mention that something had happened to the console? No, well, now it looked a lot softer and it was throbbing.

This just didn't seem right. I was still on a high from my hot piloting, so while I was interested at the intellectual level, I was more than willing to carry on with the mission profile.

"What the fuck is going on?!"

That was what the shift controller was screaming into the scenario array. Which, I guess was a good thing. I mean, it was nice that somebody out there was actually paying attention.

(irony and the death of the sense of wonder…)

Anyway, the controller hits the master switch and shuts down all the sims. So I'm sitting there waiting for the techs to show up and unscrew me from the capsule. Meanwhile I sit there and watch the console controls kind of sigh and shudder, like somebody had just let all the air out of the electronics. (Yes, I know that makes no sense!)

Then I pulled my hands away from the controls and saw the gooey pink tendrils that linked the insides of my fingertips with the wiring of the sim's hardware.

Definitely one of those Cronenburg Moments.

What was even weirder was the fact that while this hurt like ten simultaneous root canals, it also felt quite wonderful. Rather hard to explain, really.

So they cranked all of us out double quick, used some tiny lasers to cauterize the tendrils and wheeled us off to the medicos. Once we got there they jammed sensor probes up every orifice you can imagine and put us on 24/7 monitoring.

So I lay there with a wire up my ass until Sunday. The good news is that they say we get to go back to the sims tomorrow.

Toodles to you, too…

* * *

Andrew:

I guess this is a big week for transformations.

My skin has wrinkled up and turned green and my eyes are all puffy and yellow. I look like one of the Incredible Intergalactic Turtle People.

Maybe that's not a joke.

Maybe I really am one of the intergalactic turtle people.

Really hard to say these days.

My doctor says that my Evolutionary Transformation Process has pretty much spiked and very soon I will start to get comfortable with some new superhuman abilities.

I don't know what qualifies him to make a statement like that but I actually think he's right. Every time I have a bowel movement I spontaneously factor quadratic equations while experiencing powerful flashbacks of the last time my neighbours had sex.

Which I'm sure will come in handy in the office environment at some point in time.

Best,

❋ ❋ ❋

Stephen:

I received my official briefing today. Here's the short version:

The software we've been running in our simulators is turning me into an alien organism. Not just me, the whole team on my shift.

You can imagine, how as I watched new tendrils slither out of my fingertips, what a big surprise that was.

Gosh, doctor, I said, the gill slits in my cheeks making my voice really wet and sloppy, I thought it was just a case of the flu.

No, they aren't that stupid. There must be some legal reason they gave me the news in this way. And sure enough, the medico opens up my file and takes out a document that I must have signed when I accepted the job.

"It's important for you to understand that, even though this is an unexpected development," the guy says, "you gave us full consent at the outset of the project."

That's an interesting medical opinion.

The chair in this office is making what passes for my ass these days really uncomfortable. All terrestrial furniture is bad these days. I only feel good inside the sim. I really don't care what the Company doctor is telling me. All I want to do is get back to my sim runs.

"We're shutting down the project," the doctor says. "We're just not sure what directions these transformations are taking."

Shutting it down? No runs?

Shit. Shit, shit and shit.

The doctor peers at some notes. He sounds a little uncertain because this communication was written by people with different education.

"And apparently the missions you've been training for are for some part of the galaxy that we're not likely to access for another two or three millennia."

I should have said something at that point. Raised some objection. I didn't.

Maybe my mutant lisp was making me feel self-conscious.

"We just don't see any practical applications."

Bullshit. They just don't feel like spending any more money.

Now at that point, I do remember standing up really fast. Then I remember the flash of the doctor's needle and the last thing I remember was noticing how quickly the floor was approaching my face.

The tranquilizer must have worked very fast. Guess my physiology hadn't changed that much.

Take care,

* * *

Andrew:

Sounds like we had very similar weeks.

At least as far as needles and the lecture on "informed consent" were concerned. They have a better case with me. Unbelievable as it sounds to me now, I actually signed up for all this nonsense.

They called me up from my cubicle, on yes, a *Wednesday.* I was doing lateral data matches from different Company divisions and I actually thought that I was doing some good work there. So I didn't appreciate the interruption.

It's hard to get back on track when you're on a good telepathic roll.

Elwood was waiting for me. In an office with a window.

Big domed forehead, brain the size of twelve supercomputers, bulging purple bloodshot eyes. As I recall, Elwood had those ugly eyes before he underwent the Process.

I never liked Elwood. I didn't like Elwood when he was an intern in human resources, I didn't like him when he had xeno-plasmic goo oozing from his ears and nose, and I didn't like him on that particular Wednesday.

Even though he was a highly successful super-being.

It's interesting to discover what changes in a person and what doesn't.

"Stephen," Elwood spoke very quietly, very carefully. "We've been accessing your Actualization."

Yeah, tell me something that wasn't completely obvious, you ultra-craniated moron, I thought.

Then I briefly wondered if empathic telepathy was one of Elwood's evolved skills.

Oh, well. He might as well know the truth.

"We feel that the synergy between your poteniated self and our corporate objectives..."

This was not going to be good. They never call you into an office if they want to talk to you about a good thing.

"...isn't yielding the sorts of benefits we had hoped for."

Like you, maybe I should have said something. I could have tried to argue this point. Maybe I wasn't as smart as Elwood but my functional I.Q. was probably pushing 350 and I had been charted as a much more creative thinker than he'd ever be. So what if I had slimy gray skin, a perpetually running "nose" and breathing pores up the sides of my body that emitted gases that made me smell like a dead raccoon most of the time.

Small price for progress, right? I was one of the courageous few who had accepted the challenge of the (apparently) slimy, sticky and smelly space people.

None of these revelations were going to help with my discussion with Elwood. Alas, he was the one with the astonishingly advanced bean-counting abilities. If I had dropped 0000.1% below some arbitrary performance criteria, I'm sure that chrome-dome here would know all the math behind it.

"We're going to have to terminate, Stephen."

Could be worse, I thought. With all my brainpower and creative genius I could go freelance. Be an amazingly annoying consultant.

Then I guess it was my turn to get a piece of paper. It was a section of my original consent form, something that I'd signed back when I was a lot dumber.

"You do understand that because we paid the costs for your

intellectual improvements, we can't allow anyone else to profit from them."

Okay, maybe it could get worse.

Here's an interesting historical factoid: do you know that they will use the same substance to burn out my mutagenic agents that they used to treat venereal disease? I mean before they discovered penicillin.

Mercury.

That's right, they're going to inject me with heavy doses of brain killing, blood poisoning mercury. It will definitely sharply reduce my intelligence, it might make me go blind, but at least it won't kill me. Which, by the way, was the other option that Elwood mentioned.

I can even go home eventually. I wonder if there'll be anybody there waiting for me?

Maybe they've already started with doses in my food. I feel stupider these days. I'm beginning to think that the President of the Corporation is Really a Good Guy Underneath It All and I notice that I'm watching a lot more sports on TV.

They don't seem to mind us exchanging these letters. They say it seems to keep us calm. They even say that eventually I'll get to come and visit you at Fort Fuck-Up. Did you know that's what they call the containment facility for Unplanned Evolutionary Manifestations? (Okay, at least my vocabulary isn't shot yet.)

We'll make quite a pair on visiting day. I'll never be so far gone that I won't be happy to see my baby brother.

You can tell me about the wonders of the universe and how you dream of visiting all those fantastic civilizations that drift beyond the stars.

And I'll just be wondering what stars are.

THE WISDOM OF THE ROAD-TRIP

There are a couple of things to keep in mind while you read this companion piece to "Sticky Wonder Tales":

- Canada is very big. Not Douglas Adams space big, but sizable even so.
- Some places in Canada are accordingly quite far apart from each other.
- If you're not using an aircraft or (an as-of-yet-not-built) Hyperloop, it can take a very long time to get from one place to another.

Hence the road-trip. Not an exclusively Canadian institution, but one that we have perfected to high art.

It is true there are challenges to the road-trip such as: wrestling with your bladder as you wait for a socially acceptable place to urinate; feeling the entire lower half of your body going numb; or struggling to digest gas station food.

Even so, it is vital to appreciate that the road-trip is also a unique educational setting. In fact, it is often more accurate to think of the road-trip as a 100 km an hour rolling Chautauqua where drivers and passengers are able to share all manner of knowledge, ideas, memories, dreams, fears, ideals, and aspirations. Sometimes what people say as the landscape passes by can be poetry or story-telling as powerful and primal as any creation myth shared over a Cro-Magnon campfire.

One road-trip completely transformed my consciousness. I was 13 and my father and I were on an eight-hour plus trip on a prairie highway; one of my sisters had just had a baby, and we were headed out to meet this new human. It was night, and there was a steady but light flurry of snow racing towards the windshield. In the car's headlights and with the pitch-black sky, the snowflakes looked like stars racing towards us at faster-than-light speeds.

I think I must have shared my impression with my dad because he started to tell me the plots of his favourite 30 or 40 science fiction stories. His narratives were a stunning revelation to me. First, the stories were almost all really good—and his summaries did nothing to dull my enjoyment when I eventually read them for myself. Second, this was shocking evidence that *my dad actually read things for fun.* Which in turn suggested that he was a human-type person in his own right. (gasp!)

You learn the most interesting things on road-trips.

THE MEANING OF STEEL

Originally published in:
Opal Magazine
August 2017

DINNER

"So what do the good people at Progressive Apparatus want to talk to me about?"

Most days of the week PA wouldn't acknowledge that a micro-operator like me even existed. "Nothing as complicated as your last assignment."

Fuchs seemed like the usual corporate lifer: round glasses, bowtie, slicked back hair and too much gray flannel. I figured that Fuchs didn't like "complicated" very much. Fine, neither did I.

"So what's the gig?"

"Location and delivery," Fuchs said.

"What and where?"

"Irradiated steel."

"Ah, Hamilton then."

Our food arrived.

I was having my favourite, mutated exo-bass-liver. Fuchs tried not to look disgusted.

COFFEE

A. Karx's Digital Archaeological and Meta-Cultural Consulting Services, looked like somebody took a museum of historical electronics and dropped it from a great height. But what could I do? With so much new tech and apps slipping into our brains from the Great Ether, it was hard to keep stuff organized.

"Pull up your pants, Milton."

"These are an aesthetic statement. Hipsters. They're supposed to ride that way."

"When they're down to your knees, I imagine I'll be seeing you on the cover of GQ."

Milton took another swig of 'coffee'.

"So what does a swanky outfit like PA want with a shitload of steel?"

"*Irradiated* steel," I said. "And watch the language."

"Fuck yeah, sorry," Milton said. "Radiation? That's even weirder."

"How so?"

"It's just that *steel...*"

"*Radioactive* steel."

"...is a little too *terrestrial* for PA, isn't it?"

"I can only assume that they're acquiring the stuff on behalf of one of their clients."

"Sound dodgy to me."

I nodded.

LUNCH

Stan (my shotgun) was digging into a plastic bag of synthetic meat strings.

"Why do you eat that crap?" I asked as I eased up a little on the accelerator. Milton had fixed me up with a custom-made eighteen-wheeler with a couple of huge movable storage tanks. It had a custom-made cab that looked like an old Apollo command module lying on its side.

"Got to stay strong." Stan slapped one of his biceps, which was about the size of the trunk of a redwood tree.

Stan was a nice kid but he was perpetually angry. His parents kept getting laid off, getting new physio and skill mods (courtesy of our ever-so-subtle exo-friends) and then getting laid off again so they had to get more mods.

As he grew up, Stan's parents kept getting weirder and weirder. The more you got your body altered, the less human your psychology got.

"How's your sister doing?" I asked.

"She's bizarre."

Stan stuffed another mass of pseudo-protein in his mouth and looked out the window.

"Sorry," I said eventually.

"Thanks."

"Transformation isn't going well?" Maybe it would do Stan some good to talk about it.

"She's mostly neural tissue now."

"Like a big brain?"

Just after I asked that question, it occurred to me that it might be just a little insensitive.

"They have to inject her with this suspension fluid just to keep her physically integrated."

Physically integrated?! "That sounds pretty serious," I said.

"It is."

On the up side, the traffic was improving.

"Is there any possibility that… they… might…" I realized that I was venturing into dangerously sensitive territory. "…consider…" I hesitated.

"Termination?" Stan finished the sentence for me.

"Yeah…"

"I wish they would."

Another long pause.

"But she's the best systems-analyst they've ever had."

Now there was some kind of fighter-sedan trying to pass me in the slow lane. I resisted the urge to ram him off the road.

"Trouble is…" Now he started aiming his rifle out the window in the general direction of the sedan, checking the sights.

"Careful, buddy," I said softly.

"Trouble is she can access my cell phone. She calls me up. Talks to me for hours."

"About what?"

A very big, very armoured burb-wagon rolled by. I bet Stan would have really enjoyed putting a hole in the side of it at that moment.

"Most of it doesn't make a lot of sense, but I understand enough to know that she's in a lot of pain."

Stan put down the rifle. This was probably a good idea.

"So what do you think?" Stan asked me finally.

"About what?"

"What the hell does a bunch of desk-sucking dorks like PA want with half a tonne of hot steel?"

"Haven't a clue," I replied as we passed an RCMP tank. "Do you have any ideas?" I asked.

"Silver bullet," Stan said.

"You mean somebody has werewolf problems?" I'm not afraid to ask the occasional stupid question.

"I figure that the aliens have finally showed up in person."

"You figure?"

"The ETs must have said or done something, or are threatening to do something, that's really p-o'd the government. And some idiot scientist has told the moron politicians that the only way to off these aliens is to shoot them with radioactive bullets."

"No."

"No?"

"One hundred thousand science fiction movies can't be wrong. Salt water is the only thing that really kills monsters and aliens."

I looked out at the darkening sky. Didn't look like anybody was going to be landing soon.

DINNER

The methane station smelled like pig shit.

Fortunately, the restaurant had its own air supply and the food was reasonably good. Almost like real fish and meat.

"So what's your theory?"

"My theory?"

"About the irradiated steel?"

"Don't know." I tried and failed to pick up some tofu cubes with my chopsticks. "Don't care."

Just to irritate me, Stan picked up one of his tofu cubes and ate it. "You care about everything."

I gave up and scooped the remaining cubes with the emergency plastic spoon they leave out for incurable wilos.

"How about quantum computers?"

"You mean the computers that are supposed to calculate at faster than light speeds?"

A kid Stan's age probably had nine or ten of the damned things in his bedroom.

"Well, maybe the radiation has changed the molecular structure of the alloy…"

"Can radiation do that?" Stan was starting to look bored as he started foraging around in his bowl of bean sprouts.

I decided to skip any of the scientific details, which I would have been making up anyway.

"...and makes the steel useful as possible circuit components?"

"But what do a bunch of bozos like PA want quantum computers for?"

"One of the things my brother was working on, before..." All of a sudden I found myself feeling very sad.

"It's okay," Stan said quietly. We had some similar family issues.

This dose of understanding allowed me to recover some. "He was looking at Earth-based equivalents to extraterrestrial technology, in case—"

"—somebody at Galactic Central, or the Ghost Planet, or whatever, decides to shut off the magic data tap?" Stan was smiling but it wasn't a happy smile.

Most people I knew had a similar expression when they considered the fact that the most innovative period in human history was the result of various interstellar daydreams leaking into our brains through a myriad of subliminal wavelengths.

Idle thoughts.

Somebody else's idle thoughts.

"Andrew figured that quantum tech was our best bet so far," I said.

"How's he doing these days?" Stan pushed his chopsticks through a layer cake of many colours.

"He's okay," I answered as I leaned back in my seat and looked over at a pack of subnormals pushing a load of crates onto the back of an automatic cargo blimp. Robots work a lot faster but the price of two-digit IQ labour was definitely more competitive.

"His controller says he might be able to live in a dorm soon. Work off some of his debt."

"Bastards."

I stuffed a piece of cake into my mouth. "Andy knew that the gig was dangerous when he took it. So did I."

"Yeah, but—"

"I was lucky, Andy wasn't."

BREAKFAST

Big detour.

Some kind of nanotech leak onto a mild patch of Wild.

We copped a freebie at the Regional Temple of Mentotechnology and Personal Transcendence at the outermost outskirts of Hamilton. If you show up, you aren't allowed to leave hungry and you're made aware of your right to access the "hardware to heaven" process that made Mentotechnics the leading faith of the last century's leading celebrities. You also got to wear a shiny silver hat and they play a lot of vintage synthesizer music.

Kind of fun.

Besides, we weren't freeloading. We had been mugged that night and were definitely in need of a bit of aid.

The problem was that unless your vehicle is registered as high-priority automated industrial traffic, you'll never get anything like a direct route.

We weren't, so we didn't.

I swear we must have orbited Hamilton 50 times that night.

So at about three in the morning we were in this holding pattern and even with the filtered methane engines we must have been pumping out a massive carbon footprint.

Suddenly there was a big "THUMP!" Then there's a bigger "BUMP!" and then this really huge net drops over us.

I figured that it was a good idea to stop the vehicle at that point.

More than 30 guys decked out in crash helmets, hockey pads and baseball bats walked up and started hammering on the sides of Space Truck. Stan rolled down the window and pointed his shotgun in the direction of our new acquaintances:

"What do you want?!"

"What do you got?!"

Obviously these guys didn't think Stan was going to shoot them. Or maybe they didn't care.

"*Nothing!*" I yelled out into the darkness.

The pounding on the sides of the truck resumed. I didn't think they could rupture the storage tanks but the noise was irritating.

"*Nothing?!*" another voice cried out in disbelief.

"We're going in for a pick-up!" I replied.

"A pick-up?" It was the same voice, sounding even more skeptical. "In Hamilton?"

An isolated batter took a swing and smashed one of our headlights.

"*If we ever get there!*"

I knew that the residents of this particular ideological zone didn't think random violence and destruction were big deals. In fact they were almost expected forms of interaction. But our truck was a rental and my damage deposit had just flown out the window.

"What's there to pick up in Hamilton?"

Most of the guys were getting bored, and so they got back to work with their bats.

The hammering on the tanks got louder.

"Stop that!" yelled Stan. "You want your skin to melt?!"

"*Stop!*"

It was the lead guy.

One of the batters stopped just before he connected with one tank's containment valves.

"What the hell are you talking about?!"

This batter was not as smart as the lead.

"We're just off the Rochester hovercraft with a fresh load."

"Thought you were here to pick up?"

"We got an exchange going," Stan said. "Whole load of stuff from the old Kodak plant. Don't know what it is, but it sure smells weird."

At this point most of the bats were leaning on shoulders and their owners started wandering away.

"That convinced them," I said quietly.

"Not completely," said another voice.

He was an old guy (about my age) and he was standing next to the front wheel well. Instead of a bat he was holding a three-foot length of metal pipe.

"You two look way too healthy to be toxic-loaders."

"We work out a lot."

"You must be after irradiated steel," the old guy said.

"Now why would you think that?"

"Only thing they got left that ain't nailed down in there is steel." The old bastard peered at us. "What the hell do you guys want with a truckload of irradiated steel?"

"Wish we knew."

The old guy nodded his head. "You probably don't."

I shrugged. "What can you do, eh?"

"Probably got something to do with construction," the old guy said. "That's what they used to do with most of their steel."

"Good solid stuff, steel."

"They probably need it to be radioactive so they can build up north."

"Up north?" asked Stan.

The old guy nodded. "The hot steel will melt into the permafrost; it'll let 'em build really deep down."

"You think?" Stan was impressed by this theory.

"Sounds pretty plausible to me," I said.

Actually I wasn't sure about the physics of that proposition but I was not about to disagree with a man who was culturally-habituated to violence and has a metal pipe in his hand.

"You two had better be careful. It won't be an easy pick-up in there."

"Thanks for your concern."

Then the old bastard took our wallets.

BREAKFAST

Just anti-radiation capsules this morning. We didn't have much appetite. I wasn't sure if it was nerves or the steadily rising Geiger clicks on the dashboard.

Not many people would describe the former Municipality of Hamilton as beautiful but that's always how I've thought of the city. When I moved to Hamilton to study at the university back before it converted itself into a cluster of self-aware AI complexes, I was just pumped to rent my first bed-sit in the academic district. I had to tutor engineering students but I never went near their department and I never would have even considered venturing into the industrial core.

How times change.

I guess my naive country-mouse ways must have had some charm because Lucy, who was easily the coolest and sexiest grad student in our department, had decided to talk to me at one of the departmental parties.

"You don't have a clue, do you?" she asked.

"Clue about what?" My response must have confirmed her remark.

"About Hamilton." Lucy laughed and sucked back on her bottle of beer.

"I'm pretty new here." I was clutching a can of fizzy something which the bartender at the Student Union pub looked embarrassed to serve me. I felt like I was eleven years old.

"Let me take you for a ride." Yes, Lucy's blood alcohol level was probably over the legal limit but I was not going to turn down an opportunity like this because I wasn't really eleven years old.

We stumbled out of the pub, piled into her boyfriend's prehistoric Volvo wagon and thundered off into the night.

I had kind of hoped that Lucy would suggest a change in plans that we might end up at her place without her boyfriend around. But no, I wasn't exuding that much charm. She really did want to show me what she found interesting about her home town.

The steel furnace firing away against the night sky was definitely the highlight of the tour. Imagine Fritz Lang working in Technicolor and Cinerama. Or maybe 3D IMAX. The whole plant looked like a monstrously complex machine city with a metal volcano at its heart.

Talk about your prophetic visions.

Sometimes we don't like to think about how little control we have as the ol' Cosmic Paradigm Shift "progresses". Toronto got the Wild. And people, like my ex-gf's son, got good money by going into the old city centre and trying to blast out all the beasties that live there.

On the other side of the lake like Buffalo and Rochester, it got very weird and toxic and the life expectancy dropped to age 32. But at least part of that was due to the state laws about extreme sports and roller derby eligibility.

Hamilton, like Saskatchewan, got robots and automatons. Lots and lots of automatons that were always busy doing something. It would have been reassuring if we actually knew what they were doing all the time.

If you had any kind of industrial aesthetic you would have agreed that Hamilton got the best out of the new developments. The place was bizarre, totally de-humanized and absolutely amazing. I could still recognize many of the spaces and structures of the City. Except that the parks and streets were now filled with metal and plastic pods rolling around on huge inflatable wheels or ambulating about on jointed tripods.

I remember reading somewhere that some Paradigmists believed that these were apparently the best mobility configurations for materials handling.

We saw a couple of human-controlled vehicles crawling along those big one-way streets. The automaton pods would occasionally roll up beside the drivers, extend some sensors and peer at them. Eventually the pods would go away and let the humans go about their business.

"Now we're cooking with gas!"

Now where had Stan picked up an ancient expression like that? Somehow he'd managed to negotiate through all the construction and we were now on what used to be Barton Street.

Not too far now.

The warehouse was essentially a big black box, sort of like a Wal-Mart that had gone over to the Dark Side.

"You sure this is the place?" Stan pulled on the brake handle and eased the truck to a stop.

We must have activated some kind of sensor because there was a sudden burst of light and now the big black box was a big silver box. A shape was visible in front of the silver box. Then there was some movement.

We could make out what looked like an inflated heavily-articulated trench coat. It got closer, and we saw that the trench coat was wearing a multi-valved gas mask with bulbous lenses topped off with a wide-brimmed rain/radiation resistant hat.

Whatever it was—was now standing next to the passenger door.

"Progressive Apparatus?" it asked.

"Yeah," I replied.

Trenchcoat was growling those words out through some kind of speaker. It was holding what looked like a nuclear-powered TV remote in a rubber-gloved hand. It pointed the unit at the ID chip in our truck's front wheel-well.

"You seem to be who you say you are," Trenchcoat said.

"We're just contractors," Stan spat out. "We're not a part of that organization."

Trenchcoat shrugged its tube lined shoulders. It turned and pointed the remote at the warehouse door.

The irradiated steel was sitting there, waiting for us: a big semi-regular pyramid of irregularly sized girders. Somebody had dropped a translucent sheet over the stack. I sincerely hoped that the tarpaulin was made of some kind of lead-impregnated fabric.

LUNCH

We skipped it.

I prayed that the lack of appetite wasn't an early symptom of radiation poisoning. Stan and I were encased in surplus EVA suits as we used a manually-powered forklift to load the steel into the containment tanks. Fortunately the battering-boys hadn't managed to crack the tank.

"Ever wonder how this stuff got contaminated in the first place?"

"Must have been an industrial accident."

Stan was grunting and sweating up his visor as he pushed one of the girders towards the back of the tank.

"With all those bots and mechs rolling around out there, there's bound to be some screw-ups."

"Yeah, probably."

Chances were that Stan was correct. If there were constant ambient radiation levels here, that meant that the wireless control systems were probably breaking down fairly regularly.

We were down to the last girder.

"How are we doing on weight?" I asked. We did not want our truck's suspension to go when we were halfway down the I97.

Stan leaned his helmet down so he could check the meter on the rear hydraulic spring.

"We're good," he said. "Gauge says we could manage at least another 2500."

2500? That sounded like a lot.

I used the last iota of my muscular energy to slam the containment tank shut and seal it.

My face plate was almost completely fogged up.

"Are we done yet?" Stan asked.

"Almost." I twisted open one of the valves at the base of my helmet. At that point I was so hot and uncomfortable that I didn't care if the air was toxic.

We divested ourselves of the EVA suits and found Trenchcoat in an office at the back of the warehouse. It was sitting perfectly still, behind a desk, ram-rod straight.

You couldn't even tell if it was breathing.

"Somebody stole our wallets." I thought I might as well try to communicate. "We don't have any ID."

Trenchcoat stared at me with those huge glass lenses. "Why is this my problem?"

"We have to take this load across the border." I swear I could hear something clicking inside its head. "We need paperwork to do that."

A heavy sigh sounds pretty weird through a vocoder.

Trenchcoat plugged some jacks into its palms, made a few sharp gestures, and paper started scrolling out of a printer. There was a lot of paper involved so we had to wait around for a while.

"Say, are you one of those humanoid robots?" Stan sat on the edge of Trenchcoat's desk.

"What?" Trenchcoat asked without turning towards Stan.

"Or are you some kind of radiation accident survivor who has to stay in that suit to stay alive?"

"Stan—" I began.

"That's a pretty personal question." Trenchcoat pulled the jacks out of its palms.

For a second I wondered if Trenchcoat was going to fasten a chain saw on the end of its arm and use it to explain how it felt about Stan's lapse in manners. Fortunately, no.

"But the answer is yes." Trenchcoat pulled the mass of paper out of the printer. "And get off my desk."

Stan wiped his nose and walked out of the office.

"Young people these days," I said. "So high strung."

There was another, this time quieter, sigh from Trenchcoat's speaker. It reminded me of deep space static from a radio telescope.

I flipped through the print-out and spotted a few Ottawa addresses and the Fedgov logo here and there. "Any idea what they want all that hot steel for?"

"Yeah." Trenchcoat was putting more jacks into the sides of its head.

"Well?"

Trenchcoat looked at me. "The price of mercury has gone up 20.23%."

And yes, Trenchcoat did have a bunch of wires stuck in its head.

"What?"

Trenchcoat turned away from me. The jacks were probably providing a video feed so he was watching something much more interesting than me. Most likely extreme curling or naked roller derby girls.

Mercury?

SNACK TIME

There wasn't much between us and the outskirts of the city. I noticed a few subs in their yellow rubber coveralls poking their heads inside some overturned mechs. Sub-normals and Trenchcoat were probably the only humans who didn't object working long-term among all that ambient R. That is if Trenchcoat was human.

There was something about mercury…

We were both eating something that had been deep-fried and freeze-dried in the last century when we drove up to the massive wall at the other end of the Peace Bridge.

"Can I ask you a personal question, Stan?"

He hadn't said much since he left Trenchcoat's office. The kid was probably getting very bored with this gig.

"Why not?"

"Do they think your sister's transformation was a success?"

"I guess so."

"My brother's process didn't pan out too well."

"I know."

"Did they ever tell your sister what they do when they decide to terminate a transformation?"

"Company's legal position is that since they invested in the technology, they own all the results."

"Even if the transformation doesn't provide them with any profit?"

"Yeah, *obviously*."

"And how do they protect their investment?" I was as much talking myself through an unwelcome chain of thought as I was asking Stan questions.

"They inject the subject with…" Stan began.

"…mercury," I finished.

We stopped at the customs booth. The officer was a sub-normal because the Americans considered border patrol work to be particularly hazardous.

I handed him the stack of printouts. The poor sap obviously couldn't read but he was able to see the big arrow on the cover sheet and that told him that he needed to feed the sheets into the big ugly machine next to him.

"And of course, those mercury injections…"

The customs officer must have sensed something because he looked up and gave us a big goofy smile.

"Do you know the price of mercury has gone up 20.23%?"

Neither of us said anything for a while. Eventually the officer handed us a pair of U.S. entry passes and gave us another one of those tragic smiles.

We didn't start talking again until we'd cleared the Buffalo Burn-Out Zone.

Stan finally spoke: "So you figure that PA has been contracted to…"

"…find a cheaper alternative."

There was more silence.

Then: "I have an idea."

We kept on driving.

BREAKFAST

A 'power breakfast' as our lawyer liked to call them. We figured that was because Ms. Ruby likes to eat a lot in the mornings. Since she always seemed pretty sharp, it seemed to be working for her. Getting us out on bail was nothing short of brilliant.

"Let's review this once more." Ms. Ruby speared some honeydew cubes with a small fork. First fresh fruit we've had in town in five years. "You claim you had no criminal intent in mind when you launched the containment tanks?"

"Absolutely none," I replied. "I had personally supervised the truck's spring release system because it was essential to the aesthetics of the creative project."

Ms. Ruby took a sip of her smoothie and looked over at Stan. "You can confirm this?"

Stan pointed his thumb at me. "This guy's a real perfectionist."

"So when the two tanks flew through the front window of the corporate headquarters of Progressive Apparatus…"

"I prefer to call the experience as Impact Art…"

"…you meant no harm to any of the employees of said organization."

"Of course not. I didn't want to hurt my audience," I said. "Simply engage their imagination and aesthetic sensibilities."

"What about all that radioactive steel inside the tanks?" Ms. Ruby looked at us skeptically.

"We're really familiar with the tolerances of the tanks," Stan said.

"As long as no one attempts to touch them there should be no leakage," I finished. "At least for the foreseeable future."

Of course, I hadn't been sure at all. Not with all that hammering from the baseball bats.

"And we blew the horn real loud before we released the tanks," Stan added. "So everybody could get out of the way."

Ms. Ruby finished her smoothie and set the glass aside. She glanced down at her notes before she spoke again. "I don't have a note of this… I suppose I should have asked earlier."

"Asked what?"

"What is the name of this work of performance art?"

"Impact Art, please."

"Whatever. What do you call it?'

I looked at Stan.

"Brother and Sister."

EMBARRASSING SURVEYS

One Saturday morning, more than a few years ago, a student from the Urban Geography Program from a local college was standing at our front door. She wanted me to answer some questions about landmarks and monuments in the neighbourhood. To my embarrassment, I didn't score very well on the survey.

At the time, my work required me to spend most of my time in a different hemisphere. Failing that test made me decide that I needed to become a geographer and an anthropologist on my home turf. This exercise didn't require much of a change in my routine; it just meant that I would spend less time thinking about where I was going to be next, and more time noticing where I was at the time.

Skip ahead a few years. My job now involves me mostly staying at home with only the occasional jaunt somewhere. Instead of jets, I travel around on streetcars and subways. No complaints.

My appreciation of my neighbourhood has deepened, but the observations also make me very sad. Many of the places and people that were once a regular part of our lives have become obsolete and have disappeared. The local video store used to be a community hub. Ain't no such beast now. Sometimes it feels like we're all being picked up and housed in some obscure archives. And I don't know if anyone will ever be interested enough to look us up.

Yeah, I know. Change happens. Sometimes change is even good. I don't even object to being replaced by something new. I just hope there's something out there to replace us.

AMMONITE CITY

Originally published in:
Latent Image Magazine
August 2019

Do you have any questions before we begin?

"Hey! Are you crazy?"

The guy was standing just about right in the middle of the street, apparently oblivious to the end of the morning rush-hour traffic.

I yelled again: "You are going to get killed!"

Not paying attention. The guy was peering into a tiny box, probably some kind of camera. It looked like he was trying to get a shot of an oncoming streetcar.

Okay, at least this made partial sense. We're one of the few cities in North America with an active, authentic street railway system. The red rockets are very exotic and they have their fans. Still they were not worth going two-dimensional for.

The guy took his picture and leapt back onto the sidewalk. "You get what you wanted?" I looked the guy over. He was wearing a Gore-Tex parka, heavy jeans and winter training shoes. Not stylish but functionally appropriate for late November. The most striking thing was his headgear: it was one of those furry hats with big earflaps.

Clarence of the Yukon.

If they ever did a movie about this guy, that's what they would call it.

Clarence of the Yukon Who Never Got North of Sudbury.

"Oh, yes!" He was delighted. "I was able to capture an image of the cable unit sparking off the wires."

"I'll bet that's very visually interesting." I took off a glove and started fishing around in my pocket for my keys.

"Better yet," the guy answered. "It illustrates the electrical power source." So in addition to being risk-assessment-impaired, this guy was some kind of technical nerd.

"Great," I said, pushing my keys into the lock of the shop door.

"I'm glad you agree," the guy said. Then he looked at the storefront. "Do you work here?"

I looked up at the sign over our display window.

Video Portal.

A.K.A. the last video rental store in Canada. Or at least this part of Toronto.

Even though I've put in six days a week at this place for over 17 years, it's never a bad idea to check and see if you're at the right place.

"Yeah."

"Do you mind if I come in?" He moved pretty fast so I didn't get a chance to say no. I pulled off my coat, turned on the lights and booted up the cash and inventory computer.

"My name is Clarence," the guy said.

Hey, synchronicity. I dimly remembered that as some mysterious concept from my university days.

The guy, now confirmed as Clarence, but probably not of the Yukon, started wandering down one of the aisles. "What's your name?"

Clarence wanted to have some kind of interpersonal exchange. Ugh.

"Roger."

Clarence was looking over the contents of our used VHS sales bin. Basically all the Hollywood fog and stretch that you could get for 39 cents a tape. Maybe Clarence was an old movie nut, too. Then something else occurred to me:

"The adult section is over at the back of the store," I said, trying to sound casual. "Just walk through the door with the beads." Clarence might be some kind of early-bird pervert; I mean, normal people would be downloading their porn this time of day.

"No thanks," Clarence replied. "I'm not doing any studies on sexual stunts just yet."

Sexual stunts? I guess that was not a completely inaccurate way of describing our XXX collection.

Clarence took out another camera; this one was cardboard, one of those disposable ones that you could still buy at the 7-11 across the street. He started clicking off shots of the inside of the store. I couldn't be sure but it looked like he was taking pictures of the genre titles over the display racks: "Horror... Drama... Comedy... Action... Science Fiction... Family... Foreign..."

"Clarence? What are you doing?" I wasn't particularly nervous; if he was casing out the joint to rob it later on, he was going to make about 78 bucks.

Now he was taking pictures of my counter.

"Clarence?" Maybe this wasn't dangerous but it was pretty strange.

He put down his camera and looked embarrassed. "I'm so sorry; I should have asked you for permission, shouldn't I?"

"I guess so." I'd never been in a situation like this before so I had no idea if he needed to ask or not.

"I tend to get carried away," Clarence said. "It's all so exciting here."

"I can understand that." I looked past at the wall behind Clarence. It carried a poster advertising the release of *The Goonies* on Betamax and VHS for Christmas 1985.

I really should update that display.

"I've been observing your establishment for almost a month now."

"Really?" I mean, *why?*

"It's truly fascinating."

"Yeah?" Maybe the guy just didn't have enough to do.

"It is a sociological treasure house!"

"Sure."

Probably he was just crazy.

Please describe three public monuments within six blocks of your home:

- Do you know the approximate dates that these monuments were erected?
- What do each of the monuments commemorate?

- Do any of the monuments have personal meanings or associations for you?

One of the first things I did was get Clarence access to a better camera.

"I'm sorry," he said (Clarence liked to apologize every once in a while). "Some of my equipment hasn't arrived yet."

I lent him the little digital I bought at the drug store last year. If he couldn't be any less conspicuous then at least he wouldn't be completely embarrassing.

"I'm trying to make an interactive ethnographic record," Clarence explained. "As comprehensive as possible."

"Record of what?" I sipped on some hot coffee and took in the fairly ordinary vista offered by the front window of *Donut World*. You had to drink their coffee very slowly because it was the only fluid on Earth whose temperature exceeded that of the surface of the sun. Maybe those people who were looking for a nuclear fusion power source ought to stop by.

I suggested Clarence and I talk there because I didn't want him hanging around if my boss showed up.

"I'm generating a 360-degree record of the neighbourhood." Unlike me, Clarence was knocking back the caffeine flavoured lava like it was spring water. "Starting with the gated apartment complex over by Humber Bay, past the assisted housing units along the Lakeshore, up to the old railway workers' places on Hillside and then up past Sam Smith Park."

"You're following the streetcar line," I observed.

Clarence nodded as he swallowed. "Yes, it seems to be a kind of cultural lifeline... as well as a transportation system."

Interesting point.

"So what's so important about *Video Portal*?"

"It's a key cross-cultural exchange point in this region," Clarence replied. "People from every social class, income and age level, ethnic and educational background—they all frequent your store over the course of one week."

Clarence was right about that. There were various reasons that VP was such a social focus: cable and video on demand were getting too expensive for some people so downloading movies wasn't as prevalent here, the streetcar lines somehow interfered with satellite reception, and the former *Blockbuster* outlet just west of Kipling went under quite a while ago.

"Fine, all roads lead to the video store," I said as I watched a fresh load of passengers shuffle off the latest 501 streetcar on its way to Long Branch. "And why do you care about that so much?"

Clarence smiled. I think he was quite pleased to answer questions like that. "Well, for several reasons: First, it's quite informative to observe how people of different backgrounds interact with each other in a small but relatively neutral social space."

Clarence had something there. It was kind of cool to watch how people with BMWs parked outside handled getting stuck in line behind the single welfare moms the weekend before the Academy Awards broadcast.

"Second, because such a varied group conglomerates at your store, it allows me to track people back to their various economic and sub-cultural enclaves."

"Track people?" This was somewhat alarming news. "What's that? Systematic stalking?"

"Oh, no." Clarence smiled some more. "It's more benign than that."

My coffee had cooled to the point where mercury evaporates. I took a longer drink and looked across the cafe. I could see the smokers coming in from their morning fix.

"That's it?" I asked.

Clarence shrugged and took a squishy bite from his donut. "It's also revealing to see what people find entertaining at this point in human history."

At this point in human history? That was a big "*hmmmmmm.*"

> Please list the ages of the five people you know best, who are not members of your family:
>
> - If you have moved to the neighbourhood in the last five years, how long did it take you to make your first close friend? Within one week? One month? Six months? A year? More than one year?

- How many people on your block do you feel you could call on for help in an emergency?

A few weeks later, Clarence wandered into the store with a black eye and a bandage covering most of his nose.

"What the hell happened to you?"

"Interview didn't go too well," Clarence spoke with a muffled voice as he sat down in my chair behind the counter.

I finished slipping discs into plastic envelopes and handed Clarence some small dark brown objects.

"What are these?" he asked.

"Chocolate Buddhas," I replied. "I always order some in for the Christmas holidays."

Clarence put one of the sweets into his mouth and winced. "Hurts to chew."

"Just suck on their heads for a while." I pulled out another chair. "It is the path to enlightenment and true wisdom."

Clarence looked at me with some skepticism.

"Trust me! In a few minutes you'll feel a whole lot better."

Clarence responded by nodding and sucking on the chocolate. After it looked like some of the endorphin-like molecules had entered Clarence's bloodstream, I pointed at the bandage.

"Broken?"

"Yeah," Clarence said. "It seems that Mrs. Plauwick took exception to my research methodology."

"Really?" I wasn't surprised. Mrs. Plauwick took exception to just about everything. "Let's see."

Clarence handed me a very fat file folder. I opened it up and started reading.

"Okay..." I said. "You're asking people about their religion, politics, sexual orientation and personal appearance."

"Yes." Clarence shrugged. "What is the problem with that?"

"I don't think you've missed a single hot button here."

Clarence just put another chocolate Buddha in his mouth. Mrs. Plauwick may have had a point.

"If you were using these questions in the States you probably would have been shot by somebody."

"Really?" Clarence opened his mouth in dismay, revealing a row of brown sticky teeth.

I decided to be honest and shake my head. These days it did not help to exaggerate about our Friends to the South. "No, but some people are going to find these questions way too personal."

"That's too bad." Clarence sighed. "Because I really need that information."

"Work can be a real bitch sometimes."

Clarence looked at me. "Perhaps people would be more receptive to these questions if they came from someone they trusted."

He had a point there. Mrs. Plauwick, for instance, had a bizarre notion that I was a "nice young man", so she'd probably tell me anything.

"No, not this again…"

"I really could use your help."

Shit, I suddenly knew that I was going to do it!

"Okay…"

Now the reason that I agreed had nothing to do with the bruises and bandages I was looking at, nor was it because I was in reality a "nice young man". No, I agreed to help Clarence because I missed doing anthropology.

- Do you have children or siblings attending the local schools?
- Do you feel the teachers are well qualified and committed to education?
- Do you believe that education is important to achieving what is important in life?
- Do you believe that your children are getting what they need at school?

So a few days later, I was walking down the old merchant strip carrying my other camera and a fake leather case full of questionnaires. The weather had warmed up some and the sky was a very moist grey and the cars were spreading a thick layer of slush over the sidewalks and storefronts. Very scenic, very festive. The

Spirit of Christmas Mud was busy at every corner.

Hell of a time to be doing social science research.

I was, in fact, just about ready to pack it in. Most of the eating-places were closed until dinner, and with the holiday season approaching people were going in and out of the supermarkets and stores with more than the usual amount of purpose. Not that many of them had the time or patience to take on an interview—even with that harmless guy from the old video store.

I was thinking that I should either go to the library or take the streetcar across town to one of the rep theatres and see *2001* for the 87th time.

Good lord, I work at a video store and I want to go and see movies in my spare time. Didn't Marx or Weber or Dr. Phil say that was some kind of social-industrial pathology?

Then I saw her.

Saw Karen.

She had big permed-out hair. God only knows what colour it was originally.

And she had these big earrings and very, very black eye shadow. Like some artist had pushed her against a wall and roughly smeared charcoal on her eyelids.

I thought she looked great. Seriously.

She was sitting on a tiny step in front of a wooden door covered with flaking wooden paint. A sign on the door said, "Psychic Readings. Open."

Karen was pulling air hard through a cigarette. Even with the massive amount of blood-red lipstick she was wearing, you knew that unless her life took a dramatic change very soon, her mouth was going to be a very scary place in about twenty years.

Her look was definitely angry slut. But for whatever reason, I just didn't believe it. She was just trying too hard. Or maybe I just like that look. I'm not as nice a boy as some people like to think I am.

"You got time to answer a few questions?"

"Tell you what…" She looked at me in a magical (and terrifying) way that suggested an unexpected future. "…you get your fortune told and maybe I'll talk to you for a while."

Great offer.

So we went inside, Karen lit some short smelly candles and took out a stack of Tarot cards.

I have to say right now that I've never really liked or particularly understood the Tarot. The cards have always looked creepy and arbitrary to me.

She pulled out the first card. I think it read: "The Insurance Salesman."

"You have pressing family obligations," Karen pronounced.

Well, okay. Dad took off when I was twelve and Mom needed whatever help we could provide.

Karen flipped over another card. It was "The Farting Weasel." (Speaking of Dad…)

"But this has not diminished your intellectual curiosity."

True, and this was very inconvenient.

I had worked my ass off when I was a teenager, scraping up enough each month to get myself into university. I was the only one in the family to show any interest in an academic career so we had no idea how to work that system. Which meant that I pretty much had to pay as I went. Which turned out to be a pretty expensive approach.

Another card: "The Boot to the Head."

"You have experienced numerous frustrations in your plans and disappointments in love."

That's about as hard to predict as saying that a stone will fall down after you let go of it.

So I eventually had to drop out of school. I was working two jobs, which still wasn't enough to pay the tuition, and my grade point average was just under what I needed for a scholarship (funny how less than four hours of sleep a night will do that to you). And the people at the university weren't all that keen to lend money to someone who wanted to major in social anthropology.

"I mean, *realistically*," the guy from the student loans office said. "How soon do you think you'll be able to start paying us back with a degree like that?"

So why the fuck did they offer the damn program then?

One more card.

"Mighty Mouse."

"But you are a determined individual. You do not give up easily."

Maybe that was why I agreed to help Clarence. What he offered was at least a little bit like real research.

Karen put away the cards and took my hand. "I sense that we need to explore these findings in greater detail."

Okay. I wondered how much this was going to cost me.

"Do you mind if I employ other methods?"

"Such as?"

"Palmistry."

She started tracing my wrists and palms with her finger. While I doubted the insight of this process, I had to admit that it felt good.

"Yes... yes... "

This went on for a few minutes. I wasn't objecting.

"You are indeed troubled. I sense that you need deep spiritual comfort."

"Could be." Well, my life was pretty miserable these days.

"Would you like any form of special service?"

Special service?

As in: Handjob: $40. Nude massage: $60. Nude reverse: $80.

No wonder Karen looked kind of angry all the time. She probably didn't like providing, or even suggesting, such services. But times were tough in the neighbourhood.

I wasn't terribly shocked by the implications here but I've never had the spare financial resources to seriously consider such offers.

"Am I right in saying that this has been a very slow day?" Sometimes it was better to answer an awkward question with another question.

Karen couldn't stop herself. She smiled.

"After you've answered my questions, would you like to see a movie?"

"A movie?" Her expression suggested that she hadn't had this experience in a while.

"How do you feel about Stanley Kubrik?"

Karen looked thoughtful. "In spite of *Barry Lyndon* and *Eyes Wide Shut*, I think he was one of our most important film-makers."

I was too smart to raise the matter of *A.I.*

- Could you please name your three favourite books? Films? Musical compositions?

- If you could be an artist, what medium do you think you would work in?

One week after Christmas and both of my jobs were pretty brisk.

The holidays are usually good for us. Sure, people get lots of movies under the tree and there were lots of new releases at the cinemas but all that empty time between December 25 and New Year's meant there were a lot more opportunities for additional conversation between family members. Sometimes that is just not a good thing.

So some of us seek a technological solution. We go out and rent a whole bunch of movies, or if you live in a technologically more advanced part of town you download them. Then we watch them, thereby containing a great deal of dangerous interpersonal communication.

My other line of work also involved the direction (and recording) of some of the speech in my neighbourhood. As well as some digital photography. I like to think striking up conversations with people about how they live and why they think they live that way is a more positive way of handling the complexities of the holidays.

By the last week of December I had collected over two hundred interviews and I had so many pics that I had no idea where I was going to find time to organize them all. I now had two cardboard file boxes over-flowing with data. One of them was in my bed-sit and the other on the floor next to the cash register. I was going to have to do a delivery run over to Clarence's place pretty soon.

It was just before seven in the evening, so it was pitch black outside, and there were eight people waiting in line to rent games and movies. The front door swung wide open and a wall of near-arctic air rolled in.

Karen stood in the doorway. She was wearing these incredible high-heeled leather boots and one of those Gore-Tex things like Clarence's that could have been a holiday gift from Neil Armstrong's tailor. High fashion in space.

But she had tears in her eyes and was carrying a bundle of red and blue flannel.

It was a kid dressed in superhero pyjamas. The PJs didn't have those built in feet—I could see that the kid's toes were black and purple.

"I found him behind the parking lot," Karen sobbed.

"Over here, over here!" I put my parka on the counter top. (Okay, it was Gore-Tex, too). Karen laid the child inside and I wrapped up everything except his head. By some miracle it looked like his nose and ears weren't that badly frostbitten.

He was in the parking lot? Good god, with the wind chill factor, it could have been over minus thirty out there.

The reactions of the people in the store were varied and interesting. Two of them started arguing about whose kid it was, somebody started to quietly cry while somebody else reached over and started rubbing the boy's arms and legs through my parka.

"He's so cold."

"It doesn't look like he's moving."

"Is he breathing?"

"…so cold…"

Some other people put their DVDs back on the racks and quietly left with different degrees of irritation on their faces. I made a mental note to be particularly rude to those ones when they came back for their next entertainment fix.

By now Karen was blowing small puffs of air into the boy's mouth. I was about to dial 911 when Clarence was suddenly… just there. He bustled out of the adult video enclosure, not looking even slightly embarrassed. Perhaps his research methodology had reached the part where he needed to investigate "sexual stunting".

With a very smooth and gentle motion, he took the boy out of Karen's arms and headed towards the front door.

"I have something at home that can help."

Then he and the boy (and my parka!) disappeared into the night.

Karen hesitated, just for a moment, and only because she was completely surprised by Clarence's actions. She opened the door and charged after him.

"Call me—" the door pushed more frigid air inside as it shut, "—if you need help."

And I just stood there, behind the counter. Feeling completely useless.

What is your occupation?

How long have you been engaged in this occupation?

On a scale of one to five please rate the reasons that you carry out your occupation.

Please note that the Number One means "Not at All" and the

Number Five means "Most Definitely".

• Subsistence:	1 2 3 4 5
• Social Advancement:	1 2 3 4 5
• Personal Interest:	1 2 3 4 5
• A Sense of Duty or Family Obligation:	1 2 3 4 5
• To Socialize with Others:	1 2 3 4 5
• Because my job is a lot of fun:	1 2 3 4 5

Things ended up being pretty slow for the rest of the evening, so at about twenty to ten, I muttered "the hell with capitalism," closed up and headed over to Clarence's place. Things were warming up outside—I figured it was now only minus twenty-five.

To keep myself from worrying about whether the flesh on my face was going to snap off or if I was going to freeze to death without my parka, I started thinking about how little I actually knew about Clarence. I knew where he lived but I'd never been inside his apartment. We did all of our coordination meetings at the doughnut shop or one of the meeting rooms at the local library.

I didn't even know his phone number—he always called me. Hell, he could have been calling from a booth; he might not even have a phone. I think there were still one or two public telephones in the neighbourhood.

I found his building and buzzed the intercom. I didn't wait in the cold too long, it felt like just four or five hours.

"Come in." Karen's voice crackled out of the old wire-mesh speaker.

Clarence's place was a total surprise. But after I gave it a moment's thought, it wasn't a surprise at all. The first thing I noticed was the transparent rose-tinted sphere in the middle of the living room. The child was stretched out inside the sphere and he was glowing slightly.

The next thing I noticed was the decor. It was like every piece of

1970s yard sale electronics you could imagine caught halfway through the process of transforming into some post-modernist crystal. Sort of like Sears Hardware colliding with Frank Ghery. It could have been fascinating but it really was just messy.

"What the—?" I said. (So, I'm a creature of my era and sometimes under stress I lapse into comic book dialogue.)

"He'll be fine." Karen was standing over the sphere.

"Where's Clarence?"

Clarence walked out of the bathroom holding an extremely complicated mass of joined metal cables and plastic tubes. It must have been his night for entrances with flair.

"Hi," he said. Clarence didn't look at me as he started connecting all this stuff to some nozzles and slots into the base of the sphere. Then he plugged it into what looked like an eight-track player on steroids.

"Hypothermia," Clarence said eventually. "I think the boy must have been out in the snow for quite some time."

"Sounds likely," I replied. I looked over at Karen. "Do you know who he belongs to?"

"Yes," Karen said.

"The damage from the cold was relatively simple to treat." Clarence started pressing more tubes into the membrane of the sphere. This operation generated a high-pitched farting sound. "But I also picked up traces of fetal alcohol syndrome."

What the hell could anybody do about that?

"Clarence, are you some kind of doctor?" I asked.

Karen rolled her eyes.

Clarence pressed a surface on one of the crystal shapes and turned a knob on the eight-track amplifier. The boy started glowing a bit more and Al Stewart started singing *The Year of the Cat.*

"Nope," Clarence laughed. "I can barely blow my nose without help."

Clarence walked over to the kitchen and turned on the kettle. "But it's relatively easy to correct that kind of genetic damage. Even without all my equipment."

"There's more?"

Karen smiled as Clarence pointed to his techno-clutter.

"Do you like it?" he asked. "I had to make some local adaptations."

I sank into what felt like a fourth-hand beanbag chair.

"Adaptations?"

Karen shook her head which suggested that she suspected that I was less mentally resilient than she had hoped.

The kettle started whistling.

"Do you want tea or hot chocolate?" Clarence asked.

- Please name three people, who are not family members, whom you see every day:
- What workers and professionals have you interacted with in the last week?
- Did you feel that they were competent to do their job? Why or why not?

The aftermath of the Frozen Kid Incident is so complicated and hard to explain that I'm tempted to pull the page out of the typewriter and forget the whole thing. (No, I don't have regular access to a computer. I'm part of the working poor, remember?)

What I heard the next day was that about 22 seconds after Clarence and Karen left the store with the kid, people were phoning around trying to figure out who the child belonged to, where he lived, and how on Earth did he end up barefoot and frozen in a parking lot on one of the coldest days of the year?

The next morning, a very young and very tired looking guy from Child Services walked into the store and started asking me questions. He told me a few things as well:

The kid's name was Dougie and he was just a little bit over three years old. He and his mother lived in one of the rent-assisted apartments just down the street. No surprises there—actually it wasn't a bad place.

Dougie's mom was 20 years old and his dad was absolutely nowhere to be seen. Not much surprise there, either.

It turned out that the mom had over-spent on Dougie over the holidays (easy to do) and so she had to pull in a few extra shifts at the dollar store. Including the shift on that insanely cold night.

The mom didn't have any spare cash to pay for a real babysitter so she left Dougie with a neighbour lady who was in her fifties who lived with this guy who seemed cheerful enough.

What the mom didn't know was that neighbour and her boyfriend were actually in their early thirties and were total alcoholics. The guy seemed cheerful all the time because his blood chemistry was 65% gin.

"You know," the social worker said as he ate some of my chocolate Buddhas. "They didn't seem to be bad people—just not the best choice for caregiving."

What happened next was the lady and the guy cracked open various bottles (as they did every night) and turned on the TV. Pretty soon they were into their usual routine and forgot that Dougie was even in the apartment. Like most kids would, Dougie gets bored, starts fiddling with things, finds the door unlocked and wanders out—first down the hall, then out the door. The front door of the building locks shut behind you, so once Dougie was out, he was out to stay.

He probably headed toward *Video Portal* because he remembered it as the most interesting place in the neighbourhood.

"What happens next?" I asked. "Are you going to put the kid in a foster home?"

That seemed appropriate. I mean maybe those two drunks weren't evil but the poor little guy could have died.

The social worker sighed. "SOP in cases like this is that we have to go around and check out the home situation."

"What did you see?" Normally, someone's home life is none of my effing business, but damn it, the kid was found outside the store on *my* shift.

"We dropped in fast, so the mom couldn't change much. And it was spotless."

Spotless? Was my room spotless when I was 20? Was it now?

"There were also lots of kid's books and educational toys in there. I figure she's trying hard to be a good mom."

"You think?"

"Yeah." He smiled. "And when we were interviewing her, it looked like she was about the duct-tape the poor little guy to her leg."

"So Dougie won't be taking any unescorted walks any time soon?"

"Probably not."

The social worker nodded goodbye and went off to do another

550 things before lunch.

Okay, that part of the Dougie story was sort of complicated but well within the realm of normal human experience. The *really* complicated and unusual part is how Clarence had all this strange technology that allowed him to completely unthaw and revive a kid who was essentially frozen solid and had major brain trauma and tissue damage.

> What is your annual income level?
>
> Has it increased or decreased in the last five years?

Karen got a new job.

Oddly enough she was working at the same dollar store as Dougie's mother. Maybe there had been some information exchange resulting from the kid's rescue.

Her new situation was much less lucrative but at least she didn't look like she was going to bite the heads off parking meters when I saw her for coffee. Both of us figured that she'd traded up.

One Saturday morning we were both off work so we took the streetcar downtown. We took in some bookstores, a few small and interesting galleries, and a reading at a science fiction convention. The author, "Robin the Robot" she called him, used to be one of her regular clients.

"Sad little man," Karen explained. I think she insisted we attend because she was worried that the guy would commit suicide if no one showed up.

She needn't have worried. Lots of people were there. Robin was not the saddest guy in the room after all. I thought the passage he read was a little tedious but the crowd seemed to like to hear long discussions between intelligent amphibians from an alternate Triassic Era. Afterwards, someone asked Robin if there was a sequel in the works.

"Yes." At least seven, I figured.

We said "hi", "nice job" and all that and left early. We ducked down a hallway and found ourselves in one of the hotel ballrooms. It was a big one and it was filled with gamers. Hundreds of them, mostly boys and men, hunched over coloured boards and intently moving little fragments over the surfaces. I wondered if there was some way to harness all that mental energy we could bring about world peace. Scratch that, these people liked to wage imaginary wars.

Karen was much more direct in expressing how unimpressed she was: "Fucking waste of time." Her Russian accent got stronger when she was annoyed.

It might be more exciting to say that Karen and I were off to find some secret place with romantic intent. Not really.

"Let's see what's playing at the Paramount. We might be able to catch a late matinee."

Just in case you're interested, I did (and do!) have feelings for Karen. We had been spending quite a bit of time together and she was definitely passing what I used to call the "Room Test". For those of you who don't know—the Room Test is when a person steps into your room and you involuntarily feel better. That means you are probably either in, or falling in, love. Whether you like it or not.

I didn't want to get too intense or physical at that point. I was in no hurry and she'd had enough of that kind of thing for a while. It looked like Karen was pretty happy when I stepped into the room, so I figured we had some leeway in working things out.

We headed for the movie theatre—and we had to cross the lower section of University Avenue. Which is where you find the American Consulate. Unfortunately we had forgotten that this was not a particularly good route today.

It was the same day as yet one more expression of "festive" geopolitical dialogue. Maybe there was a new pre-emptive war going on, or maybe it was a fresh bombing program or invasion of someplace. As usual, a sizable segment of the local population had shown up to explain to the American government how they felt about that.

Yeah, I respected some of those activist types (I could always count on them to rent my old tape of *REDS*) but were they achieving anything? I noticed that some of the protest signs were dissing Orbital Missile Defence. That made me laugh. In a nasty way.

Eleven-thirty in the morning on September 11, 2001, the first radio interview on the radio I heard was some senator talking about how all these tragic events meant they needed a giant ballistic defence shield around the United States.

Absolutely. Nothing like targeted hydrogen lasers and multistage nuclear warheads for helping out with airport security. Vaporize those jerks as they walk through the metal detectors.

Attack Iraq? No brainer. Follow through and invade Iran? Got to do it. Carpet-bomb Luxembourg? Feasible. Could play well for a while on TV. Exterminate the Canadian Football League? Make that a priority, we hate that extra down!

No wonder all those people out on the street were pissed.

Something bad was going to happen.

Doesn't matter what you think.

What you say.

How you vote.

Doesn't matter how nicely designed your signs are at the rally.

Bad stuff is going to happen.

I suppose that if getting out in the fresh air and exercising your feet and lungs made you feel better, then go ahead.

Things were getting ugly.

There were about a dozen snipers squatting on the top of the Consulate building and the city cops were on horseback, pacing back and forth in front of the main entrance.

Meanwhile a group of protesters started to throw things at some other cops in riot gear whose assignment seemed to be to protect the sidewalk. Then the snipers started aiming their rifles at the crowd and some of the protesters started to hit the Mounties' horses with their signs.

Now we have lots of swearing and yelling.

Karen growled. I mean she *growled.* Guttural noises. I'd never seen her so angry. She was probably remembering something from her childhood.

I'm not exactly sure what happened next—whether the plumes of tear gas appeared first or the big Hummer hit that concrete barrier first. All I can say was that it was suddenly very loud, very foggy and very busy.

Then the cops in riot gear and the Mounties started to push in on us. A young woman was trying to get her baby of the way of an advancing horse.

Baby. Mother. Mob.

This was getting way too *Battleship Potemkin* for me. It didn't look like the mother and baby were going to make it.

Karen hit berserker mode. She jumped out ahead of me, and pulled the mother and child towards her just as two sets of half-ton hooves thundered past.

A massive figure in body armour lumbered forward and at that point it was difficult to determine which was louder: the yelling of the crowd, the gun shots from the roof, the wailing of the terrified baby, or Karen's scream of rage.

Then Karen did something that I didn't know was physically possible. She grabbed the riot cop by the helmet and literally ripped the faceplate off. Both Karen and cop were screaming as she dug her fingers into the guy's face.

At this point my over-stimulated and badly inert nervous system finally kicked in and I ran over to Karen as three more cops grabbed her and threw her onto the pavement.

I was now aware of a minor nuclear explosion on the side of my head. I felt a piercing sound in one ear as I was suddenly surrounded by complete darkness expect for a very tiny but very bright point of light at the very center of what was once my field of vision.

Ouch.

Good night.

- Who are your three best friends in the neighbourhood?
- Please briefly describe how you first met them:
- How long have you known each other?
- What are your three favourite things to do together?

The first thing I saw was Clarence's face hovering over me like the planet Jupiter.

"You're conscious now," he said.

"Are you sure?"

Clarence nodded and pulled some kind of plastic pouch off the side of my head. "I've always been an advocate of greater awareness."

What the hell did that mean? I sat up and realized that I was on the couch in Clarence's apartment. Karen was there too. She was on an air mattress in the middle of the floor with some kind of half-blanket, half-bubble covering the top of her body.

"She'll be fine."

She still had her winter boots on. Her feet were moving a little so I was pretty sure she was alive.

"Although she had some pretty serious injuries." Clarence made a few adjustments on what looked like an over-sized mood lamp and the membrane around Karen started to throb.

I could feel blood oozing between my teeth. "She saved a kid's life!" I felt I had to explain this to Clarence—it seemed important to defend her character.

"She seems to do that sort of thing."

"Do you have anything to drink?" I asked. Sobriety was not the way I wanted to face the remainder of the day.

"You mean something alcoholic?" Clarence got up and turned on the gas under his kettle. "They say you should never drink when you're doing field research. The combination of an unfamiliar culture and inebriation makes you lose your discipline."

"Then I'll have some of that tea."

Clarence said as he crouched down and peeled the membrane off of Karen's face, "Your girlfriend's had a pretty terrible life."

"Maybe that's why she moved to Toronto," I said. Was Karen my girlfriend? I mean really? Had Clarence used some analytical criteria to scientifically prove this? I hoped so.

"It's a pity that the violence is following her here."

The kettle started whistling. Clarence went over to fill the teapot.

"That's kind of extreme, things aren't that bad in the city—" I looked over at Karen again and just stopped talking.

Clarence handed me a weak cup of tea—more of a cup of boiling hot water. "It's all very sad," he said. "But you mustn't feel responsible—"

"I don't!"

"—because most of the evidence suggests that this social disintegration is part of an overall inevitable process." Clarence sipped his tea. "Sort of like five billion years from now when the sun will finally burn itself up and explode. Damn shame but not much you can do about it."

Now that was an inspiring thought.

The last of the membrane fell to the carpet. Karen whimpered a bit—probably her body was remembering the pain of today's, or maybe some other day's, beating.

I took Karen's hand and that seemed to help.

Clarence drank his tea.

I looked up at him. "Okay, it's your turn."

"My turn?"

"To answer some questions."

- Who are you?

Two hours and five cups of tea later, Karen was up and we were still in Clarence's living room.

Clarence folded his arms and looked very thoughtful. "Okay," he said quietly. "But you can't tell anybody."

As if anybody was going to listen to fringe-dwellers like me and Karen. Clarence opened the side panel of an old La-Z-Boy vibrating chair and started turning the fake brass knobs on the control panel. "I made these modifications myself."

"Really?"

Clarence sat down in the chair as the timer started ticking. "Yes, you might as well be comfortable while you're working." A door-sized gap opened at the far side of the room. We could hear the sounds of traffic and exhaust fumes wafted toward us. University Avenue just outside the American Consulate.

"Looks like they've cleared up a lot of the mess."

The barricades were still up but there were only a few cops walking around in front of the wire mesh barrier.

"Holyeee…" Not the cleverest thing I've said, but come on!

"I've been tracking the broader social patterns. It was quite likely that there was going to be some serious unpleasantness in the city today."

"You can predict that kind of thing?" Karen asked.

Clarence looked at me as though I had asked an extremely obvious question. "When I saw that you were there and in trouble I thought I should bring you here."

"You just stepped through that thing and grabbed us?" I asked.

Clarence looked proud of himself. "I was able to angle the fold so that it was almost impossible for anyone to see me pull you through."

"We really appreciate that." No irony was intended there. None at all.

The view through the door/fold was now of a cluster of stars.

"Don't worry." Clarence smiled. "There's an automatic gas-valve with this unit, so Earth's atmosphere won't be sucked out through the fold."

Oh good, because I hate it when that happens.

Clarence pointed at one of the brighter points of light. "That's where I come from," he said.

"You mean you aren't from the Sociology Department at the University of Kiev?" asked Karen. Sometimes I couldn't tell if she was joking or not.

Clarence laughed. "No. I am a Senior Museologist for the Galactic Superculture."

- Why are you here?

Clarence widened the fold and moved it so it was floating just below the ceiling. This really was the best home theatre system I'd ever seen.

We looked at more outer space. Lots of long, long shots of what were probably solar systems and what were definitely galaxies. You couldn't help noticing how much was just pure black, pure emptiness.

"You see it, don't you?" asked Clarence.

"The void?" asked Karen.

"More and more of the universe is becoming empty."

"Some astronomers think that this effect is evidence of reality collapsing in on itself," said Karen. "These are, in fact, vast fields of black holes."

Did I mention that Karen was a grad student majoring in astrophysics and philosophy before the society she was living in imploded? No, I was probably too busy describing how she looked in stiletto heels and Gore-Tex.

"Given the current state of knowledge on this planet, that is not an unreasonable way of describing the effect."

"But it is incorrect?" I saw more than a flash of intellectual curiosity pass through Karen's eyes.

"Oh, yes." Clarence stared playing with the dials on his mutated eight-track player. We saw a gush of light bisect the largest void. "Life is amazingly dynamic." The light grew brighter and wrapped itself into a massive sphere at the centre of the void.

Hey, Lazerium.

"But also very unstable."

The sphere grew larger, almost completely obscuring the void.

"Sooner or later, and with remarkable regularity…"

The sphere darkened and started to shrink.

"…all life is destroyed…"

The sphere disappeared.

"…or destroys itself."

I swear I heard the void burp. Well, maybe not.

"When you see those huge fields of dark matter you are actually seeing the remains of imploded life. The debris of physical reality."

Okay…

The void was rapidly growing.

"Unchecked, this effect will eventually result in the complete disappearance of the physical universe."

And isn't that a cheerful thought, Mr. Science?

- What does all of this have to do with us?

"What does all of this have to do with us?" asked Karen.

Clarence leaned back in the easy chair. "To be blunt, your world is doomed."

"Doomed?"

"At least its physical manifestation."

- So what happens now?

We finished our tea and Clarence took us through the fold for a walk.

"You're absolutely sure?" Karen was taking in the view.

"Well, nothing is *absolutely* certain, I suppose." Clarence shrugged. "But we've seen this sort of thing happen a lot. It occurs when a planet's level of technological advancement and moral retardation intersect."

Oddly enough we were not on the Planet Xegon. It looked like we were walking along Lakeshore Boulevard. I could even see *Video Portal* from here.

"There's nothing you can do?" Karen asked.

The store was much brighter and cleaner than I could ever remember.

Clarence smiled. "That's what my research project has been all about."

"How were all those questionnaires going to save the world?" I asked. Not that I didn't enjoy administering them, but let's get real here.

I couldn't get over how all the buildings and trees were glowing—like everything was held together by an inner luminescence.

"Saving the Earth is beyond our capacities," replied Clarence. "We've been collecting data to recreate your community."

Karen looked at Clarence like he was crazy. "Why?"

"To serve as a new gallery in our Central Museum." Clarence smiled with pride. "It's going to be a really great exhibition."

I insisted that we go inside *Video Portal*. There I saw myself, methodically filing DVDs in plastic sleeves while a few of my regulars were wandering around the aisles. My doppelganger's posture was better than I think it really is and my complexion hasn't been than good in a very long time.

Kind of creepy really.

"Point at the signs," Clarence said. "This is an interactive display."

I stuck my finger at the Action Adventure section. A graphic window pop-up appeared in front of me. It read: 'High Speed Revenge Fugues.'

Okay. I pointed over at the Martial Arts rack. The pop-up read: 'Asian Aerial Dance-Collisions.'

Now I just couldn't resist. I walked over to the XXX alcove and pointed at the door: 'Intense Fluid Exchange in Unlikely Social Situations.'

All these statements were to some extent true, but there was something definitely odd about the intellectual perspective. But as I recall from my own museum experience, sometimes the thought processes of curators were a little difficult to understand.

Karen took us over to the tarot parlour. The reader inside was not Karen, which I interpreted as Clarence being nice. He knew how much she hated that job.

For some reason, the customer was another representation of me. Maybe I was a good marker of some sociological trend that their curators found useful.

We stood there and watched the reader take "me" through a session that I never would have sat still for: career, love, health—such ordinary stuff! After five minutes, Karen walked over and took "me" by the wrist and examined "my" palm.

"I can't see the lines properly," Karen said. "There isn't enough detail to do a proper reading."

Clarence nodded. "Yes, there are limitations to the resolution."

"So how real is any of this?" asked Karen.

"Very real." Clarence folded his arms in what was probably a universal symbol of professional pride. "As the physical universe disappears all around us, we are increasing our efforts to transform it into information."

"Why information?" asked Karen.

"It's a much stabler form of existence."

I got this concept pretty quick. After all, I worked in a video store and I had only rented out *The Matrix* movies about 100,000 times.

Clarence took us to the doughnut shop. The food and drink were much too good.

"I've come to understand how wonderful all of you are," explained Clarence. "And you don't have to die."

"Everybody dies," I said as I dunked my simulated doughnut into my conceptual coffee.

"And it sounds like we'll be doing that quite soon," added Karen. Those Eastern Europeans. So direct.

"You can choose to become information."

"We'd be directly translated?" Karen was a lot faster on the uptake than me.

"Yes. We could have a much better record if you were alive and actively participating."

Avoiding the apocalypse and looking as good as my replicas did have a certain appeal.

"Clarence?" Karen looked uneasy as she spoke. "Are you…?

"Information?" Clarence laughed. "Just the kind you get from natural DNA and RNA. But eventually…"

"Eventually?"

"Is this another one of your inevitable processes?" I asked.

Clarence nodded. "Everyone, everything alive will have to be translated into data. It's a good thing; as data you get to live forever."

"Live forever?" Karen looked as though she couldn't decide whether to be delighted or horrified.

The idea had some appeal to me. While Karen and I were getting along reasonably well I figured that I was going to need about 250,000 years to get anywhere close to intimacy.

We got up and went back to the street. The way the golden light was suffusing everything... it made the places and people you see every day quite incredible, quite wonderful.

Living forever among ordinary wonders.

Then Karen and I looked east toward the downtown because we wanted to know how much of the city had been re-created. We saw something unexpected.

Massive curls of mottled shell, vast tubes of pulsing mollusc flesh. Glistening wrinkles the size of river valleys leading to huge crude eye-orbs.

Ammonites.

There were half a dozen of these giant ammonites sitting among the city's skyscrapers. The biggest one was roughly two-thirds as tall as the CN Tower.

Clarence looked a little embarrassed. "That's a problem we're trying to work out."

"It is a bit inaccurate," said Karen. "Ammonites have been extinct for at least 70 million years."

"And I don't think they were quite so large," I added. God, what brilliant powers of observation I had.

"It seems to be something about the re-constructive software." Clarence tried to sound casual about it. "When we load in the geological and palaeontology background data into the setting, we get the manifestations of prehistory."

"Why ammonites?" I mean they looked really cool but there needed to be some kind of reason for them to be there!

"We think it's some kind of visual indicator of the overall biomass of the region. The software may be telling us that there were a lot of ammonites and maybe other prehistoric sea creatures here—and please don't forget them."

"So there were more ammonites than any other ancient species?" Karen asked.

Clarence looked uncomfortable and sighed. "No. That's what we can't figure out and probably why we can't fix it yet."

"You can't fix it? Make it more accurate?"

"No." Yet another sigh. "I suppose we're lucky that we aren't looking at representations of giant cockroaches or algae."

"So your software, your whole system… it's not perfect?"

Clarence smiled again. "No, but we know that some day it will be."

- What would you do differently if you could?
- If you had to live somewhere else, were would that be?
- Why?

A couple of months later, Clarence finished his research project and it was time for him to leave. By coincidence, we were also closing down *Video Portal*. The cable company had also dropped its prices and so everybody was staying at home and downloading their movies now.

My boss let me keep the store open late one night and we had a party for Clarence and everybody in the neighbourhood. Clarence and I had hundreds of photographs of different people and places so we enlarged some and hung them everywhere.

Lots of people showed up, they drank lots of red wine that came from boxes and ate lots of crackers and processed cheese and some chocolate Buddhas that I was trying to get rid of.

And while everybody had seen Clarence running around the neighbourhood, nobody knew that much about him. They were understandably curious:

"Where is your family from?"

"Um, up north. Not too far from Timmins."

"Is that where you got that funky hat?"

"I honestly don't remember."

"Do you know the Lovatts? I stayed with them when I was working near Timmins."

"I don't think so."

"Where are you going to next?"

"Singapore. I've got some work waiting for me there."

"Do you know the Chias? I think they're from Singapore."

There was some unintentional justice happening here. After

months of bombarding the locals with questions, Clarence had to give them some answers.

"So where do you think you'll be getting doughnuts in Singapore?"

"Gosh, I really hadn't thought that far ahead."

None of these were particularly good answers, I might add. Then Mrs. Malcom's daughter came up to Clarence. Her name was Betty and I liked her. She was always renting foreign films and asking me to stock more. Smart kid, in her last year at high school hoping to get into college, keeping her grades up, working part-time at god-knows-where and wondering where she was going to find the money.

I was afraid for her.

Afraid that she was going to turn out exactly like me.

Betty folded her arms and leaned on the counter next to Clarence. "So was it worth it?"

"Was what all worth it?" (Oh good one, Clarence!)

"Your research project. Did you get any interesting results?"

"All kinds," Clarence nodded. "Very new perspectives on this type of community."

Betty smiled. "So you'd say the project was a success, then?"

"A success?" Clarence looked a little sad. I noticed that he was looking at me and Karen as we were knocking back plastic glasses of red. "Actually, no, not completely."

"That's too bad."

Clarence realized that he had to smile and look reassuring—because he didn't want this young lady to give up on her studies either. "That's the way it is with research. Things just go that way sometimes."

- What time is it?

With the store closed I had nothing but days off now. I spent most of this one in bed listening to war news.

It was getting pretty bad. Too much fighting on too many fronts. Every time a conflict would stop in one spot, something new would flare up somewhere else.

The Americans were debating whether they needed to use tactical nuclear weapons and there were rumours that the other sides had already used them against some of their more helpless populations. And now there was a different kind of fighting happening at home.

It was like the whole world was tightening into a huge tense knot that some maniac was going to try and slice open with the nearest red button.

Enough of that. I switched off the radio, took a couple of Tylenol (hangover? War nerves?) and called Karen. We decided to go over to Clarence's place and see if he needed any help moving his stuff.

His apartment was unlocked.

Clarence was gone.

His weird stereo equipment, his books and records, his habitually inappropriate clothing. All of it, gone. Even the outer layer of paint was missing.

We decided that he must have flicked some combination of toggles on that mutated chair, the whole place folded in on itself and everything disappeared into Intergalactic DataLand.

See you around, Clarence!

Standing there in that quiet void made us feel pretty sad. But we'd probably made Clarence feel pretty lousy, too, because we had declined his invitation.

One of the reasons for our decision was because we had some doubts about what would happen to us when were translated into the realm of pure information. The ammonites were a pretty clear indicator that the Superculture's software was at least a little buggy. We had no idea if we would be anything resembling ourselves if we entered that simulation—no matter how detailed and interactive it was. That bothered me a lot—Karen is definitely unique and while I'm not nearly as interesting, I'm still the only me I've got.

Our concerns about the translation process weren't the main reason we decided to stay. Maybe the war situation was going to settle down. Maybe not. But even if this particular war didn't happen, it was likely that within one, five or ten years another one was going to start up and finally escalate into something that kills off all physical life on the planet.

Karen and I knew that if that was going to happen, we had to be there. To see it through.

"Nothing is inevitable," Karen said in that wonderful accent that always raised my body temperature in a very agreeable way. Then she touched my arm.

I nodded and closed the apartment door as we left. We went downstairs to the street.

We looked up at the city's horizon, looking for ammonites that weren't there.

IS IT UTOPIA YET?

I'm not going to go into the details of the mass murder-suicides at Jonestown, Guyana in November 1978. There's lots of information about it out there, but be warned, you'll likely learn a great deal but you may wish that you hadn't.

At the time, one of the consequences of the Jonestown deaths was intense scientific and historical interest in so-called "new religions", or "cults" as they were usually referred to in the popular press. It's not accurate to pin all this research onto the career of Reverend Jimmy Jones[3], as there was a widespread growth in religious activity at the time. Not just truly weird groups like the Unification Church or Scientology, but more mainstream movements like evangelicals, born-agains, and moral majorities (that actually weren't majorities but said they were). I do think it's fair to say that extreme events like Jonestown did accelerate the investigation process.

When I started graduate school, I somehow got the Social Sciences and Humanities Research Council of Canada to fund some kind of anthropological study of the cultural impact of science fiction. So, when I learned about new religions and "cult-like" manifestations that originated in the SF community, the direction of my scholarly work was pretty much set. The fact that McMaster University had great resources on science fiction history and religious movements, plus being a 45-minute train ride from the amazing reference resources at the Merril Collection of Science Fiction, Fantasy and Speculation, made it seem as though my thesis topic was ordained from above. Yes, that might be a contradiction, isn't it?

Anyway, if you go to my Retrograde Mentor website at https://www.fantasticwriter.net/—you can even read the results. Even though I later moved on to different pursuits, the sometimes-conflicting issues evident in my thesis (Religious freedom VS

3 I hardly ever describe people as evil, but I believe it is a completely suitable designation for Jones.

individual rights? / Public safety VS nonconformity? / Etc. VS etc.?) troubled me; I felt the story of how religions are born and evolve, and what they can end up doing in the world needed to be better understood by more people. So I wrote what would eventually become an audio dramatic comedy (or comedic drama) titled *Amazing Struggles, Astonishing Failures and Disappointing Success*, which was broadcast by the brave and talented people at Shoestring Radio Theatre. If you're interested, you can listen to all eight episodes also at my Retrograde Mentor website.

Because I continued to be troubled by this historical/sociological narrative, I also wrote "Cult Stories", which takes its jumping off point from a scene in the Disappointing Success phase of my radio play. It was also a way to work through how I felt about some of the truly unusual people and events I encountered at graduate school.

Growing up LDS, I never felt justified in being too critical of other people's religious beliefs. It seemed to me that there was lots of strange to go around for all faiths. As a youth, it also seemed to me that believing something doesn't give you licence to push people around, no matter how right you think you might be. As a not-youth, my opinions have been informed, but they really haven't changed.

There is one thing that still bothers me about some of these religious groups. They often claim that once we all accept their teachings, the world will be transformed and saved. We either all go to Heaven or we create Heaven on Earth. And a very few say that the faithful will all become super-successful, super-evolved celebrities. Which got me wondering, what if they were telling the truth and the teachings and practices of these groups actually worked?

Would we finally achieve a utopia? Or would we get something else?

CULT STORIES

Originally published in:
Tesseracts 16: Parnassus Unbound
2013

1979:
Young Love, Strange Love(s)

INTERVIEWER:	How long have you been practicing Mentotechnics?
SUBJECT #3:	Just about two years.
INTERVIEWER:	Have you noticed any benefits?
SUBJECT #3:	You bet! Back when I started, I could barely read.
INTERVIEWER:	You had literacy problems?
SUBJECT #3:	Big time!
INTERVIEWER:	But you think Mentotechnics changed that.
SUBJECT #3:	No kidding! Now I can read really fast and I really love reading!
INTERVIEWER:	What was the last book you read?
SUBJECT #3:	Ummmm…

* * *

The phone rang. It was just past three in the morning.

Although Ethan had been in a deep sleep, he answered by the third ring. He lived in a small apartment.

"She doesn't live here anymore," Ethan spoke without waiting for the person on the other end of the line. He had the routine down pretty well. "She" was Gabriella, a young call girl from Quebec City who had rented the apartment before Ethan.

He'd only met her the one time when he'd first come to see the place. She was pretty, very quiet and was surrounded by a cloud of strong, but not altogether unpleasant, perfume. Gabriella also wore a T-shirt with a lace-up front that showed off a little more cleavage than usual.

Ethan had wondered whether these pleasant sensations were the reason that he agreed to buy all Gabriella's furniture as part of the move-in deal.

Meanwhile, nobody said anything on the telephone.

Anybody calling this time of night was probably very drunk.

Drunk, and possibly very desperate.

I'd better help this guy out, Ethan decided. "She hasn't lived here in over a year."

After five or six of these calls he had figured out what line of work Gabriella was in. Soon afterward, he persuaded the landlord to fumigate the furniture.

Still nothing on the phone.

It was a shame that the landlord refused to change the phone number in the apartment.

Nope. Just some distant breathing.

From previous experience, Ethan knew that this could either go reasonably well or very badly.

If it went well then the poor sap would just hang up and find some other cryptic listing in *The Hamilton Spectator*'s personal section.

If it went badly, this drunken moron would decide that Ethan was one of Gabriella's clients, or worse yet, a boyfriend. This would usually stimulate the idiot-competitive lobe of the guy's tiny brain, which in turn would trigger a stream of abuse.

It was no use hanging up either, Ethan knew that. When these guys got this way, they'd just call right back. If it was one of Gabriella's old regulars, he might even threaten to come around to the apartment.

It was all very weird, maybe a bit scary, but kind of fun. One of the few forms of entertainment that an anthropology grad student could afford.

"Is this Ethan Daniels?"

It was a quiet voice. Very young, maybe a girl, probably a boy. Twelve, thirteen at the most, Ethan concluded.

This was different.

"Yes," Ethan replied. "Can I help you?"

"*You better stop what you're doing.*"

The voice didn't project a lot of confidence. In fact it was squeaky and sounded like it might go out of control at any second. Ethan couldn't tell if this was because of extreme nervousness or the onset of puberty.

"Stop what, exactly?"

"D.H. Evanston is the greatest man who ever lived."

That's what this is about! Ethan realized that this exchange was now making some kind of sense.

"He certainly is a remarkable person," said Ethan. "But you must admit—"

"*He's going to save the world.*"

"That's a really interesting opinion." Ethan felt that this could be an opportunity to gather more data. "It would be great if you could come by to my office and we could dis—"

"People like you are working out of fear and ignorance."

"I don't know about the fear part. But you're right, there's lots about Mentotechnics that some of us don't understand."

I don't believe it, Ethan thought, it's three in the morning and I'm about to start a lecture on social science methodology. "That's why we conduct research."

"Bad things will happen if you don't stop."

Dial tone.

Strange, Ethan thought as he rolled back onto his folding couch. That was probably the least effective threatening phone call in recent history. Somebody should tell these people that kids whose voices haven't finished changing aren't particularly menacing. Still, the kid's vocabulary was pretty good for someone that age.

Maybe there is something to the training after all.

* * *

When Ethan woke up (at a more agreeable time) that morning, his first thoughts were not of his mysterious phone call.

He really had to break up with Nina.

He went through this every time he was just about out of condoms.

For such a scientific optimist, Nina was strangely nervous about the Pill, so she insisted on alternative forms of contraception. However, she was also an affectionate person, so she suggested that they use condoms made of 100% sheepskin.

"They transmit our body heat," she explained. "It's so much nicer."

Not if you're a sheep, Ethan thought.

Nina's theory was good, but unless you had the genitals of a sperm whale, it was pretty hard to get a snug fit. They were always dealing with air pockets in the membrane and the constant fear that the damn thing was going to slip off at the wrong moment.

The net effect was that the regularly emptying box made Ethan very conscious of this aspect of his relationship with Nina. This in turn called to mind what he felt was going wrong with the whole situation.

Nina—Ethan decided to use the appropriate folk-culture term—was going seriously nuts.

He marked the serious disintegration of her personality from the day that they attended the premiere showing of *Star Trek: The Motion Picture*.

* * *

If *Star Trek* had been a church back then, Nina Brown would have been one of its most devoted saints.

Ethan met Nina in a second hand bookstore. She was almost glowing with joy because she'd found a copy of the, then rare, paperback edition of James Blish's novel *Spock Must Die!* She explained that this was the climax of a rather lengthy literary quest.

Therefore Nina was in an incredibly good mood, which made her very attractive to Ethan.

When she invited him to a marathon screening of episodes at the local art-house cinema, he accepted. He felt a bit of a sociable buzz set in as they sat through six hours of burnt popcorn odors and the whispering of well-known and well-loved dialogue from the audience.

Nina had more respect for the quality of Ethan's cinematic experience. She let him watch without interruption. In turn, Ethan had to admit that the direction, writing and even the acting wasn't bad. Especially if you considered the overall state of episodic television in the 1960s and 1970s. It was a period when the cost and quantity of recreational drugs had gotten so small and so large (respectively) that most programs were essentially unwatchable.

About two in the morning, Nina and Ethan found a coffee shop in Westdale where Nina spent another two hours explaining that she was an activist. She was a passionate member of the "Bring Back *Star Trek*" movement.

Hamilton, Ontario had a university and it had a lot of big steel mills, so it had lots of politics. Therefore Ethan knew quite a few activists but most of them were not involved with helping William Shatner and Leonard Nimoy get their old jobs back.

Ethan briefly considered whether Nina and her friends might be good subjects for anthropological study. Probably, but he was enjoying her company too much to raise the question.

By four, they realized that the buses weren't running anymore, so there was no way for Ethan to find his way home. Nina invited him to her place.

When they got there, Nina poured him some beer. This was Hamilton, after all.

The drinks didn't make them sleepy, just a bit stupid.

Nina took out a very thick binder filled with loose-leaf papers. "I've never shown anyone this before." The pages were covered with line after line of expansive handwriting. "You might find this interesting."

It was Nina's fiction. Fan fiction. Incredibly pornographic fan fiction. Throughout, there were three or four characters of Nina's creation who did some unlikely but enthusiastic coupling, but most of the stories focused on a long-standing homosexual affair between Captain Kirk and Mr. Spock.

Context is just about everything.

That must be why (at the time) Ethan didn't find the stories to be funny or pathetic (which he ordinarily might have); or deviant or perverted (because he hadn't had much experience with gay relationships or other people's sexual fantasies back then); or typical of a new expression of folk culture (which professionally, he really should have). No, (at the time) Ethan just found reading the stories rather arousing. Which was convenient, because Nina happened to be in the same mood.

And these events ultimately led to Ethan's current dilemma with Nina. When they first got together, Ethan didn't think that Nina's passion for *Star Trek* made her crazy, it just made her more fun.

He had been forced to revise his opinion.

This was quite sad. The sadder thing was his realization that he didn't love Nina enough to stick with her or help her through her craziness.

* * *

SUBJECT #18: I'm pretty sure I shouldn't be talking to you.

INTERVIEWER: Why do you say that?

SUBJECT #18: Because you could be writing something that's hostile to Mentotechnics.

INTERVIEWER: No, this will be an objective study.

SUBJECT #18: I guess I should just look on the bright side.

INTERVIEWER: You mean that Mentotechnics will benefit from objective study?

SUBJECT #18: Hell, no! I mean that I can use the money you're paying me to buy more therapy sessions.

* * *

Ethan liked many things about McMaster University.

What he really loved about the institution was that the library system had an outstanding collection of science fiction studies material, including some oral histories about the early years of American fandom.

In Hamilton, Ontario. It was a surprise that saved Ethan's academic career.

There were a couple of things about McMaster that Ethan wasn't quite so excited about. There were huge engineering and medical programs, and this of course was a big challenge for anyone doing tutorials in anthropology. The classes were filled with big, smart and ambitious kids in a hurry to get into their chosen professions. Most of them got quite unruly after the first set of midterms, when they discovered that social anthropology wasn't a bird course after all. It was just one more damn useless complicated thing to study.

But there were some amusing consequences to this effect. One kid offered him a car, another on-demand blowjobs, if Ethan could find some way to nudge their grades up just a little bit.

No go, of course. Ethan didn't like driving very much and Nina, even with her intrusive contraceptive practices, was enough for him at the time. Still, on a graduate student's budget, free entertainment was always most appreciated.

McMaster was also a very populist school back then. Faculty members were directed to find any, and all, opportunities for their work to contribute to the well-being and improvement of the wider community. This mandate included the activities of any students under the tutelage of the faculty members.

Ethan's thesis supervisor, Dr. Sirkowski, was a chain-smoking, bearded, ex-American, ex-Marxist activist. He was also one of the architects of the University's community service policy.

When Sirkowski learned of Ethan's interest in science fiction fandom and so-called "marginal religious movements", he immediately became interested. It was just after the events in Jonestown, and the images of Kool-Aid-induced suicides still troubled the professor's conscience.

"This will be your opportunity to contribute something of true value to the greater public," the respected academic growled through his saliva- and tobacco-stained beard. "Even before you've completed your doctoral studies. You are very fortunate!"

So Ethan ended up doing community service just because he wanted to study groups like Mentotechnics. Every time somebody showed up at the department asking about "cults" and "wacko religions" they were sent up to Ethan's office.

At first Ethan tried to incorporate these confessionals into his research, but usually the results were too weird and pathetic to be very useful. Most of the time he was just talking to people who wanted to vent. The best thing to do was be polite, sympathetic and try to pass on a bit of accurate history.

* * *

MILGORE: I heard that you're carrying out a research project on Mentotechnics.

DANIELS: Yes, that's true.

MILGORE: My daughter has joined the Temple.

DANIELS: I see.

MILGORE: I'm so worried!

DANIELS: Mrs. Milgore, aside from offering my sympathies, there isn't much I can do.

MILGORE: There's *nothing* you can do?

DANIELS: Some people would say your relationship with your daughter was a regrettable, but necessary, sacrifice to living in a free and open society.

MILGORE: *Oh, thank you very much!* I suppose I should try and find one of those deprogrammers.

DANIELS: You probably respect your daughter too much to have her kidnapped.

MILGORE: So what can I do?

DANIELS: Well, here's something, wonder where I put it…

MILGORE: (sniffs) Yes?

DANIELS: It's an article published in an old science fiction magazine by a writer named Bob Clyde. He used to know Evanston and he's quite blunt about the man's ethics and where he got his ideas for a new religion.

MILGORE: What am I supposed to do with this?

DANIELS: Read it. Let yourself know what you're dealing with.

MILGORE: Isn't there anything else I can do?

DANIELS: Just the simple stuff—keep in touch with your daughter—don't give her very much money.

* * *

It had started out as a good day. Saturdays usually were good for Ethan because the department offices were just about empty, which made it a great time to catch up on transcribing his interviews.

That particular Saturday was even better, because he was able to finish the first draft of his thesis. At about 1:15 in the afternoon, Ethan typed in the last entry from his index cards, boxed the 300-plus pages and left the whole package in Professor Sirkowski's mailbox. All he had to do now was wait for comments.

Unexpectedly, Ethan had some free time.

Nina had mentioned that she was going to be at her place filing some punch cards from the Physics Department's mainframe. He'd missed lunch, but maybe he could persuade her to go to that new Greek cafeteria and take in a movie at the Student Union building. Which left a few hours before that to do stuff that Ethan wasn't feeling particularly guilty about at that moment.

The department secretary had forgotten to lock the main office, so Ethan made a quick phone call and, thank god, Nina said yes!

The weather was quite nice for late January, so Ethan decided that he'd forget the Hamilton Public Transit System and walk to his apartment. The fact that he'd reached a milestone in his studies, and the prospect of a certain amount of fun with Nina, filled Ethan with all kinds of energy. He felt like he was radiating photons and almost bouncing all the way home—as if McMaster had suddenly been teleported to the moon.

Maybe that was why Ethan didn't hear the car roar up from behind, turn and head towards him. At that point, Ethan did notice that something was happening, but there wasn't much that he could do about it.

He turned, and the car was bearing down on him—at maybe 70-75 miles an hour.

I'm going to be liquefied by the front end of this vehicle; Ethan heard a curiously calm voice inside his head. Then he was impressed by the speed and complexity of human cognition. How can I be having such complex thoughts in the less than a microsecond that I have to live? How can I be having such complex thoughts?

Ethan was most amazed by the reason why he had time for all this interesting thinking.

Just before what was definitely going to be an inevitable collision, the car swerved, missed Ethan and took out a mailbox instead.

It took two or three minutes to figure out what had just happened. Ethan's brain must have been working very slowly at that point; perhaps it was some kind of existential relativity thing going on.

The mailbox was seriously flattened and the car was extremely bent.

Pity, thought Ethan. It was a nice car, a Triumph TR7, one of those sports cars that academics could dream about without guilt because there wasn't a chance in the universe that they'd ever own one.

Well, maybe Ethan could now afford the one sitting in front of him.

Help.

Another thought was germinating, forming, taking solid form and rising through the turgid mass of Ethan's consciousness.

You should.

What was that, he asked himself.

You should help.

Oh god, yes! Ethan realized that whoever was inside that car was probably horribly injured.

He should try and help.

Moreover, the poor bastard behind the steering wheel probably hit the mailbox because he was trying to miss Ethan.

Now he felt as though he weighed 30 tons, as if he was suddenly trapped in Jupiter's gravitational field, or he was being sucked deep down into some primordial tar pit.

Ethan dreaded what bleeding, flayed mass of human suffering he was going to find crushed behind that steering wheel.

Behind? Hell, this was an import here, maybe the steering wheel went right through the poor sod.

So it felt like a geological age before Ethan reached the car. Maybe his subjective perceptions slowed down to give him some scope for reflection, some kind of psychological cushion, a period of "fake time" to help him prepare for what he was going to see.

It didn't work. Ethan was not prepared for what he saw on the other side of that shattered windshield.

Nothing.

Nobody.

Not a thing was behind the wheel of that car.

Ethan's first thought was that somehow the driver's body had gotten wedged below the dashboard. He took a deep breath, and peered over the empty frame.

Still nothing.

There was no sign of a driver.

So according to the evidence of his eyes, nobody had been driving the car that had almost run him over.

At this point, things started to get very spotty. Ethan couldn't quite remember walking the rest of the way home, but he did recall lying down for most of the next two days.

He sort of remembered a not very satisfactory telephone conversation with Nina.

(Well, even more unsatisfactory than most of their communications.)

Ethan most certainly did not remember talking to the police about the accident, but he must have at some point. After all, he was a very responsible citizen when it came to that sort of thing.

Ethan definitely remembered feeling *completely* exhausted for the next three days. Lying there on the mattress that he and Nina had long since crushed flat, Ethan pieced together what must have happened.

It was selective amnesia brought about by random trauma.

Of course he had tried to help.

Of course he had seen a body.

And of course, it must have been something absolutely horrific.

Of course, Ethan had gone somewhere and called an ambulance and of course he had waited for the police to arrive and made a complete statement.

And of course, Ethan had absolutely no memory of any of this because his conscious mind just wasn't able to process all these events right now.

This kind of stress reaction was something that Ethan was familiar with, but as a social scientist, Ethan was annoyed that he was a participant in this pathology rather than an observer.

By Wednesday morning, Ethan was able to move around his apartment. Maybe by the end of the day he might be able to take the bus to his office.

The phone rang.

It wasn't Nina this time. No, it was Professor Sirkowski.

"Outstanding first draft. Lots of revisions needed, mind you, but you may have something publishable by the end of the process."

Ethan was never able to explain just why he said what he said next.

"Forget the whole thing, sir. I'm changing my thesis."

But Ethan was certain that he meant it.

1993:
"Pictures at an Exhibition"

INTERVIEWER: Were you ever concerned that D.H. Evanston was a science fiction writer before he founded the Temple of Mentotechnics?

SUBJECT #40: No, not at all.

INTERVIEWER: You mean it didn't raise any doubts?

SUBJECT #40: Why would it?

INTERVIEWER: Well, to some people it might be like finding out that John the Baptist was a contributor to *Cousin Mort's Flying Saucer Quarterly.*

SUBJECT #40: Your statements are more biased than usual today. You must be tired.

INTERVIEWER: Yeah, I'll watch out for that.

SUBJECT #40: In answer to your question, once again, no. Evanston's work as a science fiction writer didn't bother me at all. I thought it made a lot of sense.

INTERVIEWER: Made sense? In what way?

SUBJECT #40: It takes tremendous vision and imagination to apprehend the enormity of what Mentotechnics really is.

INTERVIEWER: I guess that's one way of looking at it—

SUBJECT #40: And besides, science fiction is the only truly relevant literature left!

INTERVIEWER: But you told me earlier that you had some concerns about the Temple, that some people were there for the wrong reasons.

SUBJECT #40: Yes, some people, like ones at the Celebrity Training Centres, were just there for personal advancement.

INTERVIEWER: And there's a problem there?

SUBJECT #40: They're missing the big picture. While they're worrying about ways to win auditions they can't see that the human race is evolving into something new and wonderful!

INTERVIEWER: Sounds terrific.

SUBJECT #40: It's beyond terrific! It's beyond infinity! We're on the verge of a new relationship with the very being of the universe!

* * *

"We need you to go to Los Angeles."

It was an unexpected request from a very unexpected source.

Ethan hadn't seen Nina in over ten years.

"I'm flattered," he said into the telephone receiver.

Ethan eyed the pile of third-year term papers, all grappling with that eternal problem of human existence:

"*Compare and contrast economic behaviour models in three hunter-gatherer monographs*".

Ripping shit. Ethan hoped that Nina didn't hear him sigh.

"But I haven't been researching minority religious movements in quite a long while."

"I know you, Ethan." He heard laughter at the other end of the line. It wasn't particularly nice laughter. "You're a determined man and you're a sneaky bastard."

Thank god, you're not bitter, Ethan thought.

Actually, he was surprised that Nina wanted to remember anything about him. Particularly after the last days of their relationship.

Way back in 1979 as the weeks, the days, and finally the hours counted down to the *Star Trek* movie premiere.

Nina had been collecting every newspaper story, any fanzine that mentioned it, and absolutely all the gossip she could possibly absorb. Back in the pre-internet era, this was actually quite time-consuming.

But she seemed to be enjoying it. The more *Trek* data she collected, the more excited she got.

"It just goes to show," Nina would say with increasing regularity.

"*Star Trek* really does live."

Like a lot of other Trekkers, Nina took a lot of pride in the movie. She believed she was part of a worldwide grass roots movement, motivated by love and idealism, that had changed the course of the monolithic American Entertainment Establishment.

"It's going to be incredible," she would say.

Ethan decided that after Vietnam and Wade versus Roe, that all that activist energy had to go somewhere.

He had to admit the sex got more and more incredible as the premiere got closer.

But as Ethan lay there in bed, his hormone levels returning to something approaching normal, rational thought would set in and he got a little scared. Yeah, he didn't like to use simplistic Freudian concepts, but they seemed to apply here. There seemed to be some incredibly powerful cathartic psychosexual link between the *Star Trek* Universe and Planet Nina.

He really ought to do something about it. Maybe talk to her.

But the pathology was so much fun.

* * *

REPORTER: What do you say to those who are critical of you and your organization?

EVANSTON: I'm always surprised by critical people. Who are they?

REPORTER: Those people who say that your work is a lie and that you are a fraud.

EVANSTON: What can I say, Mike? We have measurable, scientifically proven results. There's hard evidence.

REPORTER: *Scientific* evidence that Mentotechnics works?

EVANSTON: Absolutely. Astonishing evidence. People are changed in ways that are miraculous.

REPORTER: Scientific miracles?

EVANSTON: Beautifully put, Mike.

* * *

"You must be doing some kind of research."

Nina was right about that, too. But really all he could manage these days was to check out the microfiche files at the local library and save clippings whenever he found a story about Mentotechnics in the newspaper.

This time Ethan knew he sighed out loud.

"What do you need?" he asked.

There was a note of triumph in Nina's voice. "My division is in the middle of a long-term investigation. You might be able to give us some context."

"Context?"

"That's right," Nina replied. "We need you to make an assessment of the criminal potentiality of the organization."

Ethan smiled. There was some consulting money coming down the line, maybe he could even get a publication out of it.

"You want me to write you a report."

"We want you to go and look at something and tell us what you think."

* * *

REPORTER: If you have "hard evidence", why is the Department of Justice raiding your offices and impounding your files and therapy machines?

EVANSTON: Good question, Mike.

REPORTER: Do you have a good answer?

EVANSTON: I don't think the Department of Justice would say we don't have evidence… they just don't know what it's evidence of…

* * *

It was a Friday in early December.

The great day had arrived.

Nina appeared at the door to his classroom—about half an hour before the end of the tutorial.

Ethan saw her expression and knew that he had to take preemptive action.

"Okay," he said to the twenty second-year students. "We've

been talking about marginal social states and liminal conditions in a range of different societies…"

The undergrads nodded in that polite, gentle way they always did when Ethan had just said something very obvious or very boring.

"…so let's have an unscheduled research assignment."

Ethan felt a sudden spike in the collective tension level. If you added in Nina's current Strange State of Being, the risk factor in the classroom was getting extremely high.

"…I want you to write up a paper, at least ten pages long, for next Thursday…"

Flushed faces, flashing eyes, tight lips.

Danger, Will Robinson! Danger!

"…analyzing your weekend as a liminal state where you encounter and practice different mores and social expectations."

The slightly thick keener in the front row started to raise his hand. Ethan knew he had to prevent all discussion.

"I want you to make a log book of all your activities for the next forty-eight hours," he said quickly. "Then compare the notes in that log with your behaviour on Monday and Tuesday."

The students were now nodding their heads and making notes. Perhaps the implications of what Ethan was saying hadn't quite sunk in yet.

Documenting twenty sets of two days of undergraduate depravity? It would be fun to grade.

Ethan thought that it was a real pity that Nina was so fixated on the movie opening that she didn't appreciate how brilliant he was at that moment.

"I know that this is quite a challenge to spring on you so suddenly," he continued. "So we're going to adjourn a little early to give you more time for your assignments."

Game, set and match!

One hour later, Nina and Ethan were standing in line outside the Tivoli Theatre waiting for the five o'clock showing. There were about thirty people in front of them.

Ethan was feeling the early December wind, but Nina seemed oblivious to any physical stimuli. She was busy chatting with her Trekker friends as they arrived and took their place in line.

Speaking of liminal states, Ethan thought. These Trekkers are definitely existing outside of normal social space and time. This was definitely an instance of "communitas"—the breaking down of social barriers and distinctions as part of the celebration of a greater ideological or spiritual collective expression.

Except that this wasn't a holy communion or the right of passage for the youth of a west African village, or even a sacred ritual orgy. No, this communitas involved people wearing rubber ears.

Ethan wondered if he should share these witty anthropological insights, but then he looked over at Nina and decided that it probably was not a good time.

The dramatic climax of the queuing experience came when a van pulled up to the box office and a man wearing a denim boiler suit got out. He rolled open the back of the van and started hauling out massive film canisters. The letters "S.T.M.P." were stenciled on the sides.

The trekkers looked both relieved and excited.

"That's it? That's the movie?"

"It's here? On time?"

The deliveryman nodded. "Goddamned prints are still wet. I heard they the pulled things right off the editing machines at Paramount."

Nina had told Ethan what most of the trekkers were worried about, many times.

There had been some problems with the special effects. The original SFX studio had been fired and two new technical teams had to start work just a few months ago. There had been a lot of speculation that the film just wouldn't be ready for its scheduled release. Or that the special effects would look really terrible, especially in comparison with *Star Wars*.

Things like that were really important to Nina and her friends.

But it seemed as though the artisans of Hollywood had come through after all. Ethan looked at Nina as she watched the last of the film canisters disappear through the glass doors of the Tivoli. He wondered if she would look as happy at the birth of her first child.

Inevitably, Nina's mood was going to change that evening. It did so, fairly soon after the thumping orchestral soundtrack propelled the audience through the hastily superimposed titles into what Ethan loosely considered the "dramatic" portion of the film.

Frankly, he was more of a group systems and collective manifestations person. Ethan wasn't very good at identifying individual emotional states. That made it difficult for him to be precise in determining what Nina was going through as she watched the film.

The only qualitative assessment that Ethan felt comfortable with was to say that he believed that *Star Trek: The Motion Picture* was not quite the experience that Nina had expected.

After the show, Ethan suggested that they stop by the Student Union Pub, figuring that a couple of beers would improve Nina's state of mind.

She snarled at him. Literally.

And to his regret, Nina then didn't deal with her despair in isolation. Hours later at his apartment, in the early morning, she was still weeping, calling up friends from across the continent.

"The world has lost a great opportunity," she sniffed at some shocked fan in New Mexico.

Ethan thought about his phone bill and wished that they really did have transporter technology. That way he could just beam Nina around to all her weird friends and they could commiserate in person.

Instead he went to bed.

Alone. Which was how it was going to be for a while.

* * *

REPORTER: How do you respond to rumors that D.H. Evanston really isn't dead? That he's gone into hiding to avoid legal difficulties?

SPOKESPERSON: That's just not the case. The death certificate is a matter of public record and some of us were present at the time of his passing.

REPORTER: Who was present?

SPOKESPERSON: Close family members and senior Temple officials. Myself included.

REPORTER: This must be a tremendous loss to all of you.

SPOKESPERSON: A loss to all sentient life.

REPORTER: Uh, yes. So how are you all coping? Will this lead to the end of your organization?

SPOKESPERSON: Not at all. We're completely prepared for this and our movement will continue to flourish.

REPORTER: Is this a time of great change for Mentotechnics?

SPOKESPERSON: There's been some change and there's been some continuity.

* * *

The World Center for Mental Technology is located in what was once a Navy blimp hangar in Orange County. "One of the world's largest wooden structures", a brass sign read on one of the highways leading to the main gate.

Contrary to popular belief, not all of Orange County is fabulously wealthy. The neighborhoods surrounding the Mentotechnics World Center were most definitely not of the fabulous type; in fact Ethan thought that the houses and roads looked as though they had sustained repeated bomb damage.

But it was just protracted poverty. A quieter but no less damaging form of warfare.

Popular belief is correct in the assertion that it is essentially completely impossible to get around southern California without a car. Ethan hated driving, but there he was stuck behind the wheel of a Kia rental, trying to find his way to the Center.

He had been driving around the general area for over an hour. He could see the huge golden spire that marked the building, and once in a while he could even get a glimpse of the great wooden hump of what was once the hangar.

But drive as he might, Ethan could not find the actual entrance. If he had believed Mentotechnics doctrine, Ethan would have concluded that this was some kind of telepathic defense system, that someone knew he was coming and was using the power of illusion to prevent it.

Really, it was just the unique quasi-urban geography of Orange County. Finding the historical marker from the Parks Department was Ethan's big breakthrough.

* * *

"I advised my people that you have a unique combination of experience." Ethan was sitting in Nina's office at the Ottawa headquarters of the Canadian Security and Intelligence Service.

"Thanks," Ethan said a little nervously. "But you probably know as much about this phenomenon as I do."

Nina's face turned red.

Perhaps she's trying to put things behind her. But Ethan didn't think she had much to be upset about. After they broke up, Nina had left the computer science department and entered McMaster's law enforcement program. And after that, she'd become very successful.

She looked at her hands and continued speaking. "I emphasized that you are a highly credible source."

"Thanks."

"A portion of the World Mentotechnics Center is now accessible to the general public."

"That's… unusual."

What else could he say? Given the Temple's paranoid attitude toward any criticism, it was extremely unusual. "What are they doing? Guided tours?"

"Yes," Nina replied. "They put up an exhibition honoring Evanston on the anniversary of his death."

Ethan was a little embarrassed that he hadn't heard about this. Now that he knew, it seemed obvious that the Temple would want to use Evanston's passing as an opportunity for some kind of promotional event.

"Exhibition?" The second he said the word, Ethan knew that he'd scored a 9.5 on the moron scale.

Nina didn't seem to notice. "The U.S. Department of Justice has run into some political problems with the Mentotechnics organization."

"They made an exhibition about Evanston?" What was wrong with his brain?

"Yes." Okay, now Nina did seem to notice the cloud of stupidity surrounding him. "The Americans have asked us to take over the investigation."

That didn't sound quite right to Ethan but he decided that he wasn't likely to get any explanation from Nina.

"You want me to go and see this exhibition?"

"*Yes,*" Nina said, attempting to sound patient. "All you have to do is show up and tell us what you think."

* * *

The young woman at the reception desk looked like some kind of a sexual newt. Artificial blonde, pale—almost transparent skin. She had an astonishingly thin body that looked like it might topple over from the sheer magnitude of what must have been surgically enhanced breasts. This was Orange County after all.

She frowned at Ethan. Naturally he was staring at her chest but he didn't think he had been that obvious.

"What do you want?"

Good god, thought Ethan. It's not my fault that she has such weird tits. Or worse yet, was she *expecting* him?

"I, uh, I—"

Ethan had this terrifying thought; maybe the Temple had some kind of vast enemies' list on a database. Was the nearly-clear young lady even now sitting there calling up his life history on her terminal?

"*Well?*"

"I, uh, just came to see the exhibition."

Ethan briefly wondered if he could get CSIS to cover half his travel expenses even if he couldn't get admittance.

"I can leave if I'm not welcome."

The young lady looked puzzled, then a little upset.

"Do you mean you're not a mental technologist?"

"No," replied Ethan. For some reason he felt hurt and rejected. "The man at my hotel said that the Temple was open to the general public."

"*Yes!* Yes, it is!" The young lady said with great intensity. "I thought you might be part of a bus tour of members from our Albuquerque branch."

"Oh…"

"But I guess they must be late."

Ethan wondered how super-evolved beings with hyper-developed mental powers could let things like traffic jams interfere with their day. But he decided that it probably wasn't a good idea to mention anything.

"Is it okay for me to see the exhibition?"

"Of course!" The young lady seemed relieved, possibly even eager to make up for her earlier rudeness. "I'll give you the guided tour."

Ethan was fascinated as he watched the young lady totter out from behind the reception desk. She was wearing six-inch heels and a metallic mini-dress that looked as though it had been applied with a spray can.

She looked like one of Captain Kirk's girlfriends from the third season. Ethan was slightly disgusted with himself because he liked the effect so much.

Stop it, he said to himself, as he followed her to the entrance to the exhibition. Ignore your life-long weakness toward lechery and at least try and stay objective. You're supposed to be some kind of a social scientist.

The first display was pretty validating—the scene was almost exactly as Ethan had imagined. It was a recreation of the offices of *Tremendous Stories of Super Science*. There were two figures: one represented the editor Stewart D. McReady, and the other the then-youthful D.H. Evanston. They were leaning over McReady's large oak desk, presumably discussing Evanston's latest submission.

"It was at this stage in his career," the young lady said, "that Donald Evanston quickly became one of the most popular and prolific writers in the Golden Age of science fiction."

She spoke very well, thought Ethan. As though she'd memorized every word but wasn't bored with the material yet.

"People say that Donald Evanston could produce at least three short stories a day."

The young lady pointed to an artifact display: a very early model electric typewriter connected to a hefty roll of newsprint.

"He wrote so quickly that he didn't want to wait to change pages."

"Sounds like real creative flow."

"Yes." The young lady sounded very pleased that Ethan seemed to be taking an interest in her presentation. "I've never heard it put that way, but yes."

They left the office reconstruction and walked down a huge tunnel, a collage of four-colour print. The walls were lined with thousands of science fiction magazine and paperback covers. The floor and ceiling were lined with mirrors that created a room-sized kaleidoscope effect. It was sort of like the trip sequence from Kubrick's *2001* but with much worse art direction.

"Donald Evanston went on to become a major influence on the

genre," the young lady said as they walked toward the far end of the eye-splitting tunnel. "The Temple is still a patron of important new work."

They entered a room that looked like another set from a movie or a TV show. Maybe something like the *Time Tunnel* or *Lost in Space*. There were flashing lights everywhere with lots of reel-to-reel tapes and shelves of electrode-covered skullcaps.

"And this is our Therapy Machine Timeline." The young lady gestured at the old technology with pride.

"I've heard of these," Ethan said, trying to sound as innocent as possible. Actually, he was so excited that he thought he might wet himself—nobody had seen this much Mentotechnic paraphernalia. It was the Holy Grail of post-modern religious/popular culture studies.

"The T-Machine is the foundation of everything we do in Mentotechnics."

Damn right, Ethan thought.

"And this is a complete collection of every unit issued by the Temple. From the 1952 prototype to next year's model."

"How do they work?" Ethan knew the official story very well, but he was interested in how his guide interpreted the belief system.

She didn't hesitate: "Well, T-Machines operate on the principle that we can monitor and record every human thought." She pointed to an antiquated oscilloscope that showed a single illuminated line gently curving up and down.

Of course, that is not possible, Ethan thought. You can measure various clusters of electrical activity in the human brain but nobody can track specific interior meanings.

In terms of accurate, provable science they were essentially in a room full of animated Etch-A-Sketches. Ethan tried not to smirk.

"Could you stand over there?" The young lady moved Ethan over so that he faced one of the T-Machines. It looked big and comfortable.

"Once we've traced a thought," the young lady said, "we can repair it and eventually enhance the abilities of the thinker."

What a lovely, and hopelessly naïve, thought. But "Gosh" was all that he said.

It was the only thing he felt he could safely say.

"And in some ways we find ways to more effectively think together."

Ethan started a bit. He didn't know anything about collective telepathy in Mentotechnic doctrine.

"Would you like a demonstration?"

Ethan nodded. Not just for academic reasons but also because it would be good colour commentary for his report to Nina.

The electrodes went on very quickly.

"At the advanced levels we believe that we can record entire human personalities and sustain their intellects in artificial environments."

Ethan would have to think about the significance of what he'd just heard. He would also have to think about whether it was actually true that the vocabulary of his guide seemed to be growing as they continued the tour.

She clicked a few switches on the T-Machine.

"This is how we've been able to maintain continuity of leadership in our organization."

"Huh?" Okay, thought Ethan, he could have been more eloquent there.

"*Huh!*" Ethan's spine snapped rigid as a not-insignificant amount of electricity ran from the T-Machine to the skullcap and into his body. He realized that he would only be speaking in monosyllables for a while.

"Would you like to meet the living mind of D.H. Evanston?"

He's been dead for years, thought Ethan.

"*Duh!*" was what Ethan said.

Then everything went very dark and for an indeterminate time Ethan felt like he was floating weightless in the presence of something very ambitious with an Arkansas accent. A lot of words were floating around with him but he could only understand one. It was a direct, powerful message, meant only for him:

"*MORON.*"

Then Ethan woke up. He was lying next to a very cold lake, on a pile of leaves, twigs and some rather bouncy soil. When he eventually found his way to a human community, he discovered that he was in Prince Albert Provincial Park, somewhere in central Saskatchewan.

2009: Dish and Saucer

Arrangements were running a bit late, so Ethan had a couple of hours to kill. Not the easiest thing to do in central Alberta.

He decided to take in the local museums and attractions.

There was the obligatory Royal Canadian Air Force museum with the rusting Avro CF-100 stuck on a pole in the front yard. The rather subdued cases of uniforms and medals were housed in the former Royal Canadian Legion Hall.

That experience was good for about twenty minutes. Ethan then crossed the street to the local history museum.

In this part of the world, local history was essentially agricultural history. Ethan had never seen so many ancient tractors and combines—all reverently positioned on illuminated plywood pedestals.

This was definitely farm country. Even the docents were dressed in those denim bib overalls that nobody makes anymore. Ethan felt as though he was in a very grounded culture, one that was focused on very practical and concrete things, stuff that grew out of the earth and that you could eat.

But according to Nina's briefing notes, Ethan's perception was not accurate. This part of western Canada was a "hotspot"—a region with numerous UFO sightings and encounters. His favourite CSIS memo about the town started: "RE: ROSWELL NORTH".

Ethan decided he'd test the reports by talking to one of the docents.

The man was a volunteer and a retired farmer, with a mass of wiry white hair and cracked sun-blasted skin. He looked like a part of the museum's agricultural collections.

They talked about the usual sorts of things: where the old man had farmed, the kinds of crops he grew, and why it was a shame that so many young families couldn't make their living in town anymore.

The conversation started getting a little strange when they started talking about the weather. Ethan appreciated that the weather is a topic of passionate interest in agrarian communities; after all, the variations in temperature and rainfall could have an enormous impact on your livelihood.

Even so, Ethan was surprised when the old man started talking about how many of the harvests in the 1970s and 1980s had been seriously damaged by giant Soviet weather manipulation satellites.

"Wow."

That was all that Ethan felt it was safe to say.

"Guess they must be still up there, workin' away," the old man said. "Because even though the commies are gone, the weather hasn't improved much."

Before they could get to the topic of cattle mutilations, Ethan pointed to the picture windows at the far end of the gallery. Through the glass they could see a ragged cluster of rotting wood in the field next door.

"That's the McArty Ranch," the old man said. "That's what's left of our Centennial project."

Ethan suddenly remembered something from a magazine he'd read when he was a kid. "Is that the…?"

The old man grinned. "That's right, that's the flying saucer landing pad."

The details of the article were coming back to Ethan now. The landing pad was the town's way of welcoming everybody in the universe to come in and celebrate Canada's 100th birthday.

The old man laughed. "Some people swore they did see a couple of spaceships over there."

"Did you ever see anything?"

"Naw." The old man forced his hands into the pockets of his coveralls. "The furthest visitor we've ever had was from Halifax." Then he smiled and looked beyond the plywood heap. "Of course, I'm not counting those folks over at the Mentotechnics Institute."

"What are they like?" Ethan tried to sound casual.

"They're okay. Very polite," the old man replied. "Must be real busy because we don't see them very much."

Ethan looked out the window and noticed an unmarked van parked under the suspended jet. He excused himself and left right after he dropped five dollars in the jar designated as the fund for the restoration of the landing pad.

* * *

"Meet me at Vulcan."

Ethan wondered how many times Nina had wanted to say that to him. Or anybody.

But the circumstances and the meaning were very different from what she might have imagined all those years ago. Nina meant Vulcan, Alberta, not Vulcan the planet. This Vulcan was a fairly small town a couple of hours drive from Calgary.

Why here?

True, it was reasonably close to the Mentotechnics compound, but there were lots of other places to meet.

Maybe Nina was just trying to be ironic, somehow trying to let Ethan know that she was beyond all that *Trek* stuff now.

That didn't feel right. By now, Ethan had figured out that Nina had changed quite a bit; he doubted that she really cared what he thought about her beliefs.

Still…

Ethan parked his rental car next to the Vulcan Visitors' Centre and looked at the giant sculpture of the USS Enterprise looming over the highway. The centre itself was modeled after a United Federation of Planets Space Station.

Maybe Nina was trying to say something here.

She was inside waiting for him, sipping blue Romulan Ale.

"You're looking well," Ethan said as he took a seat in the booth.

"You're still a terrible liar."

"Truth is relative." Ethan smiled feebly. "And we're all getting older."

He waved at the Andorean waiter to bring him a blue drink.

"Drink? A blue one like my friend's."

Nina was right. She really did look awful.

Pale, red-eyed, and her business suit was hanging off her like combat fatigues. She looked the way Ethan felt when he'd woken up in northern Saskatchewan almost 15 years ago. But he'd been drugged and shipped halfway across the continent while he was unconscious. He had an excuse.

"You've been here before?" Ethan asked.

"Couple of times." Nina smiled a little as she stared at her half-empty glass. "The Klingon group from Great Falls comes up here every spring. They do a nice music festival."

"Oh."

Ethan and Nina watched as the tube of blue beer was deposited in front of him.

"So, are you getting back into that sort of thing?"

"No."

Nina emptied her glass.

"You can't recapture that kind of a feeling." She gestured for another drink. "But I still respect what they're trying to do." Nina looked around at the information desk and all the displays that carried facts and maps from the local chamber of commerce—all themed as *Star Trek* sets. "What this whole place represents."

"A positive vision for the future?" Ethan still remembered that phrase from the many earnest late night conversations.

"A *human* vision for the future." Nina got quiet and they both watched as her beer materialized in front of them.

Slightly odd turn of phrase, Ethan thought as he watched her take another drink.

He decided that he had better help Nina get to the point.

"I assume you want to talk about what they're doing with that radio telescope at the compound?"

She smiled, which was somewhat scary.

"Do you know that they think they're picking up intelligent signals from outer space?"

"Probably from a confederation of star systems from the galactic core," Ethan replied matter-of-factly. "Completely consistent with Temple doctrine."

Her smile got slightly scarier.

"And what do you think they're doing in the aircraft hangar?"

"Most likely building a flying saucer." This discussion seemed to be getting a little cryptic for Ethan. "Every once in a while one of their branches builds a mock-up spacecraft, hoping that they can get out there and commune with their maker."

Nina downed two-thirds of her latest drink.

"Yeah."

"It's not a big deal, Nina. Ask the Vulcan Chamber of Commerce." Inexplicably Ethan felt that he had to convince her. "It's like those cargo cults in the south Pacific that used to build airplanes out of palm trees."

Nina burped menacingly. "Palm trees?" she said. "You think this is all about *fucking palm trees*?"

Ethan pushed back into his chair a bit. He hadn't seen Nina this angry in almost three decades.

"I'm just saying that..." Ethan spoke as carefully as possible, "... that there's precedent for this in the ethnographic literature."

And Ethan noticed that after almost thirty years, he sounded just the same.

But Nina either didn't notice, or didn't care.

"Ethan, I have three pieces of information that you might find *somewhat interesting*."

Ethan was pretty sure that he would probably not welcome new information.

"Really."

Just then Ethan remembered something important; Nina could be really annoying sometimes.

"First." Nina stopped and ingested another large portion of her latest beer. "They have two connected super-computers in there."

"So?" This still didn't seem terribly serious to Ethan. "Maybe they have picked up some interesting astronomical data and need something to process it with."

"Do you really think so?" Nina laughed.

"Why not, there's nothing in Mentotechnics that precludes some kind of legitimate scientific inquiry. Even if they've come across the data accidentally."

"That's mighty liberal of you, Ethan." Nina ingested all but a millimeter thick ring of blue from her glass. "But there's more news, and it goes from bad to worse."

"Let's hear it."

At least when they were dating, Ethan could tolerate these moods because he knew they'd be having sex at some point afterwards.

"We also think they've got some plutonium in there."

Ethan's reaction was nausea. He was briefly thankful that he'd only had one beer. Then he felt nothing, probably because he didn't want to consider the implications of what he'd just been told.

"That's terrible," he said finally and rather weakly at that. "But..." He paused for a moment, hoping that he wouldn't whine when he asked the next question:

"But, what do you want me to do? I'm no expert on nuclear bombs and—"

"I want you to go back there with some of my people and pick up one of their members."

"Why?" Ethan felt his back stiffen as the old ethical reflexes set in.

"I want you to interrogate that person. *Thoroughly*."

Ethan folded his arms. "Nina, I'm a social scientist, you know I don't do de-programming."

"*This is serious shit, Ethan!*"

Nina then noticed that the Andorean waiter, as well as a few other staff aliens, were now looking at them.

"This is plutonium!" she whispered. "And I'm not asking you to de-program anybody. I doubt that's even possible."

"So, what do you want me to do?" Ethan couldn't imagine how he could be of any use in this situation.

"Just try and behave like a real anthropologist and get us some information about what's happening in that compound."

Ethan studied his half-glass of fantasy beer, then he studied the glass that once held Nina's fantasy beer.

"Okay," he said.

"Okay." Nina seemed to be calming down.

"Nina?"

"Yes?"

"What's the worse news?" Ethan noticed that his voice was trembling a little. "What could be worse than a bunch of crazy Mentotechnologists having the makings of an atomic weapon?"

"Oh," Nina replied. "Nothing much. We just think that Mentotechnics—or some aspects of it—might actually work."

Okay, Nina had convinced him. She'd gotten really bizarre in the last twenty-five years.

* * *

Even though she was the one going progressively crazy, it was Nina, not Ethan, who had walked out on the relationship.

They had another fight when Ethan mentioned that he was thinking about making her *Star Trek* friends the subject of his revised thesis project.

"Ethically, I have to tell you that I'm planning this." Ethan handed her a few pages of typed notes—his revised research proposal. He was confident that Professor Sirkowski would like it.

"*In your mind, you have capacities you know...*"

She read the proposal for a few minutes and handed the pages back.

"You are such an asshole."

Then she left.

Evidently she did not like the proposal. Possibly she was

offended at the idea of being the subject of anthropological study.

"...To transmit thought energy far beyond the norm."

Two days later, Nina called him on the phone, and in an apologetic voice told him that she felt badly about leaving things like that. She knew how important his work was to him, that she believed that this kind of social scientific research was important to human progress, and that she knew that he really didn't mean to sound condescending.

"...Please close your eyes and concentrate with every thought you think...

Well, two out of three, Ethan thought. But missing that one point did not stop him from inviting Nina over for dinner the next evening.

"...Upon the recitation we're about to sing..."

Ethan went to a certain amount of trouble getting ready for that dinner. He actually cooked a chicken, bought some wine that wasn't from Ontario and even bought her a record album.

The clerk at Sam the Record Man had recommended it: "If she's into sci-fi, then she'll love this one."

The record was by a Canadian band called Klaatu.

"Some people think that these guys are really the Beatles," the clerk added as he took seven of Ethan's dollars. "The first cut is the best one on this album."

After dinner, Ethan put the record on his used Viking stereo while he and Nina made love on the sofa.

"Calling occupants..."

The first time around, Nina really seemed to like the music, but when they played the LP again, Ethan noticed that she was getting a little distant.

"...calling occupants of interplanetary craft..."

She said she couldn't stay the night. Ethan slipped the vinyl disc into its sleeve and handed it to her.

"Keep it," she said. "It's just some silly stuff about UFOs and alien contact." Nina opened the door. "That's not what I care about."

"Yes, but I thought you might like the music—"

"I guess you really don't understand me."

Then she left.

And as Ethan eventually deduced, that was essentially the end of the relationship.

"...We are your friends!"

* * *

Nina's crew showed up in the van, and after that it was pretty easy to carry out the plan. But they seemed a bit nervous.

"Just remember," the team leader growled at him. "Keep that toque on your head at all times."

It felt as though the black wool hat had kevlar earflaps.

Canucks in space, Ethan thought.

"Why?" he asked as the van rolled to a stop in the parking spot behind the local Tim Horton's.

"Orders, Professor." The team leader held up an air gun. "If you lose your hat, sir, I'll have to give you one of these darts."

"No thanks." Ethan had experienced enough forced unconsciousness for one lifetime.

But in spite of the hats, maybe because of the hats, the operation went very smoothly. After about two hours of waiting, somebody in a pick-up from the compound pulled up at the front entrance to the shop. It was a kid, maybe 17 or 18, probably going in to get something for their morning shift. Apparently even highly evolved superbeings like their daily fix of doughnuts.

When the kid walked out with his box of bakery goodies, the team leader aimed his air gun and squeezed off a shot.

There was a tiny puff as the kid caught a dart in his ass.

Two of the team members dashed over to the kid and held him up before he could drop a single banana cream-filled.

The kid was in the van before anybody in the doughnut shop could peer through the coffee steam and notice that the kid hadn't made it to his truck.

* * *

SUBJECT X: Oh, it's you again.

INTERVIEWER: I don't think we've met.

SUBJECT X: We know all about you.

INTERVIEWER: Really?

SUBJECT X: Really. We've been keeping tabs on so-called "researchers" like you for quite a while.

INTERVIEWER: Pick up anything interesting?

SUBJECT X:	Not from you, but some people have been making surprising progress.
INTERVIEWER:	What do they know?
SUBJECT X:	You, on the other hand, provide entertainment.
INTERVIEWER:	Thanks.
SUBJECT X:	Don't worry about it. None of it matters any more.
INTERVIEWER:	Why doesn't it matter?
SUBJECT X:	We don't believe we'll tell you right now.
INTERVIEWER:	*We?*
SUBJECT X:	That's what "We" are. The Therapy Machines, the hypnotic training processes, all those expensive courses, everything in Mentotechnics was designed to bring us all together.
INTERVIEWER:	All together? With a collective political ideology?
SUBJECT X:	You're thinking too small.
INTERVIEWER:	A unified consciousness?
SUBJECT X:	Very good! You remember the doctrine!
INTERVIEWER:	But that's scientifically impossible.
SUBJECT X:	All minds at the compound are governed by the recorded thought patterns of D.H. Evanston… and we say you're wrong.
INTERVIEWER:	Do you know that you're part of a profoundly delusional community?
SUBJECT X:	Do you know that you're really pissing us off right now? Not a great idea, Professor!
VOICE:	(off mic, partly unintelligible):—*about the plutonium!*
INTERVIEWER:	These gentlemen want to know why you have plutonium on the compound.
SUBJECT X:	I'm sure they do. But they already know more than you do.

INTERVIEWER: What do you mean?

SUBJECT X: Those silly hats you have to wear. We can read minds if you don't have telepathic protection.

INTERVIEWER: (sigh) Fine, since we're protected and we have you here, why not answer the question? What's the big plan at the compound?

SUBJECT X: You're supposed to be the expert. What's the ultimate goal of Mentotechnics?

INTERVIEWER: To bring about the total transformation of the human race.

SUBJECT X: By creating the ideal consciousness.

INTERVIEWER: And that's a hive-mind, based on its founder's personality?

SUBJECT X: Sort of. But you forgot the most interesting bits. We also plan on transcending the boundaries of this tiny world and taking our place among the stars!

INTERVIEWER: Okay, but what does have to do with plutonium?

SUBJECT X: We used the radio telescope to ask for help.

INTERVIEWER: Help from outer space?

SUBJECT X: They suggested that we needed the plutonium to help things happen.

INTERVIEWER: You think you can use it to power that flying saucer and go out and see these aliens?

SUBJECT X: The saucer isn't any kind of a spacecraft. It's more of a catalyst.

INTERVIEWER: You mean it's a bomb?

SUBJECT X: Bomb is such a pejorative term.

INTERVIEWER: You—

* * *

When Ethan heard the explosion he thought that the

Mentotechnists had detonated their nuclear device.

As usual, he was wrong.

It was just Nina driving an armoured truck full of plastic explosives through the compound and blowing up the saucer.

Ethan later found out that fissionable materials need a specific type of detonation for a chain reaction to take place. Nina only wanted to destroy the supercomputers on the compound. She knew that was the fastest way of stopping things from going nuclear.

So, if Evanston's mind had been recorded in there, it wasn't any more. Neither were Nina and 22 residents of the compound.

None of the CSIS team knew about her plan. They had been told that the explosives were going to be used to destroy the radio telescope after they had made all the arrests.

* * *

One thing Ethan could do was write a report.

He was still reasonably good at that sort of thing.

"None of the events convince me that any aspect of Mentotechnic practice or belief has any basis in empirical fact," he wrote in the 312-page analysis to Nina's replacement at CSIS. "It is likely that the intensity of the operation caused your team leader to become one more subscriber in the cult's delusional world-view."

Poor Nina.

Once again she got caught up in the fantasy and went off the deep end.

"Never-the-less," Ethan concluded, "her actions were correct, though perhaps somewhat extreme, in spite of her warped frame of reference. She recognized the strong possibility of nuclear terrorism and took direct steps to stop it. If the pathology of similar 'communities of unreason' is any indicator, then we can assume that the group at the compound was planning to use the detonator as a vehicle of mass suicide. Your team leader's actions undoubtedly saved the lives of over two hundred Mentotechnologists on the compound as well as the residents in the nearby town."

* * *

Another thing Ethan could do was attend the funeral.

Nina's *Star Trek* friends had arranged the service. They all put on their convention uniforms and the organist played some really touching transcriptions from the best soundtracks.

The service was held at a Unitarian meeting hall that had been built in the early 1970s, so it looked a lot like they had all gathered in a set from the original series.

Two people gave the eulogy.

The first person talked about what a wonderful, loving person Nina was and how lucky he was to have her as his partner for fifteen years.

That statement surprised Ethan. He had trouble imagining Nina with any other significant other but him.

The second person described how Nina represented everything that was fine and noble in *Star Trek*. How she respected the unique potential of the individual. How she understood the importance of a strong sustainable world community, and how she strove for our species to create its own best possible future.

One of the speakers was dressed like Captain Kirk.

The other looked like Mr. Spock.

LIVING INSIDE YOUR TELEVISION

I embarrassed myself in a recent conversation. The topic of the discussion was favourite TV shows when we were kids. Everybody except me mentioned one or two, maybe three shows, that they really liked and why they liked them. That was about all they said—probably because when they were growing up, they had friends, played sports, had favourite subjects at school, studied dancing or took up a musical instrument, or maybe just went outside once in a while.

Not me. I went on and on about what I loved to watch, who was in them, who made them, how many seasons they were on for, what day and time they were broadcast, which were their best episodes, what the best thing to eat was while you were watching them, etc., etc., etc. And these were shows made before we were even remotely close to peak television.

It became very apparent to everyone in the conversation that while they were having normal and healthy childhoods, I had been living inside the family television set. It wasn't an impossible thing to do, our family had one of those big Marconis with the real wooden sides. Plenty of room in there.

I admit it, I wasn't just a consumer of television, I was a person who lived and loved his television. It was one of my fondest dreams to write for television, but I never figured out how to get invited to that particular party. I guess television didn't love me back.

Later, I also got into movies and live theatre, and it was learning about a combination of TV and the stage that sparked "John, Paul, Xavier, Ironside and George (but not Vincent)" into existence. I came across a news report about how a community theatre in the United States was performing classic episodes of *Star Trek* on stage. My first thought was whether people would pay to see a live re-enactment of a script they had already viewed dozens and dozens (possibly thousands and thousands) of times before. The next thing I wondered was how much would it cost me to fly down there and see a performance? Which pretty much answered the first question.

I kept obsessing about the idea of old TV serving as the text for stage plays and I started thinking about what sort of circumstances would make this the only way for people to enjoy their re-runs? Hence the villains of the story and a new form of digital contagion. Parts of the story remind me of how in 2020, we are making targeted and "strategic" efforts to contain the spread of biological viruses. And as the U.S. Presidential election approaches, I also wonder how many informational viruses are swarming around us.

JOHN, PAUL, XAVIER, IRONSIDE AND GEORGE (BUT NOT VINCENT)

Originally published in:
Ominous Realities: The Anthology of Dark Speculative Horrors
2013

I was sitting in the bus station lobby watching the disintegration of Hong Kong. The big monitor was tuned to the news channel and we had a ground-level view of Wan Chai as it was being chewed into micro-ash.

Micro-ash being the final form of all matter that has no further use.

Very sad. Wan Chai was made up of lots of old narrow skyscrapers with huge neon signs advertising dancing, food, booze and massages. The sorts of things we humans tend to consume when we're in places like that.

Not what the Meanies consume.

We kept on watching as the swarm reduced a sign for a strip club into light gray powder. A neon cartoon sailor with squinty eyes and bulging forearms vanished forever. I felt a wave of despair because I would never be able to visit "Cockeye's Go-Go Bar and Night Club".

Stupid Meanies.

Goddamned AIs.

Artificial Intelligence.

Machine Intelligence.

The ground feed shut down so the news channel cut to some

LANDSAT images. It looked like Hong Kong was under some kind of violent weather system, engulfed by a swirling vortex of clouds.

Looked like?

Hong Kong *was* being engulfed in a swirling vortex of clouds. Very smart, very determined and very hungry clouds.

Son of a bitch.

Machine Intelligence?

More like Machine Appetite.

I wondered if the Meanies enjoyed satisfying their appetites as much as we liked satisfying ours.

Just about every plastic seat in the bus station was occupied but the place was almost completely silent. The TV announcer couldn't think of anything to say either.

Time to hook up my therapy box and do equilibrium check.

> **Quantitative:** It is 20:30 Eastern Standard Time. I am mid-way through the trip to start my new job. We are 32 minutes behind schedule and in spite of the age and crappy ergonomic design of the seats in the bus I've managed to sleep for seven of the last 15 hours. I will likely arrive at the Care Facility on time, relatively alert and well rested.
>
> **Qualitative:** Anger gives way to numbness as I watch the clouds consume the Asian coastline. Now I'm worried. Why have I stopped feeling? Maybe I'm turning into a Meanie.

After the broadcast someone tried to change the channel to something more entertaining. The plasma in the monitor screen bubbled and the casing started to melt around the edges. One of the janitors ran out and pulled out the cable hook-up.

By the time my bus was ready to go, two technicians wearing old Animal Control uniforms showed up to take the monitor away.

"Gonna have to pulverize it," one the techs told the ticket-seller.

"And you'll have to replace all the electronics in the station," the other tech added.

The station manager's face turned the same color as micro-ash.

"Happening all over town," the first tech said. "News broadcast spread the infection."

*   *   *

I was going to start the first day of my new job with a runny nose and no tissue paper. Legacy of my old job.

In old science fiction movies, they show the brain-computer interface in ways that are kind of elegant or at least relatively mess-free: retina scans, helmets with video visors, a few electrodes neatly taped to the forehead. Maybe in the edgier productions you might see a jack in the temple or the base of the skull.

Big deal.

In my world, they do use wire-jacks to hook you to a machine but since they need a quick means of connecting to the higher cognitive functions, they put the link as close to the frontal lobes as anatomically possible. That is without poking a hole through your eye and making you go blind.

Therefore, they drill in the jack and insert the wire at the base of your left nostril. Your right nostril if you're left handed. This is an incredibly painful procedure and once they do it, you will always be more susceptible to colds, allergies and sinus infections.

So the price of being a Big Time Design Actualizer is living with these constant rivers of snot. And you get to keep paying this price even after you stop being a Big Time Design Actualizer.

There was nothing as unsanitary as a box of tissues at the Care Facility's information desk, so I did a quick dash to the men's room. I ducked into one of the stalls, found some toilet paper and wiped my nose.

Ah, simple joys!

Then I stuffed some T.P. into my pockets in case of future need.

It's okay, I told myself. Soon such indignities will be a thing of the past. I'm a working person again and if supplies permit, I might even be able to buy some antibiotics.

I noticed that my hands were trembling and sweat was on my forehead. I am either getting a fever or very nervous. Maybe both.

Wash your face in cold water. That's always good.

Now I feel nauseous. The ghost of that powdered egg and synthetic strawberry jam muffin I had for breakfast was manifesting itself.

Sorry to take you through all this slightly gross minutiae but I think it's good for you to have a sense of how thrilling life in the 21st century has become.

Time for another equilibrium check:

> **Quantitative:** It is 07:45 on Monday. My physiological state is far from optimal but at least I am ahead of schedule. I figure that my chances of successfully navigating the day have dropped from 70 to 55%. I've managed worse odds.
>
> **Qualitative:** Mild panic and disgust. Panic with having to deal with something new. Disgust, not with my surroundings, but with my own weakness.

She was waiting for me as I emerged from the washroom. Doctor Somebody; the nametag was partly obscured by her lapel. She handed me a very thick, very heavy plastic binder and pronounced my name to rhyme with "failure". The markings on her shoulder indicated that she was with the Ministry of Information Defense.

MID scares me almost as much as the Meanies.

She pointed to a corridor and we started walking.

"I'm not a medical doctor," she said.

"Neither am I." Dr. Somebody (who is not a physician) did not laugh at my little joke.

"I'm a specialist in complex biologically-embedded data ecologies."

"Sure." What else can you say to a statement like that?

"That is the field of scientific inquiry most relevant to your client's condition."

"Okay." Sounded daft to me but if MID was behind this it was usually a bad idea to ask too many questions.

"There's a number on the last page of your binder," she continued. "You call it if any bits start to drop off him or if he catches fire or something."

How scientific. How sensitive.

"His physical condition is very stable so any health issues are very unlikely."

Dr. Somebody pushed the door open.

"Your job is to help your client do whatever he wants to do, listen to whatever strange things he has to say, help him go wherever he wants to go."

I could see a massive shape sitting at the far end of the room. It looked like a mountain of dried and cracked clay sitting on a nuclear powered forklift.

"Oh, and he'll want to play Flipper Crutch," she added.

Before I could respond with some intelligent and perceptive questions like: "What the hell is Flipper Crutch?" and "What bits of him are most likely to fall off?"—a low voice growled out of a set of large vocoder speakers:

"You here to take me out of this old fool's home?"

* * *

"One more game before we leave?"

The Flipper Crutch gaming space was a mini-spectacle. My client had taped at least ten different board games together: Risk, Parcheesi, Sorry, Clue, Chinese Checkers, Chess, Careers, Life, etc. into a vast wonderful pattern. There were at least two dozen playing pieces including the race car and top hat from Monopoly, some checkers and chessmen, a spool and some of those little gin bottles from the old airline days. Also some *Star Wars* action figures.

My first week working at the Care Facility was spent playing Flipper Crutch. To be more accurate, my client was playing. I was moving pieces around while being told how much I was losing.

"Very bad move," my client said, as he snatched one of my pieces off the board. Damn, he took the race car (my favourite piece).

I threw the three irregularly shaped dice.

"Should I move there?" I asked, pointing to a section of board.

My client tilted his huge deformed head at an angle that I took to be an affirmative.

I moved my piece (Obi-wan Kenobi, my next favorite piece) down the number of allotted squares.

My client's pseudo-mandibles stretched into a really ugly grin and he used his left hand, the one that was more like a lobster claw, to crush my hapless action figure.

"Terrible move."

I had to protest: "Now why was that so bad a move?"

"You keep moving the same number of squares as there are on the dice," he replied. "You shouldn't do that too often."

"No? Why not?"

"Much too obvious."

At that point I decided that my client had either invented a game of near-infinite complexity or else he was making it all up as we went along.

Possibly both.

I was very glad that this would be our last game of Flipper Crutch for a while.

> **Quantitative:** It is 14:07 on Wednesday. I'm ten days into my new job. My client is an early victim of self-induced Bio-Information Disease, a.k.a. Data Cancer. Apparently he has no name but judging from the money the Ministry is putting into looking after him, he must have been Someone Pretty Fucking Important. That's an official designation: or S.P.F.I. Replaced V.I.P. about ten years ago. Sorry, I'm slipping out of quantitative mode here. I'll start again.
>
> The information disease is quite advanced. His mind is as eccentric as his body. Let's start again.
>
> My shift ends at 20:00. I will then go to my room and try to make some progress with the verbiage and number columns in the binder. Then I'll stick a wire up my nose. Nothing recreational about that. It is a legally authorized therapy to prevent my hypothalamus from exploding.
>
> I won't bother starting again, I'll just move on to the next section.
>
> **Qualitative:** Aesthetic stuff really. The physical manifestations of my client's data cancer are hideously beautiful. His skin is more mineralogical than organic—like ceramics made from the clay of Mars. There's hundreds, maybe thousands of nodules and vast fractal landscapes of scab tissue.

What I've read in the binder repeats the commonly accepted theory that some early researchers injected self-actualizing information into their bodies when the Meanies started making our super-computers unreliable and potentially hostile.

Most of these scientists died. In pretty horrific ways. The few who didn't die had pretty horrific lives.

* * *

Our extended field trip.

Good thing that my therapy box is portable enough to be carried around in my duffle bag.

I've read most of the binder and there's still no clue to who he used to be. Not even a first name.

He needs a name.

Joseph Merrick.

No, what would be unkind.

Captain Flipper Crutch?

That's not very nice either.

My mood is not good.

How about John? Short, easy to remember. Not unkind.

Fine, John for the time being.

John and I were traveling inter-city.

"Square twelve?"

"Uh... roll four?"

"You lose again."

John was playing Flipper Crutch in his head and forcing me to play along.

"You got me there."

The train's membranes changed color to something slightly less putrid and more transparent, so we had/saw a view of an ocean of high rises and the distant haze of Meanies obscuring the sun.

Minor Meanies. No real danger unless you flew into them.

So nobody flew anymore.

"Square 49!" John declared.

"Okay," I replied. "How about Square 93?"

John was wearing a pair of protective goggles (partly to protect his eyes from the sun, partly to protect the general public from getting a good look at him)—even so, I could see him blink in surprise.

John's voice was barely visible through the vocoder. "You win that one."

> **Quantitative:** The train is ugly (with photographs I could objectively prove this) and it smells of rotting bio-control matter. However, we are 13 minutes ahead of schedule.
>
> **Qualitative:** I am irrationally pleased with myself. No one should be proud from the results of what is probably complete randomness, but there you go.

One of the more surprising things I found in my binder was a functioning Über-Card. It was in a little ringed plastic pouch at the back.

My ex-wife used to fantasize about us getting an Über-Card: "Unlimited goddamned credit!" she'd say. "No interest charges. Make payments whenever you feel like it."

Before I could explain that financial tools like that tended to cause global economic meltdowns, she would have fallen asleep. Probably so she could dream about buying things.

Even in those heady pre-Meanie times when the two of us were re-purposing seven, maybe eight major product designs a week, we couldn't afford to be in the ÜC Zone. I was thankful for that.

Now I finally had an Über Card. Which was going be very helpful in getting Paul across country. (I had decided that John no longer suited him.)

The irony being that now that I could get, to quote my ex-wife: "any goddamned thing I wanted," I was at a stage in my life when I didn't really want all that much. Anything that I couldn't stuff into the duffle bag was pretty much a pain in the ass.

However, I did enjoy the expressions of awe and fear the Über-Card evoked when I handed it to the ticketing agent at Union Station and the clerk at the hotel registration desk. Both of them held it gingerly like it might be slightly radioactive and stamped the paperwork very quickly as if the card's raw power might melt the mechanism.

* * *

It took two days to get to our destination. A middle-sized city in the middle of the continent.

One nice thing: the skies were so big you could actually see real cumulonimbus clouds.

Very nostalgic. Cue Joni Mitchell.

The cars drove ten kilometers below the speed limit which placed them at the same speed as most of the pedestrians. Most of the buildings weren't more than six storeys tall except for a few banks at the city core, a huge cathedral across the river, and a rather strange tower which also could have been a cathedral but for an extraterrestrial faith community. I asked the hotel desk clerk about the tower.

"That's the tower from the Museum," he said. "Been closed for years."

The elevator pinged. We rolled towards our room. Get your tip ready, I told myself.

What the hell were we doing here?

The binder warned me that:

"Clients with this condition are prone to erratic behavior and tend to gravitate towards extreme situations."

Extreme situations? In this burg? I should drop someone at the Care Facility a note.

Paul and I were going to share a room; that way I could keep track of him at all times. You never know, he might actually find some extreme situation and gravitate towards it while I was busy in the other room.

The elaborate growths around Paul's nostrils made him such an outrageously loud snorer that he managed to break his vocoder with the feedback effect.

My fault, I was so tired I forgot to turn the unit off.

"Stupid thing," he muttered, half-asleep.

Actually his non-assisted voice wasn't all that hard to understand.

In the morning, I decided to sit on the bed, stick the wire up my nose—really deep—and do my quantitative and qualitatives. Try and get some equilibrium going.

Paul hadn't said much since his defeat at Flipper Crutch. He had positioned himself in front of the TV and was watching a documentary about changes in the Indian Ocean's ecosystems.

Nothing really new here. The producers just found a way to present the material in an even more depressing way. Australia and

New Zealand were the first places to be reduced to a very fine powder and these were very large piles of powder indeed. Big and horrible implications for the oceans surrounding them.

Throw away your blue box, folks!

Paul pushed the remote which mercifully made the TV show go away.

"TV outside," he growled.

"Yes, you turned off the program," I said in that annoying tone I assumed whenever I was trying to humor him.

"TV outside," Paul said a little louder this time.

Okay, I hadn't interpreted his statement correctly.

"Paul," I said. "I really don't think we need to take the TV out of the room."

"*TV outside!*" Paul yelled.

Wow. He really didn't need that vocoder.

"If a client is not placed in any danger," the binder said, "it is usually best to agree to any requests or demands they make."

Fine.

I sighed, pulled the wire out of my nose and walked over to the TV. It was one of those big cathode ray jobs and it was going to be a mother to get it off its stand and out into the hall. I supposed I could call the hotel staff to help but by then Paul might be completely apoplectic.

Never mind.

I wrapped my arms around the molded plastic and started to lift.

Paul snarled in disgust and handed me one of those free "What's On in Town" magazines they leave in hotel rooms.

"TV outside," he said.

The cover of the magazine read: "Mass Culture Nostalgia: Classic Television Performed in the Park."

TV Outside.

Now I got it.

Quantitative: After about five minutes of miscommunication, my client successfully expressed his desire to attend a summer theatre festival. I will make appropriate arrangements.

Qualitative: I was never keen on the idea of having children. Looks like I've got one anyway.

The last time I attended theatre in the park, all you had to do was show up with a blanket and a few bucks to make a voluntary donation.

"I'm very sorry, sir," the concierge said over the phone. "There just don't seem to be any spaces available."

"You did mention that we've traveled quite a long distance to see the festival?"

"Square 18!" Xavier called out.

Xavier was my client's new name because of his wheelchair and his uncanny mutant ability to spontaneously generate inconvenient situations. Like starting a new game just when I started talking on the phone.

"Yes, I did, sir," the concierge replied. "They said they were deeply sorry."

"Page 890!" Xavier called out.

Square 890? That was just dumb. Even Phantom Flipper Crutch didn't have that many squares.

"*Page 890!*"

Did he say "page"?

The binder.

"Hang on," I said into the receiver. I grabbed the binder and flipped to page 890. A passage near the bottom had been marked with yellow highlighter:

"Always keep in mind that the Über-Card provides a range of different forms of access, not just financial. Do not hesitate to apply its power to change your circumstances."

Okay…

"Do you have the number for the box office?" I asked the concierge.

"Sir, I doubt—"

"You're probably right of course," I said, anticipating that he was going to tell me how useless my call would be. "Still, I need to tell my client that I've tried every option."

Xavier leaned back in his chair and farted loudly. Then he smiled at me.

"Page 890."

A minute later I was dialing the box office.

Dialing.

Mechanical switchboards were back in a big way. Nobody wanted a bunch of nano-Meanies streaming out of your cell phone, so the simpler the telecom the better.

"Hello?" A subtle, analog voice said to me.

All I said in reply was the 34-digit number on the back of the Über-Card. I didn't even get a "one moment please"—just a click and almost immediately another voice introduced itself.

"This is the House Manager. Would you like us to send a limousine to pick you up at your hotel?"

"7:30 will be fine." This card was great! "We'll need a vehicle with wheelchair access."

"We will purchase an appropriate conveyance this afternoon."

Okay…

"And would you like me to dismiss the box office staff?"

"That won't be necessary," I said quickly. "Simple misunderstanding."

I ended the call before I could do any more damage.

Xavier didn't feel like going out during the day so we sat around and watched more TV.

Another stupid news report.

A low altitude super-colony of Meanies was heading towards the west coast. Very serious Meanies. Had to happen sooner or later. In about six hours (more sooner than later), that cloud was going to hit Seattle and Vancouver.

"Square 19."

I'd forgotten that we still had a game going. Might as well get back to it.

"Square 50?"

Late in the afternoon some technicians from the hotel came around to take away our TV. Apparently some of the sets in the other rooms had started to act up after the last news broadcast so now every TV in the building had to be destroyed.

Quantitative: Fuck this.

Qualitative: Fuck that too.

The program notes stated that the themes of the festival were "Mystery, Integrity and Science."

Tonight was mystery night.

The play was an adaptation of an episode originally broadcast in

1973 from a series called *Ironside.*

My mother had the DVD set and I remember her watching it. The show never made a huge impression on me, although it did have great theme music by Quincy Jones and the actor who played Ironside had one of those "crack of doom" voices like Orson Welles or Lorne Greene. Like most American TV shows from the mid-20th century, everyone drove around in enormous cars. Except for Ironside, he was driven around in a huge van that had been adapted to carry him around in his wheelchair.

Oh yeah, that was the main premise of the series. A San Francisco Police Chief (nicknamed Ironside) had been shot by a sniper and lost the use of his legs. Now he headed a special task force and fought crime from his wheelchair.

I wondered if they were going to show us Ironside's van on stage. They did at the start of act three, when Ironside arrived at the criminal's mansion. The back doors of the van swung open and amidst the searchlights Ironside descended from the back of his van on the platform of his personal elevator.

It was an impressive effect and the audience applauded. My mother never applauded when she watched the show on her TV.

"There's no sense in hiding in there!" Ironside called out through a megaphone.

A man, dressed in an elegant silk smoking jacket and ascot, opened the front doors of the mansion and staggered towards Ironside.

"I don't care if you shoot!" the man cried.

Alarmed police officers pulled out their revolvers.

"Hold your fire!" Ironside barked through the megaphone. "He's not armed."

"I have nothing to live for!" the man sobbed.

"You know that's not true." Ironside handed the megaphone to a police officer while two other officers handcuffed the man's wrists behind his back.

"You're going to play it smart," Ironside said. "And face those extortion charges."

"How did you find out?" the man in the smoking jacket choked out the words.

"You might control a lot of people," Ironside replied. "But only through intimidation and bribery."

A young woman pushed her way through the line of police.

"*Daddy? Daddy!*" she cried out through tears of anguish.

"You were betrayed," Ironside continued.

"I'm so sorry, Daddy!" The young woman threw her arms around the handcuffed man. "I just couldn't let you go through with it!"

Ironside looked the accused man in the eyes.

"Betrayed by the one person who didn't fear you... but who loved you."

Music rises. Ironside turns away from the father and daughter—still locked in their tragic embrace.

Curtain.

* * *

Xavier really enjoyed the play. The pinprick scars in his forehead were pulsating a little and that usually meant that he was happy.

It was a pretty good story and in the context of live theatre it felt like something that Agatha Christie or Dorothy Sayers might have written. Mostly, I think Xavier liked the play because he identified with a hero who also rode around in a wheelchair.

"What did you think?" I asked Xavier as I hooked up his auxiliary breathing apparatus to the hotel mains for the night. No sense in a repeat of the vocoder incident.

Xavier pulled the lever that moved his chair into its horizontal position. He looked thoughtful.

"Square 76," he said.

I turned down the lights.

That was a good sign. Square 76 seemed to be one of his favourite positions on the Phantom Flipper Crutch board.

> **Quantitative:** We achieved today's recreational goals. I noted 0.35% degradation in my client's health readings this evening. The binder tells me that this is not a major concern. Estimated expenditures for our outing are about 530% higher than I originally budgeted.
>
> **Qualitative:** Mixed feelings. I'm a bit worried about Xavier's slight deterioration but he seems to be in good spirits.

"Are you awake?"

"Yes I am, Xavier." Actually, I had been asleep but what the hell.

"Why do you put that wire up your nose?"

"To help keep my mind in equilibrium," I said.

"Why do you need to do that?

"So I don't get a bad brain infection."

"Why would that happen?"

Why is the sky blue? Why do birds fly? Why is the moon so bright? I had a kid on my hands.

"Because in my old job I used to rent out parts of my brain."

"You rented out your brain?" Xavier asked.

My eyes were adjusting to the dark and I could make out the mini-landscape of Xavier laying back in his chair.

"People used to pay me money so they could use some of my brain. Sort of like a creative computer."

"Why?"

Argh!

"Well, people like designers or architects or professors would run some of their ideas through my brain to see if they could make their ideas better."

"I'm not an architect or a designer," said Xavier. "Why did they send you to be with me?"

Why. Again. Sigh.

"I needed to get a new job, Xavier."

"Why?"

"After the Meanies came, everybody who could rent out their brains had to help find ways to fight the Meanies."

"Except for you?"

"Except for me," I said quietly.

"Why couldn't you help fight the Meanies?"

I remembered having the same conversation with my soon to be ex-wife.

"Because my brain isn't very good at finding ways to fight."

I could see the profile of Xavier slowly nodding his head. It looked like the Rocky Mountains were agreeing with me.

"I don't like fighting either," he said.

"Well, there you go, Xavier."

"Don't call me Xavier anymore, okay?" my client said. "My new name is Ironside."

"Okay, Ironside."

Thus was confirmed my wheelchair identification theory.

"Can we go to sleep now?"
"Okay, Ironside."
We were silent for a few minutes, then:
"Square 76."
A good place for us to be.
"Square 76, Ironside."

> **Quantitative:** Day three of our theatre festival excursion. My client is making me aware of his requirements for daytime activities.
>
> **Qualitative:** The Meanies may finally be descending on us and all I'm doing is watching live TV reruns with what may be the World's Most Expensive Failed Science Experiment. Oddly liberating.

Our replacement TV was a thing of antediluvian splendour. It was this gigantic Zenith console unit with a huge bulbous screen that only showed black and white but with really deep and sexy Hi-Fi sound. Of course when you think of television you think of life in the woods, so the whole thing was encased within these massive slabs of mahogany.

It took four bellhops to get the thing in through the door.

"They got this from the old museum's warehouse," one of the bellhops said.

Okay, here's twenty bucks.

"They sure made 'em heavy back then," one of his co-workers added.

Fine, fine. Have another fifty.

The wiring on this thing was total tubes and copper and insanely simple which made us feel pretty safe watching it for as long as we liked.

It would have been fantastic if we'd been able to find a rerun of *Ironside* but no such luck. We did tune into a low-budget Canadian daytime sitcom (talk about your worst possible combination of unfortunate cultural elements) called *The Trouble with Tracy*. It was so dumb that it made your eyes water.

Everything else was news.

The goddamn, relentlessly depressing, news.

We didn't have Victoria, Vancouver or Seattle anymore. They didn't say anything about Portland or Richmond but then they never do. Some of the footage from Victoria showed people at a farmer's market, picking through bins of vegetables, munching on fruit, listening to the street musicians even as the Meanie cloud started to block out their rare and precious sun.

The newsreader said something about "mass hysteria manifesting itself as widespread collective calm" which sounded a little contradictory to me.

My theory was that the residents of Victoria had their priorities right.

"Square 11."

Oh dear, not a good place to be on the Phantom Flipper Crutch board.

"Are you sad, Ironside?" I asked. "Is the news making you feel bad?"

"Square 11."

"Me too, Square 11."

I turned off the TV and put a wire up my nose for the rest of the day.

* * *

"It's hopeless, Vincent," the man in the dark suit said. "Even if you could escape, no one will ever believe you."

Architect David Vincent (for some reason his profession was very important) was restrained by two blank-faced men dressed in zippered green coveralls.

"Nothing will stop us, Vincent." The man in the suit pointed a large and angular ray gun at our hero.

The big speakers at each end of the stage rumbled and shook just about every inch of the park as they simulated the detonation of an alien doomsday machine.

Tonight's theme was "integrity" and they were re-enacting an episode of the Quinn Martin 1967-68 classic series *The Invaders*. It was a great interpretation of the "aliens among us" theme. The Invaders were creepy but ordinary. Mostly they dressed like members of your Local Order of Moose, the nearest Business Improvement Association or the Electrical Workers of America Union. All three of those organizations already filled me with deep suspicion and finally here was a plausible reason why.

Each week Architect David Vincent struggled to overcome continual ridicule and tremendous physical danger to outwit the Invaders' latest conspiracy to take over the planet. That's why this play represented the integrity theme: think of *The Invaders* as *An Enemy of the People* but with malevolent extraterrestrials.

An off-stage explosion distracted the "men" in the green union suits long enough for Vincent to break free and pull out a snub-nosed revolver from his windbreaker. The report from Vincent's gun was incredibly loud—like they'd loaded the prop with enough gunpowder to fire off the cannons at the park entrance.

Then an arc of electricity crackled out from one of the dying aliens' ray gun—narrowly missing Vincent.

Another blast from our hero's revolver.

And now my favorite effect of the night. In the TV show whenever one of the aliens died, they would glow with this creepy orange-red aura then vanish in a puff of super-heated radioactive vapor.

On stage they replicated this effect with smoke bombs illuminated with multi-colored spotlights. When the smoke was gone, so were the Invaders! Which was convenient because who really wants a bunch of dead aliens cluttering up the stage?

There was even an "Epilogue" (as they used to caption them in every QM series).

Vincent stood among the curling wisps of smoke, with the yellow and purple lights from the disintegrating saucer slowly fading. A young woman with helmet-like hair and a tweed mini-dress walked hesitantly towards him. Our hero looked away from her as he re-holstered his revolver.

"David… I-I'm so sorry," the young woman said. "I should have believed you sooner… before it was too late."

Vincent looked over his shoulder in the direction of the woman.

"I can't let myself believe that it's ever too late, Susan."

The young woman looked as though she wanted to embrace Vincent, affect some kind of reconciliation.

Vincent zipped up his jacket and walked away.

"None of us can."

Slow curtain. Off-stage narrator says something ponderous. Music.

Wow. It was the first time I got to watch an episode of *The*

Invaders without my ex-wife telling me how dumb she thought it was.

"Paranoia is so boring," she would say every time I turned it on.

Well, paranoia is S.O.P. for many people these days. What with the Meanies eating cites and continents every other week and nobody sure exactly why. If you managed to get past denial, paranoia was usually the next available emotional response:

Why our planet? Why our species? Why our generation? More to the point: *why me?*

> **Quantitative:** Two shows down. One to go. I sincerely hope we have enough time to finish the festival. My mathematical abilities may not be sufficient to correctly time our exit strategy.
>
> **Qualitative:** Irrational happiness.

Ironside was not as taken with *The Invaders* as I was. He was definitely interested, however there were no smiles or nod factor during the performance.

Maybe he was getting sicker. Better consult the binder when we get to the hotel.

* * *

I was pleased that they hadn't removed our monster TV while we were away. I was less pleased that the only thing on was the "We Are All Going to Die Soon" News.

Stupid news.

No more B.C. No more Calgary or Edmonton.

The Meanie cloud seemed to be picking up speed so sometime tomorrow Saskatoon would probably be a memory.

That is if you'd heard of Saskatoon in the first place.

Call Joni Mitchell.

"Square 89."

Which if my increasing body of Phantom Flipper Crutch knowledge was correct, meant that Ironside would like to watch the news for a while.

Ugh.

Time for the wire.

Q and Q.

After a few hours Ironside gestured that he wanted me to shut off the TV. We didn't have a remote so that was my job.

He looked tired.

"Square four?" I asked. Square four was a cheerful and supportive place that usually meant "do you want to play some more?"

Ironside shook his head.

"The Meanies aren't Invaders," he said. "We made them."

Some people said that space aliens were at the root of the Meanie problems. Some people said they were God's punishment for other people not matching up their genitals with the correct body openings when they had sex. Most people who weren't insane or incredibly stupid were pretty sure that we (as in human beings) had made the Meanies. Maybe it was terrorists with a nano-tech weapon that got out of hand.

"The Meanies were supposed to be like you," Ironside continued.

"Like me?" I had a sudden and irrational fear that the end of the world was now revealed to be all my fault.

Sorry about that.

"Yes, enhancers, *actualizers,*" Ironside said. "To make things better. The name 'Meanie' was supposed to be a joke."

A joke?

Big laughs.

* * *

"Square one."

> **Quantitative:** It is 05:45 on the last day of the festival. I *had* been sleeping.

"Square one." This time a little louder.

> **Qualitative:** I would really like to go back to sleep.

"*Square one!*"

Okay, okay. You're the client.

Oddly enough we rarely started our games at Square One so I'm not sure what it meant in the rich symbolic vocabulary of Flipper Crutch; I'm pretty sure it had something to do with getting out of bed and doing something.

Ironside had a point. If the city was going to get eaten in a day or two we really had to make good use of our time.

* * *

Our van dropped us off at a small aluminum building set at the top of a low hill.

The landscape was so flat that even from this very modest elevation we had a very good view of the downtown core and the Museum tower.

The metal siding of the building was pretty seriously corroded. It was one of those temporary portable shelters that someone had decided was going to be permanent and stationary. It was also a branch of the local public library system.

Still open to the public.

Amazing.

However, not open for another two hours. It was just coming up on seven in the morning.

I was expecting to see more signs of fear and panic in the city but that didn't seem to be happening.

It could have been a misplaced case of hope. Sometimes the Meanies changed directions or even stopped for while. Could happen. City still might have a chance.

Right.

Maybe it was resignation. Sure, you might go somewhere else but sooner or later the Meanies were going to be occupying the same space as you. If you had to go, you might as well go doing what you liked to do with the people you cared about and in the places you enjoyed.

Ironside motored up to the front entrance of the library.

"Void Square," he said.

Whenever you hit a void square you had to stop and wait your turn.

We waited there. Watched the sun rise, watched the city wake up, watched one of the librarians cycle up and let us in.

> **Quantitative:** We spent approximately one hour and fifty-five minutes doing absolutely nothing but looking at things.

Qualitative: I'm glad we did. This city is a lot prettier than I originally thought.

Once inside the library, Ironside rolled over to the science stacks in the children's section.

He looked at the books on the shelves.

"Not here!" he wheezed in frustration.

"If you're looking for a book that you used to borrow when you were a kid," I said, "it's probably been out of circulation for a long time now."

Ironside started to cry. Well, his eyes were leaking some kind of fluid, I'm not sure if they had the same chemical composition as human tears.

It was really upsetting, though. I really hated to see Ironside cry. I put my hand on his shoulder, felt something odd squirming under the skin, and spoke as kindly as possible.

"Let's ask the reference librarian."

We were in luck. The books *The Prehistoric Kingdom* and *Fossil Worlds* by Dr. Robert T. Hall were indeed long out of print and had been taken off the shelves before the century began. However, some industrious librarian had decided to copy the books onto microfiche and so we spent much of the morning scrolling through back illuminated text and illustrations.

"Most of this is hideously out of date," Ironside said.

"Really?" Well, I didn't know. A dinosaur was a dinosaur as far as I was concerned.

"The big picture is what's important," Ironside said.

"Why's that?"

"When I first read these books, what impressed me was the idea that fossils could tell us so much about the past." Ironside pointed a clawed finger at the screen which was now showing a diagram of a petrified bone. "When you think about it, a fossil is a message sent from prehistory across millions of years to the present. The bodies of organisms when they get turned into fossil rock become the information medium for the message."

"That's pretty profound," I said.

"That idea made quite an impression…"

So much so that you decided to use your own body as an information medium? I didn't say that last sentence out loud. It seemed unkind to remind him that his experiment was a failure and now he got to live that failure every day?

What I did say was:

"You're very lucky to remember what inspired you when you were young."

For some reason Ironside smiled.

We were leaving the microfiche room when Ironside noticed a display case near the exit.

"Good god," he whispered. "I gave these to the library when I was ten years old. My grandfather was always finding them on his farm."

I looked down at the fossils mounted in the cases. A yellowed typewritten label in the case read:

"Pre-Cambrian Ammonites. Donated by George Frances Arthur."

George.

My client's real name.

> **Quantitative:** We spent 2.5 hours reading out of print books on the library's microfiche machine. It will take at least another 45 minutes to get us back to the hotel. Odd ways to spend the minutes of what could be our last day alive.
>
> **Qualitative:** I feel sad.

On the way back to the hotel, our driver told us that we had tickets (first class no less!) on the train back east. Our bags would be waiting for us at the station. The train was scheduled to leave at 23:30. Plenty of time to see the last show.

"Square 72," said George.

A fairly neutral position on the board.

I noticed that we were back to playing the game.

* * *

The monolith TV was still in our room!

This is good, I thought. It looked like George was tired and was going to take a nap before we went out. In the meantime maybe I could catch another episode of *The Trouble with Tracy.*

Just as I was turning the channel dial, the doorbell rang.

It was the concierge.

"There's a long distance call for you downstairs."

Long distance! Another message from prehistory.

"Can't you transfer the call up here?" I asked. I really didn't want to leave my client on his own.

"Regrettably our switchboard is no longer allowed to provide that service."

It must be someone from the Care Facility, I decided. Maybe they weren't happy about the charges that were mounting up on the Über-Card.

"I really can't leave my client—"

"I can wait with him while you take the call."

The concierge was right. These days, any kind of a long distance call was pretty urgent.

"Okay," I said. "Just don't get in his way."

"Yes, sir."

"Come and get me if he seems to be in any distress."

"Yes, sir."

While we are on the topic of distress, it was not the Care Facility calling me.

It was my ex-wife.

"You're not an easy man to find."

"Are you all right?" A number of possible scenarios as to why she was calling me came to mind. None particularly pleasant.

"Oh, I'm fine."

Experience had taught me that particular phrase really meant: "Try again and look harder for clues."

"Everything okay with your folks?"

"Given the current state of the world, I suppose they're pretty good."

At least that was a halfway direct answer. Her parents lived in the Maritimes, which were still reasonably Meanie free.

But I still didn't know why she was calling.

Take two cards and wait out this turn.

Go Fish.

Void Square.

"How's Mike?" I asked. Mike was her current live-in.

Silence at the other end.

"Is Mike with you now? Can I talk to him?"

I didn't mind Mike. He was a lot less psychotic than most of her boyfriends and maybe if he got on the line I would finally find out what this call was all about.

"Mike was in Vancouver."

"Oh."

So Mike wasn't doing so well.

"I'm sorry to hear that," I said finally.

"I'm okay."

I had my doubts.

"That's good," I said instead.

"I'm in Moose Jaw."

"I'm very sorry to hear that, too."

"Why do you say that?" Her reaction was a cross between a laugh and a sob.

I was going to say something dumb like, "I'm sorry to hear that anyone is in Moose Jaw" but I decided to tell the truth instead:

"That's pretty close to the cloud, isn't it?"

"I can see it from my window."

"I think you should get in your car, *right now*, and drive over here," I said. "I can get you a train ticket the rest of the way to Nova Scotia."

Was that what this was all about? She wanted to see me but she wanted me to invite her first? She always was a very proud person.

"I'll get into my car but I'm driving in the opposite direction."

"*There's nothing in the opposite direction!*"

"I'm going to drive into the cloud."

"*That's just crazy!*"

Although to quote her, given the current state of the world, maybe it wasn't that crazy after all. Even so, it was wrong to let her do this.

I started giving her directions to find the TransCanada and she began her oral suicide note. At the end of the conversation she agreed that she would "think about what I had said" but I knew that she already had her jacket on and her car keys in hand.

Quantitative: I have just spent over 90 minutes on the telephone.

Qualitative: I still have absolutely no perspective on my relationship with that woman.

When I got back to the room I discovered that George had been behaving rather eccentrically.

"You said to let him do what he wanted…" The concierge's eyes were wide with panic.

George was completely naked. His chair was set to clean up after all of his bodily functions so seeing him in the altogether was new information for me too. I was also quite surprised to see that George could walk. Also, spin, skip and jump.

Much of George's body was too complex for me to describe with any degree of meaning, but I will say that the physical symptoms of the information disease had spread everywhere. The texture of his skin looked like an electron microscope's photograph of a cluster of exotic viruses.

His penis, and I mention it only because a lot of you are very curious, looked like a deflated sculpture by Sorel Etrog. Look it up.

"It's okay," I said to the concierge. "None of this is your fault."

George was hopping on one foot, then the next, onto different pieces of paper scattered all over the carpet. He was counting off numbers as he jumped: "17… 38… 91… 128…"

I think I said the right thing to the concierge because the expression on his face went from ten to six on the mortification scale.

I then realized that the sheets of paper on the carpet had been arranged into a giant version of George's Flipper Crutch board.

"…12… 69… 117…"

More realizations followed: not only was George playing Flipper Crutch with himself, all those sheets of paper had been taken from my binder.

Great, now I had to completely wing it.

George started jumping in a spiral pattern at the center of the room and cried: "*326! 326! 326!*"

We'd never gotten that high up in Phantom Flipper Crutch so I had no idea what "326" meant or why he was so excited about it.

George kept on spinning around which was pretty impressive for a guy who looked like a pixelated version of the Elephant Man. There was something quite aesthetic to his performance—like it was an interpretative dance or a kinetic art installation.

Then George stopped, grinned and opened his arms to the universe in general. I hoped it was to the universe in general because being hugged by him at that moment was way beyond my comfort level.

"*I am done computing!*" George announced in a voice loud enough to definitely indicate that he was indeed addressing the universe in general.

The concierge look at me with an "instructions please?" expression.

"What does that mean, sir?"

"I would say that my client, through his own unique methodology, has finished computing something."

There was a silence. So I added:

"But I'm not sure what."

The concierge responded with a "more instructions please?" expression.

"I will handle things from here," I said. "Please make sure our driver is ready to take us to the park this evening."

The concierge looked almost calm as the discourse entered more familiar territory.

"Of course, sir."

George had fallen asleep on the floor. I wondered how long it was going to take to get him dressed and back into his chair.

> **Quantitative:** We now have less than 4.3 hours to pack, dress, get to the park, see the play, get on a train and evade vaporization by a gigantic swarm of ravenous nanobots of mysterious origin.
>
> **Qualitative:** They really aren't paying me enough for this job.

In my opinion they definitely saved the best for last.

The final performance was a dramatization of *The Undersea World of Jacques Cousteau.*

The actor who played the narrator must have been channeling Rod Serling because the voice, the posture and the black suit were all perfect. Since the narrator was omnipresent they put him on a platform on top of a very tall tower; so that he could look down on the aquatic adventures below and pass judgment on their meaning.

The rest of the show was the ultimate puppet theatre. They were re-enacting an episode where Cousteau and the crew of the

Calypso were doing underwater photography of the species found in the Great Barrier Reef.

The puppets representing the tropical sea creatures were incredibly colorful and black lights highlighted the beautiful details of the coral structures.

Much of the show felt like dance—which was good because the local symphony was on hand to provide the musical score.

George and I seriously bonded during the course of the show. Each wondrous surprise in the performance seemed to bring us closer together.

Finally, regrettably, curtain.

When the stage lights went down, we could see that the Meanie cloud was approaching and it didn't look like it was going to stop anytime soon.

So much for hope.

"George," I whispered. "We have to go now."

George was silent but didn't object when I pushed him out of the amphitheater ahead of everyone else. Since I now knew that George could walk, hop and spin—it might have been even faster if I asked him to get out of the chair but I didn't feel like attempting that conversation.

> **Quantitative:** I am expediting the safe departure of my client as per my contracted responsibilities.
>
> **Qualitative:** I feel guilty as shit.

"There!" George was pointing at the Museum tower as our van approached the station.

"George, we don't really have time," I said.

"There!"

"The Museum is closed, George."

George reached out to the door handle. I put my hand on his claw and sighed.

"Driver," I said. "Take us to the tower."

It was still my job to take George wherever he wanted to go.

The next challenge was getting into the place.

George looked like he was going to bulldoze the fence with his chair. Fortunately there was enough security there to prevent that from happening.

I tried to explain to the guards the importance of our getting up the tower as quickly as possible. This was hard to do because I didn't know why we had to go up there.

"I'm sorry sir, the Museum is permanently closed to the public," the shift captain replied.

"Who's responsible for the building?" I asked.

The shift captain replied with the name of some organization that I'd never heard of.

"Can I use your telephone?"

The shift captain shrugged.

One call and an Über-Card transaction later and I owned the Museum.

I looked over to George. What next?

"Is there a viewing gallery in the Tower?" George asked.

The shift captain nodded.

> **Quantitative:** Our train leaves in 20 minutes. I estimate that the cloud will reach the outskirts of the city in just over an hour. The elevator ride to the Tower's viewing gallery will take at least five minutes each way and I don't know how long George will want to stay up there. I have no idea how the numbers are adding up in this situation.
>
> **Qualitative:** I *really* have no idea how the numbers are adding up in this situation.

We had a very clear view from the viewing gallery.

Unfortunately.

Most of the lights of the city were still on. You could see the occasional pair of headlights desperately speeding east but a lot fewer than you might expect. We even saw a few headlights heading towards the cloud. Kindred spirits of my ex-wife, I suppose.

As far as the cloud itself…

It was very big. Also, essentially featureless and vibrating. Looking at the cloud straight on was like watching an IMAX documentary about static.

George sat there and stared at the cloud. He was staring at it for a lot longer than I liked. Was this how he'd decided to commit suicide? Maybe he felt very guilty about whatever his connection to the Meanies was. Even so, it still seemed rude of him to take me along without asking.

"George, I really think we should be going now."

I would give him this one chance to come with me but I figured that I had just about reached the limit of my job description. I was not too proud to be sitting behind a set of headlights screaming east.

George didn't move.

I could try and take him with me. All I had to do was push the chair onto the elevator. No, that option wasn't practical. He'd slow me down too much. Besides, if he felt like it, he could just get out of the chair.

George reached down into one of the chair's carrier compartments and took out my therapy box.

"Hope you don't mind," he said, sticking the wire up his nose. "I made some modifications."

"What kind of modifications?" I know this was a dumb time to be offended about someone messing around with my private property but as you may have noticed by now, I'm not always rational.

George smiled. "It transmits now."

He resumed staring at the cloud. I found a folding chair, sat down and watched as George transmitted.

I assumed that he was transmitting to the Meanies. I also assumed that he was transmitting himself, all that data that he'd been incubating in his body for all those years.

We sat in the viewing gallery until the sun came up.

Hot damn, the sun came up!

No Meanies.

Later on, experts concluded that the message that George was transmitting was a command to the Meanies to start consuming themselves instead of everything else.

It was a very effective command. Within twelve hours every Meanie super colony had stopped expanding, within twenty hours they were noticeably shrinking. Two weeks later there wasn't a trace of a Meanie anywhere on the planet.

George is gone as well. I did manage to get him back to the Care Facility but he didn't last very long after that. I guess using your body as a living computer takes a toll and George ended up paying it.

George and I had some good conversations on the train ride but he never did explain exactly what his connection to the Meanies was and what they were originally intended to do. Maybe George figured that none of that was relevant anymore.

I did have to ask:

"Why Flipper Crutch?"

"It was an interesting way for me to crunch numbers." Then he laughed. "It was also fun to keep you guessing all the time."

"And why the Festival?"

"I was lonely for my home town."

"Lonely?"

"And I always did enjoy the theatre."

> **Quantitative:** With George's passing my contract has been terminated. I had no useful (or rather polite) suggestions as to what MID could do with the museum they now own.
>
> **Qualitative:** Back on the bus. Looking for a new job. Got myself an extra duffle bag to carry the Flipper Crutch board George gave me. The future is uncertain.

At least there might be a future.

THE PROGRESSIVE APPARATUS AND THE RETROGRADE MENTOR EXPERIENCE DENIAL THEN DEATH

That title pretty much describes what happens in the Progressive Apparatus story cycle. I'll pass on giving you a lecture on any possible meanings and implications that might be associated with each story. I shouldn't have to do all the work here.

However, you might have noticed when you consider all of the stories in this collection that the words "Progressive" and "Apparatus" have different meanings:

1. Is the Progressive Apparatus an invasive but slowly deteriorating piece of sentient software?
   Yes.[4]
2. Is Progressive Apparatus a vast corporate entity with definitely amoral and possibly immoral intent?
   Yes.[5]
3. Is there a connection between the software PA and the corporate PA?
   I'm not going to say. Some readers have been quite firm in their wanting to know the answer to this question but as I mentioned earlier, I shouldn't have to do *all* the work here.

There's another question that might have occurred to some of you:

4. Does the term "Progressive Apparatus" imply that I am opposed to liberal or progressive political causes?

---

4 And as the story cycle progressed, I found myself feeling sorry for the poor thing.

5 I don't feel sorry for these people at all. My sentiments are even more obvious in my novel *The Hard Side of the Moon.*

> No. Most of you must have immediately figured out that I was being ironic. However, irony is tricky sometimes, so in a few rare cases it can be good to be very clear about your intent.

I figure this is one of those instances.
Stay safe. Connect.

Hugh A. D. Spencer
November 2020

Three-time Aurora Award nominee, Hugh Spencer has been writing science fiction and cultural commentary (popular and otherwise) for longer than he cares to admit. He has been published in *On Spec*, *Interzone*, and *Descant* magazines, and has also been included in various anthologies. He also writes for radio and the stage, and has collaborated with Shoestring Radio in San Francisco, Praxis Theatre, and the Scripted Toronto Festival. He also occasionally contributes his alleged wisdom to the Gernsback Continuum, the podcast for *Amazing Stories Magazine*. Hugh's collaborations with Brain Lag Publishing include the novel *Extreme Dentistry* and the collection *Why I Hunt Flying Saucers and Other Fantasticals*.

www.ingramcontent.com/pod-product-compliance
Ingram Content Group UK Ltd.
Pitfield, Milton Keynes, MK11 3LW, UK
UKHW040005200726
13854UKWH00001B/53